CW01308767

A VINTAGE YEAR

IAN NALDER

First published in Scotland in 2017 by Cawdor Press

Copyright © Ian Nalder 2017

The moral right of Ian Nalder to be recognised as the author of this work has been asserted in accordance with the Copyright, Design and Patents Act, 1988.

All rights reserved. No part of this publication may be reproduced, stored or transmitted in any form or by any means without the express prior permission of the publisher.

Typeset in Bembo Standard

ISBN: 978-1-78808-960-9

Design: iolaire | design | edit | print Logie Steading Forres IV36 2QN
Printing & binding: POD Worldwide, Peterborough PE2 6XD

ACKNOWLEDGEMENTS & COMMENTS

I wish to thank Alison Shaw and Jim Andrews for their advice on perusing the first draft which, in retrospect, I surmise to have been a task beyond the call of duty. May I also thank the professional team at Emergents of the Highlands & Islands Enterprise based at Forres in Morayshire.

This tale is fiction but personal experience has played some part in dreaming it up. Every one of the young cricketers is a figment of the imagination and bears no resemblance to anyone I have ever met. More is the pity in some ways. As for those personalities, famous in their own field and who I either met or knew of, whether they are alive today or not their attributes are recorded as faithfully as I know how.

I recall with awe the inspiring headmaster of my Derbyshire prep school, John Roberts. A friend of the Duke of York in the 1930s, a linguist and a man of extraordinary talents, he is the inspiration for Gaffer. Incidentally, the elegant suspension bridge behind the parish church at Doveridge which did indeed break asunder, has long been repaired and is fully fit for purpose.

A year in Kenya on national service was as happy as was possible. Buller Camp was my base. A brief stay in Zanzibar was restricted just to the main island, the island of cloves.

My thanks to Jonathan Lawley whose book 'Beyond The Malachite Hills' alerted me to a number of speculative African ventures that feature as recommendations of the disgraced stockbroker Claude.

The Galle Face hotel in Colombo, built in 1864, is still family owned and is greatly to be commended. The swimming pool has to be the best in town. Due to its unique position south of Bentota on rocks above the awesome sandy beach, the Saman Villas hotel escaped the terrible devastation of the tsunami in 2004.

My friendship with Richard Chidobem stems from the early 1960s when he was studying veterinary medicine at Glasgow University. He was a good tennis player and a keen cricketer. On returning to his homeland, his assassination within the year is a tragedy beyond compare. I would like to think he had relations who later emulated his talents in some field or another. But sadly I have no idea.

CONTENTS

    Prologue 9

    The Characters 11

1: Early School Days 13

2: Teenage Years 33

3: National Service 43

4: Back Home 65

5: Working For A Living 75

6: The Feedback 89

7: Setting Up Business 99

8: The London Scene 109

9: The Underworld 119

10: The Betting Coup 125

11: Teamwork 137

12: New Horizons 151

13: Concern For Claude 159

14: Dramatic Changes 165

15: The Game Of Life 177

16: Consolidation 189

17: Ups And Downs 201

18: Caught Out 219

Jeremy – Aged 20

PROLOGUE

To say Nigel was a mite peeved would be an understatement. Due to unusually harsh winter winds, for three consecutive weeks his golf on Rye's venerable and inimitable links had been cancelled.

Retirement was all very well. But now he was doubly frustrated for he had been deprived of plying his skill in the most genial of company. Which, had it taken place, almost certainly would have been followed by strong black coffee and a shot of kummel after a simple but glorious lunch of scrambled eggs and ham succeeded by Boodles cake with Stilton. As for the house claret, that would have been a prerequisite.

One evening, after her third successive win at Scrabble in a fortnight Marilyn glanced at him. He appeared a trifle tetchy. After all he had been a journalist. So arguably he was a man of letters. Not that he thought of himself as such. But that did not mean he liked losing to his wife at a word game. Thus it was with some difficulty he sought to be gracious. Marilyn could not be other than aware of this.

'Why not settle down this winter, forget golf, and write a story?' she volunteered. 'Surely that is something you can easily manage. And enjoy doing at the same time.'

'What kind of story?' he replied with a yawn as boredom threatened.

'Well, the story of your life. How you faced catastrophe. Then through your own endeavours along with the help of your oldest friends you recovered. And just consider those friends. What a triumph most of them have made of their lives!'

'I suppose I could. But who would want to read it?'

'Think for a moment,' said Marilyn. 'Almost everyone experiences ups and downs in life. Tell it how it has been. Introduce the wonderful people you have come across. OK, granted not all were amazing and wonderful. One or two were scurrilous. Recount anecdotes, drama, success, and pathos. And don't be frightened of tragedy either. Highlight resilience in the face of adversity. Don't shy away from goings on that have been unsavoury. Titillate the readers with tales of home and abroad. Let them find relief, curiosity, and even excitement away from their armchair or deckchair. May they see sixty years or more pass in a flash, happily remote from the drudgery of the humdrum. Usher them into another world and one which you actually knew.'

'Possibly. Allow me to sleep on it. But I hear you well. At least this would provide a different test of endurance to that over eighteen holes in the perishing cold.'

The Characters

MARK	Schoolmaster both musical & solicitous
	Married to Myfanwy
THEO	"His own man", a gifted engineer and a jockey with an eye for a horse
	Married to Cressida
JEREMY	Chartered surveyor, a leader, handsome, caring, and "too good to be true"
	Married to Fiona
HARRY	Barrister specialising in criminal law, gregarious, moneyed
	Married to Veronica
CLAUDE	Failed stockbroker, rescued before becoming ultimately a kindly teacher
	Married to Maisie
OWEN	Entrepreneurial, sensitive, conscientious, successful
	Married to Penny
NOEL	Ambitious businessman, brilliant, generous, loyal to his friends
	Married to Evie
NIGEL	Journalist and PR man, slight inferiority complex, late developer
	Married to Marilyn
BART	Hotelier, brazen, industrious, good with people, far-sighted
	Married to Giselle
SLIM	Chef, dedicated, a showman and workaholic
	Married to Jessica
VINCE	Duplicitous solicitor with a clientele of doubtful repute
	Married to Leila

CHAPTER 1: EARLY SCHOOL DAYS

Imagine if you will you are just five years old. You have never attended nursery school or even pre-prep. What little education you have is from a governess who took you for rambles on the common and pointed out flower and fern, trees and birds. Then to avoid the ongoing onslaught in the skies raging during the Battle of Britain in the summer and autumn of 1940, you are bundled off from Kent to a small boarding school in Derbyshire happily distant from the Luftwaffe's feverish efforts to achieve rampant dereliction in and around south-east London. Mercifully though, thanks to the heroism of our airmen Hitler never got to launch his Operation Sea Lion whose clear but evil purpose was to invade Britain.

What precipitated my being despatched as a refugee some 150 miles away was rather strange. It was the desire of my brother and me to have fish and chips for tea. He was home for autumn half-term from Adleby Hall on the edge of Ashdown Forest since his school at Bickley had been evacuated there. That afternoon we were playing cricket by the garage back door. At least I had to endure the penance of bowling while Eric, six years older than me, took careful aim and deflected the ball this way and that. When Mother called out asking whether we wanted cottage pie or fish and chips for tea, unanimously we opted for the latter.

'Well, Eric,' she said, 'on your bike and cycle into the village. Then ask Bob Fry on the Esplanade for four helpings so that Dad and I can have that for supper too. Here is a ten shilling note. There should be plenty of change. And don't forget to ask for a generous measure of his pink sauce. It comes in a bottle so please take care. Nigel, come with me. It is time for a story. I have a new Beatrix Potter book to read you. It is called Timmy Tiptoes.'

Eric had not been gone long before the air raid siren gave warning of an impending attack. Now the ride from our home to the Esplanade involved a rutted footpath at the back of the golf course which led onto Willow Grove. At the far end lay the village school, an attractive building with a steeply arched roof and within walking distance of children attending it. By the time the siren sounded Eric had cycled three quarters of the way towards his goal. So he had to take a decision on whether to proceed or return. Slightly indeterminate, he decided to continue to Bob Fry's and so fulfil his mission to fetch our tea and Mum and Dad's supper.

As he prepared to leave, Bob cautioned him, 'Go carefully, son. There has been a siren and the Gerries may be dropping bombs at any moment now. Or you can stay here. There is a brick building at the back of my yard and you can hunker down there until the all clear.'

As he stood outside Eric listened. With the air so quiet it was almost eerie. So, encouraged to risk the ride home he declined Bob's kindly offer. It was a decision he forever came to regret. Minutes later as he was passing the village school several low flying enemy planes let drop a flurry of bombs. One of these struck the school. Two died and two more were injured accounting for a teacher, two cleaners and a handyman. Just as well that the children had been sent home at the first sound of the siren. As for Eric, he was flung off his bike which then buckled on crashing into a lamp post. In the process he broke his arm and lost all hearing in his right ear. Our tea and Mum and Dad's supper cascaded across the road.

Back home Mother and I could hear the sound of this bombing when she was halfway through Timmy Tiptoes. Halting the story abruptly, she declared she must dash off to the village to see if Eric was all right. Then realising she could not possibly leave me alone in the house whilst the air raid was still on, Mother tried phoning Molly Harding our neighbour two doors away. But, with the telephone exchange struck, the line was down. Grabbing me by the hand she promptly hustled me along the road to Molly's where she begged her to look after me while she took to her bike to check up on Eric. However when she reached our once proud village school – a sickening sight leaning precipitately with half the roof off – the siren had sounded the all clear. Eric was now nowhere to be seen for he had been rescued by the ambulance team and was being attended to in the Annunciation Church.

Mother was not the type of person to panic but judging by comments I overheard much later I guess this was the nearest she ever came to it. I rather think we had corned beef hash and baked beans for supper that night, certainly not the fish and chips that had been planned. What I am reasonably sure of is it will have been this single incident that impelled my parents to seek safety for me well out of harm's way. Clearly they did not want both their sons to be damaged or worse. So by the end of the week arrangements were in hand for me to go to Derbyshire to attend Barley Farm. This was the kindergarten for Barley Hall, a prep school run by a distant cousin of Mother's. Here as a boarder, cast off from family and totally green, on 2

November 1940 my education commenced in earnest.

Little was I to know it at the time, but from that inauspicious start my fellow five-year olds were to become my companions for the next seven years. And in the case of the cricket team which won every match in that glorious summer of '47, barring an interregnum of some six years and with arguably one exception, we would remain colleagues and friends throughout life happily willing to make use of one another's talents. For boys of that age to bond so well must be highly unusual if not unique. But, my goodness, this certainly helped me.

I had been at Barley Farm for just over a year when at the end of the winter term in 1941 we were informed Barley Hall would close. Then we would all be moving to Heathside on the westerly border of Derbyshire and Staffordshire. I had enjoyed my time at the Farm. Our single storey building was separate from the senior school the other side of the road where the bigger boys of between seven and thirteen were accommodated. This turreted late Victorian edifice had been the seat of a prosperous family whose fortune had derived from constructing bridges, banks and civic offices in the Empire. Where we little ones stayed will once have been the farm for this grand hall. We felt entirely safe as both the headmaster Gwyn Evans and his wife Kathleen slept there too as did the red haired Nurse Ethel.

That first journey to Barley Farm had been by train and taxi. Gwyn and Kathleen had kindly put Mother and Aunt Sibyl up for the night in the hope that I would settle in more easily than if they simply dropped me off at the gates. Next morning we awoke to a very different November world with two inches of snow. As a new boy I was allowed to celebrate this with Mother and Aunt Sibyl by frolicking in the fields playing Grandmother's Footsteps before their taxi took them to Derby for the afternoon train to St Pancras. During my absence the other boys created a snowman. Once I appeared, a boy to whom the others looked up to and answered to the name of Jeremy said to the others, 'let's ask Nigel to finish him off.' Handing me an old bowler hat that had formerly belonged to Gwyn's father, with a welcoming smile he invited me to top him with this. It was his way of making me feel part of the team despite the fact I had taken no part when the snowman was being so lovingly fashioned then embellished with anthracite eyes and a sturdy carrot to serve as his nose.

The previous day I had met my fellow pupils over high tea. The friendliest was perhaps the least likely. This was Bart, proud and in awe of his father the proprietor of Rotherham's Greyhound Stadium. I found him companionable. For his part he seemed glad to find a newcomer to whom he could relate, possibly because most of the other boys appeared to come from less recent wealth. I suppose they detected he was that little bit different to them. His small pal Owen was quietly welcoming too and content to act as Bart's side-kick. Owen's father was even better known. Possibly he was more prosperous for he owned Sheffield's most prominent department store. Alas for the slightly built Owen, he had poor eyesight and wore spectacles. One half was banded with horizontal stripes to try and correct this. For a term or two we three would troop around, possibly the odd chaps out but finding safety in numbers.

Once a term parents were permitted to take their offspring out for the day. But Mother and Father could only manage the journey from London when Sports Day took place on the second Saturday in June. So that I was not left alone on my own, during the Lent and Autumn terms Bart invited me to meet his parents. His Dad was bald, stout and stocky. Happily wearing well cut suits in loud checks oblivious of good taste, it transpired he was the greatest fun. In retrospect I surmise he resembled Viscount Castlerosse, the Irish peer who was then the irrepressible gossip columnist for the Daily Mail and a friend of the golfer Henry Cotton, ultimately Sir Henry, who was also then writing a column for the paper's golfers. Bart's mother was a shade taller. Not smart, she was motherly, welcoming and utterly unspoilt.

Bart's Dad had a cream and black Jaguar with a fine chrome strip separating the two colours. I thought it dashing and longed for him to race the car. But despite his flamboyant sense of dress he was a careful driver even when there was scarcely another car in sight. However, on one occasion when the road was straight and seemingly empty he put his foot on the accelerator. We shot forward to his broad Yorkshire cry of, 'Who is pushing my car?' I tried to persuade him to do this again and again but he was far too sensible to play to a little lad's emotions. Lunch would be taken in the Peak District at one of two fine hostelries after which a ramble through the dale and alongside the river Derwent was customary.

On another occasion Owen's parents took the three of us out to lunch at Derby's Midland Hotel. It seemed rather grand if a little austere with everyone talking in hushed whispers as befitting a select clientele. For a treat we boys were allowed ginger beer. Owen's father, in wearing a monocle and sporting a gold watch chain on his waistcoat, resembled one of the Western Brothers, a droll duo who spoke with a posh drawl and performed on Sunday radio's Variety Bandbox ahead of the star turn Frankie Howerd. They also featured in my favourite comic, Radio Fun. When the time came for us to say good-bye, he dipped his hand into his pocket and gave Bart and me a shiny new half-crown, sufficient to buy ten bottles of fizzy pink pop at the school tuck shop. I rather think Owen got the same too.

Mother's Welsh cousin Gwyn Evans was a man of many talents: a linguist, an accordion player, an artist, an actor and a former Cambridge University hockey blue. He was of strong religious beliefs and despite his florid complexion apparently teetotal. Later in life I learned this was because his father had drunk himself into an early grave and ruined a promising career as an actuary with a leading North Country building society.

None of us had bicycles. Walking everywhere we all acquired strong legs. On Sundays we would manage the two and a half miles to the village church in a random crocodile formation. Here the regular reader of the Old Testament was the local Duke generally attired in a brown suit. Maybe he was prey to nerves since he gabbled away in a monotone which we found hard to follow. But I suppose nobody dared point this out to him. Certainly not the rector, a gentleman with a face the colour of claret and the proud owner of a BSA drop-head coupé sports car. He had a telling way with words, lived in a fine rectory and enjoyed the company of folk looked upon as "county" and included him in dinner parties. On Mondays he visited the sick; Tuesdays he set aside for funerals; Wednesdays in season he shot with the gentry when invited; Thursdays he ran a bible class; and on Fridays he wrote his Sunday sermon. On Saturdays when not conducting a wedding he would visit schools in his parish and watch the cricket or whatever team game was being played. So all in all he sort of knew what was going on and we sort of knew him. Such then was the pleasant life of a country parson!

On sunny summer Sunday afternoons the twelve of us who stayed in the Farm would split into three and go for a ramble with the two daughters of Gwyn and Kathleen, Myfanwy and Cressida. Sometimes we would collect wild flowers which we brought back for pressing into a book. On one occasion we wore gloves to gather nettles so that Nurse Ethel might make nettle wine. Why she liked this I cannot imagine for not only was it horrible, it smelt like pee. I knew this because when we were six years old five of us were dared to taste our own. The instigator was Noel who was our dormitory head.

'Let's declare we are the Famous Five,' he said, 'and show our courage and undying friendship by tasting our own pee.' Bart, Owen and I screwed up our faces but Noel's pal little Theo bravely followed his example. Seeing our reluctance Noel chided us saying, 'last one to do so is a cissy.' Bart was the next to accept the challenge followed by Owen. Finally I capitulated but little good it did me for I felt the full brunt of Noel's tongue. For a long time we were anything but friends. In fact at one time I dreaded him. What I can say is that as far as I know none of us ever chose to repeat the feat.

When Halloween came round, at dusk we boys were sent in pairs into the surrounding woods to gather firewood for the bonfire. With the air chill and having a curious taint of mothballs and unwashed trousers, Bart and I came across two old men doing the very same but for fires in their hearths at home. Bart cautioned me to be beware and not get too close for they looked distinctly unfriendly. Both were large fellows, big bruisers, obviously impoverished and probably brothers. Each wore a jerkin over his shirt and baggy trousers that were tied with string around the waist. One of them suffered a cold and devoid of handkerchief blew his nose between thumb and forefinger to allow the snot to fall at his feet. The other then did the same. Neither was the slightest bit concerned that Bart and I had witnessed this vulgarity. They merely ignored us. Tempted to offer my hankie, I thought better of it. Without a word on anyone's part Bart and I slunk away.

That evening under a full moon it was crisp and cold. Handyman Mason lit the bonfire on four corners with the aid of Mr Gardiner our geography master. The giant pile was constructed on a base carefully laid some days earlier and then covered with tarpaulins to protect it. So when Mason chucked on our timber offerings they crackled mightily. Atop poles a little higher than us were pumpkins. Hollowed out with grinning spiky teeth, they resembled gargoyles. Also perched on poles and interspersed with these were coconut husks filled with oil which, when lit, contrived to make the pumpkins appear grotesque.

We gathered round in expectation of a warming drink. All of a sudden we heard a dramatic cackling as we were treated to a weird figure waving a broomstick. Whoever or whatever it was wore a conical hat and was shrouded in a dark cloak. This apparition circled two or three times before disappearing into the woods, all the time continuing this dreadful cackle. Those boys who had witnessed the wicked witch the previous year claimed it was Gaffer, as we called the headmaster. Maybe that was right for he appeared shortly afterwards to join us in a warming drink on wearing a green checked plus fours suit, green wellies, a light tartan scarf and a Tyrolean hat boasting a cluster of tiny feathers. He was the essence of pleasantness and a far cry from the spectre he must have impersonated. As we clustered round the fire chewing Kathleen's deliciously crunchy crackly treacle toffee Nurse Ethel fetched his accordion. Soon he was amusing us with songs that used to feature in pubs on a Saturday night. These included "Daddy Wouldn't Buy Me A Bow-Wow" and "Has Anybody Here Seen Kelly?" But we never sang "There Is A Tavern In The Town". He would not teach us that.

It was a month later that we learned in January we would be moving to Heathside not far from the Derbyshire village of Doveridge. Our junior school was to be merged with the senior school. The school building was an imposing late Victorian mansion, once the proud home of a pottery millionaire from Stoke-on-Trent whose china was still seen in countless homes throughout Britain. But if he had heirs they were no longer around. Certainly there was no boy at school with the name of Fancourt. Situated on a plateau, this fine example of Victoriana enjoyed views towards the river Dove. To its rear was a coach house with a handsome clock tower and the broadest of eaves. These afforded sanctuary to craftily sculpted nests created by house-martins who swooped and dived with verve and poise over the adjoining courtyard. As we had to cross it when leaving the gym, on pretending to be a plane and with arms outstretched we too swerved and scuttled whenever they chose to tease.

Heathside's grounds were equally awe-inspiring. There were formal rose gardens and a cricket pitch embracing an athletics track. In addition there were a couple of football fields, a walled kitchen garden and a lake surrounded by rhododendrons which was home to ducks. From time to time this sheltered water also attracted swans. But they did not appear to bother the ducks except when we chose to feed them in the depths of winter for fear that otherwise they might starve. Then they chose to squabble and, free of inhibition, displayed a show of might is right to leave the ducks foraging for titbits that had eluded their outstretched necks.

Summer of 1945 was hot. With no swimming pool in the grounds, three times a week we all traipsed the mile and a quarter to the river through pasture and water meadows scented with meadowsweet and buttercups. Here we swam or just splashed about in the waters. On our route we skirted a cultivated field in which potatoes, cabbages and turnips were growing.

One day Italian prisoners of war were working there. Just yards away was one I regarded with a suspicion. Noel saw my trepidation and teasingly urged me not to get close.

'Italians smell of garlic you know for they eat funny things like pasta, salami and snails.'

'The French eat snails too,' piped up Owen. 'Well, that is what my Dad says.'

'But Italians make super ice cream,' chimed in Slim whose father had a string of ice cream parlours in Sheffield. 'Dad had one working for him before the war called Morganti. Then he was taken away and – what they call – interned in the Isle of Man. But not to worry! Dad has his recipes. In any case he has said that if Morganti wants to return when the war is over he will take him on again. Much my favourite of his ice creams was his tutti frutti'.

'You are just a fruit cake,' intervened Noel a shade unkindly.

'Fruit cake yourself, you noodle,' replied Slim coolly.

With the bickering continuing, this handsome bronzed Italian who generations later the charismatic film star Jude Law came to resemble, ambled over and asked if anyone played the piano. Two or three boys, of whom one was Mark, said they did but were currently without a teacher as the previous incumbent had moved on to a school in Worcestershire.

Hearing this, the Italian said, 'Perhaps I could teach you – that is if I receive permission.'

Mr Gardiner, whom we christened Woodbine on account of his love of tobacco, will have overheard for he had a word with him. Gaffer must have approved for some days later he appeared at morning prayers and was introduced to us. His name was Giuseppe. But we called him Seppe for short. Not only did he teach those who wanted to learn the piano but he was also allowed to form a choir. And it was here I felt he excelled. Anyone with any musical inclination wanted to be in the choir for he was funny, sang in a glorious baritone voice, and was totally inspiring. At the end of the summer term he organised a concert which included songs from Gilbert &

Sullivan. Everyone had a ball! When Father died and I left Heathside Seppe presented me with a little silver cross. I don't know why as I was not the best singer by far. Theo Manners was. But then perhaps he felt even sorrier for me than he did for Theo.

The winter of 1946/47 was the coldest for generations. Awaiting collection on wooden platforms at the junction of farm tracks with the country road were milk churns glistering with globules of congealed ice. In places the river Dove froze. But skating was out. Sharp chunky slabs of ice in the river's centre would break away and float silently at whim as the currents chose. That term team games were abandoned due to snow and engrained frost. To have played would have been madness with broken bones two a penny. Gaffer must have feared he would lose several pupils and that furious parents would never forgive him. Instead, twice a week he sought to entertain us through arranging for the fifth and sixth forms to have dancing lessons. Joining us were girls from St Benedict's. We learned the foxtrot, the waltz, the Palais Glide and the Gay Gordons. It worked well and gave rise to much conversation in the bedrooms at night, with my fellow room-mates trying to outdo each other in explaining how the girl they fancied was equally keen on him and how they had managed a furtive kiss and a cuddle.

Jeremy's friend, Harry, was keen on a girl called Carol. 'She puts her hand on my behind.'

'What's so special about that?' called out Bart. 'Maureen is a wicked kisser. She slips her tongue onto mine.'

'Oooooh!' called out Noel and Harry. 'Who is a little pervert then?'

Laughter followed. Difficult to cap that. So I did not try. In any case Jeremy took charge.

'Hang on fellows. Give it a break. Soon Woodbine will be on the prowl and as it is a good ten minutes after "lights out" if he catches anyone talking then tomorrow Gaffer will administer the cane. Bart, if you are not careful you will end up with more stripes on your bum than a sergeant has on his sleeve.' Jeremy was respected. So after a little snigger we shut up.

Not content with introducing us to the fair sex through dancing, Gaffer also used his ingenuity to persuade the local golf professional to come and teach us. After all, he was earning next to nothing since the golf course was frozen too. With the stables in the coach house having been converted to a gym, this was now fitted out as an indoor golf school with a large mirror, two full size nets and an area where one could pitch balls from a couple of mats into mini nets acting as non-bouncy buckets. It became my very special playroom.

The professional, Gabbitas, was a sturdy fellow who stood no nonsense. We never learned his christian name for he was content simply to be Gabbitas. He taught us how to stand to the ball with flexed knees and grip the club with two Vs pointing to our chin. His method was simple: take the club away with the left hand and ensure the left hand then stayed on top of the right shoulder. He stressed the need for a pause at the top and that we then kept our left eye behind the ball at impact. He was more flexible on the follow through as long as there was one. Whenever the ball sailed away he was immensely encouraging. If we foozled the shot he would merely say, 'you will do better next time.' We loved him.

Gabbitas had served in the Great War but was considered too old to be conscripted in World War II. A formidable all round athlete, he so enjoyed coming to us that he volunteered to be our gym teacher too as long as he was not required by the Golf Club. He and I got along famously and he taught me to be proficient at vaulting the horse. His presence together with the assurance that his smooth muscular arms would catch me in the event of mishap did wonders for my confidence. That Lent term was the happiest I had had to date. Gabbitas fitted in so well that in the summer he found time to help coach cricket too as the golf course was scarcely functioning, and his wife was well able to cope with the shop for those few intrepid players prepared to accept the challenge that rustic course now presented.

It was in the gym that I first developed a real rapport with Harry Fairest and Jeremy Broughton. Both were a few months older than me. I had long admired them and not just because they were our top two batsmen. Moreover, the curly-headed Harry possessed an enviable swashbuckling attitude, something foreign to me for in comparison I was quite shy. But very kindly and not necessarily correctly they looked upon me as the top gymnast and even their equal at golf. Up to then my particular pals had been Bart Warner and Owen Gifford. However, now to be in the same company as the extrovert Harry and the handsome Jeremy made me feel good. Rightly or wrongly I considered it a step up.

Harry's father was the proprietor of a Sheffield steel mill. Among other things it made were razor blades. Advertisements for these showed three men at 7 'o' clock in the evening. The first two had descending degrees of shadow but the third one seemed to have none. The tag line was "Fair, Fairer, and Fairest". Then underneath was the slogan, "Fairest Blades Last the Whole Day Through". This campaign was aimed at their competitor who manufactured Seven 'o' Clock and whose advertisements showed a clean shaven chap above the caption "Seven 'o' Clock, Cock", so indicating the need to shave twice a day.

The Fairest family lived in a manor house set in substantial grounds. Harry's Dad ran a rare gleaming maroon Lagonda sports saloon, luxury such as I did not know. I was privileged to travel in it on the special occasion when I was invited for the weekend. Jeremy was the other house guest. A natural athlete, slim, with regular features and a little quiff above smiling eyes, he was the epitome of a "good fellow" who had the talent of making one feel valued. His Dad was land agent to the Earl of Ruabon who resided in some splendour in the nearby village of Somersal Herbert.

The Earl's family, the Eyton-Winns, had been big landowners in and around Ruabon in north Wales since the eighteenth century. In the mid nineteenth century they owned two collieries, an ironworks, and a small chemical plant for extracting oil from the local shale. Then they built a brickyard adjacent to clay pits. After World War II those old clay pits earned the Earl a great deal of money for the landfill of household waste. In addition to all this entrepreneurial activity, the Earl's ancestors had been early investors in canals before shrewdly selling out in the 1850s and reinvesting in the railways. It was then that his great grandfather, who was chairman of his local railway, was ennobled and celebrated this by building a huge Gothic pile. During World War II this was sequestrated as a training school for the Royal Engineers. I learned later the present Earl, who also carried the family name of Walter, was glad to be shot of it since the upkeep was horrific. After the War, with the Sappers gone the house was used as a setting for horror films produced by Ealing Studios.

Happily for him the Earl inherited a vast acreage of rolling farmland east of Uttoxeter fringed with may trees. Jeremy's father managed his estate with consummate ease. Preferring this to his property in damp and rural Wales that he chose to avoid if at all possible, the Earl continued to live in Derbyshire enjoying the life of a country squire who rode with the hounds and shot pheasant in season. It was a far cry from his enterprising ancestors whose fortune came from the land, the dirt and grime of industry, and astute financial deals. A considerate man and a long-time widower, aside from a brief military career he had never needed to work in his life. But this rather plump, ruddy-faced, silver-haired gentleman was honest and kindly and took an understandable liking to Jeremy.

Harry's manor house had a games room housing a full size snooker table. In an ante room were bar billiards and table tennis plus various coin-in-the-slot machines. Joining us was Claude Hanbury, our wicket keeper, son of a Liverpool stockbroker and nephew of the Earl. He also lived at Somersal Herbert to where his father returned at weekends. It was a memorable weekend to establish lifelong ties between the four of us although one could not possibly foretell that in due course one strand would become so enfeebled as nearly to shatter.

Other members of our cricket team were Mark Atherton, an aspiring pianist, Theo Manners also known as Tip, Noel Telling, Slim Marston, and Vince Winterton. Mark's father was the local doctor. Mark himself was tall, courteous and encouraging to others, and possessed of a broad forehead that hinted at intellect rather than a passion for games. He was fine in his way but I recognised he and I had little in common. Theo was totally different. The son of a successful timber merchant in Uttoxeter, he was compact and well-proportioned, wore his hair short and neat and had lively brown eyes. Ever alert, he displayed a sense of mischief, was his own man and in thrall to no one. Noel's father possessed the Rolls Royce agency in Sheffield, Derby, Chesterfield and Stoke on Trent. When Noel's parents arrived to take him and his pal Theo out – it was only in my last term that I was similarly favoured – we all clustered round to admire their glistening limousine. Noel enjoyed this but was no show-off and never bragged. Well built, blue-eyed, ebullient and masterful, he was "all boy". Slim had freckles. Not slim in any way at all, he was tubby and cheerful rather than an athlete. If he did have a christian name which I suppose he did, he was never called by it. Rather later I found out it was Albert. No wonder he did not like it! Anyhow to us Slim he was and Slim he remained. His father ran milk bars and ice-cream parlours in Sheffield so successfully that he had diversified into a handful of pubs aimed at satisfying thirsty steelworkers. He kept a wad of pound notes in a gold clip from which once a term he would endow the tuck shop with sufficient cash to ensure we all could enjoy free ice cream for a week. When I found myself in the company of Harry and Jeremy more often than with

Bart, I could not help noticing Slim had taken my place. The tallest of our team was Vince, aquiline, a loner and a shade aloof. His father was the deputy Chief of Police in, I think, either Yorkshire or Leicestershire.

I did not have much to do with any of these except, in due course, Noel. He sat next to me in form. Bright as a button, he was a tough little blighter ever ready with his hands. A year earlier he had terrified me when I must have been something of a wimp. He would sometimes remind me of my reluctance to sip my own piss and taunt me as a cissy, and in leisure periods if he was in threatening mood I would hide in the loo. In time he became my most avid competitor at sprinting. It was then that Gaffer must have spotted our uneasy relationship. Cleverly he arranged for us to be paired in the three-legged race on Sports Day when everyone's parents were present. So instead of sparring we absolutely had to combine as a partnership. Determined to win, we practised like mad and even when falling over did not blame each other but worked patiently to recover our rhythm. This forced harness together with our joint will to succeed worked like a charm. For we won in fine style. Thereafter, on gaining mutual respect we never looked back. As for that tendency to bully, he overcame it. Indeed, as the years rolled by he was to prove the most loyal of friends. In due course I was to owe him a lot. Actually more than I can say.

In the third week of that summer term in '47, on one particular day when Gaffer took our regular Morning Prayers he looked unduly solemn. He announced we would only sing the first and last verses of our hymn. Then he addressed us all in quiet tones.

'You may know that yesterday afternoon Theo Manners was driven home. The reason is a tragedy has befallen his family. Yesterday morning his father was killed in an accident at their timber mill. Theo will be away for some days to be with his mother and two young sisters and to attend the funeral. Theo will be returning to school as soon as he is ready to do so. When he does I want you all to be very understanding. Those who know him well, please show your sympathy. But to all of you I say welcome him back and offer every kind of support you can. Make sure he is left out of nothing and is made to feel part of our family. He will need kindness and consideration. That is all I have to say for now. Thank you for listening.'

Prayers were then said for the Manners family and for all in grief at the loss of any relative or friend. Next to me was Noel. He was clearly moved. A tear or two trickled down from his right eye which he dabbed surreptitiously. I felt greatly saddened too even though I did not count Theo as a particular friend since we were in different forms. However he was a sort of pal and a member of our cricket team, who at number two opened the batting with Mark. A little fellow possessing agility and a good eye, he stood next to me when fielding in the slips. Moreover, he was a spry batsman who earned the nickname Tip for his artful play and adventurous spirit in sprinting for single runs. Initially, when he was out of hearing he was referred to as Tip and Run. But in due course we did not bother. Tip and Run he became.

In contrast Mark was steady and a bit dour, understanding well that his job was to stay in as long as possible and be a thorn in the flesh of the opposition whilst the more gifted players swung their bat cheerfully and went for runs.

Jeremy looked the part as captain, being slim, graceful and well-mannered. A natural leader, he possessed a gift for placing his field tactically. Our most cunning spin bowler, he was also our star bat. Choosing to go in first wicket down at number three, he was the personification of patience and elegance for he could time the ball with stylish sweeps to the boundary. That summer he averaged fifty six so beating the school record by eight runs. Harry, chunkier than his friend Jeremy, at number four whacked the ball strenuously and when his eye was in could score thirty with ease. Although inclined to be wayward, he was perhaps our most flamboyant fast bowler. The lissom Claude, blonde and tall, was a dashing batsman who went in fifth. Like Mark a left hander, Owen at number six was plodding and careful. Difficult to dislodge, he blocked the ball and infuriated adversaries in much the same way as that famous cricketer Trevor Bailey must have done. His task was to mirror Mark always assuming Mark had performed as required. Noel was formidable at number seven and a talented if overbold player to have at such a crucial position. He opened the bowling along with Harry and was that little bit more reliable. Frankly there was not much that Noel did not do well. I went in at eight where my own contribution was pretty minor for I averaged only seven runs. As a slow spin bowler I was put on late by which time the star opposition was generally back in the pavilion. My forte if there was one at all was as a slips fielder. I was reasonably quick to react and safe with my hands. So at the end of the season I came out equal top with Theo for the number of catches. The last three places were taken by Bart, Slim – an efficient fielder at square leg – and the lanky Vince, nicknamed Spider Man. He patrolled the boundary with uncanny understanding and would pounce on the ball like a terrier to thwart a four.

That summer we won all our ten matches. A belief in one another led to loyalty and trust and enigmatic bonds of affection. It was as if a gossamer filament had become unsnappable. While revelling in being a team, our behaviour was almost too supportive for if a boundary was scored we applauded noisily. Justifiably we were cautioned on occasion not to be so boisterous. Rightly this was considered bad manners and overbearing. More to the point, we were taught to exercise grace and humility in winning. 'After all,' said Gaffer, 'pride comes before a fall.' And he backed this up with a quotation from Thomas Gray:

"How vain the ardour of the crowd; how low, how little are the proud."

It was a useful lesson to learn. For while one admires a winner, conceit and a lack of consideration for others jolly well deserves to be frowned upon.

The one match that so nearly went wrong was at the end of June against our old rivals from Monksbury. They were all out for 129. This set us a difficult target although not one that was insurmountable. However at the outset things went awry. Mark was out lbw for 3. More happily Theo was joined by Jeremy who gave a fluent display in quickly attaining 20. Then Theo was dismissed for 17 with a smart catch at gully which even he would have admired had he not been the batsman. Harry at number four was clean bowled first ball. He was furious. This had never happened before. Over confident, he took his eye off the ball. Claude was doing fine and knocked up a sprightly 18 before being caught on the boundary when he gave a "sitter" to the outlying fielder. Owen at six looked set for his usual dour stay but then when on 9 unaccountably hit his wicket. By now Jeremy had notched up 36 and there were six extras. So the score had got to 89. Noel who was our last batsman of any real talent now joined him. With 41 to win we were on tenterhooks that this well practised partnership would continue to function as it had all summer. The omens were good. Soon Noel had scored 10. By now Jeremy was on 42 and as he drove the ball to the boundary Noel seized the initiative and called for a second run. Jeremy was not so sure on spotting a fielder ready to swoop. He hesitated a moment. Noel insisted. Alas, the throw in at Jeremy's end was both fast and accurate. The ball catapulted into the stumps leaving the wicketkeeper a spectator.

Jeremy our star bat was out for 43. Noel had been complicit in being over ebullient. With extras now at 8 our score had achieved 108. That meant we had a further 22 to win. I was nervous. Batting was not my strength and I knew that Bart, Slim and Vince were equally frail too. With time for four more overs I parried the ball and prodded, doing my best to ensure that Noel faced the bowling. Then I was out lbw for 4. Next, Bart went for a duck on his third ball. Disaster threatened. Even though Noel had advanced from 10 to 16 we were still short of victory. We needed a further 12. Now Slim was to steady the ship. He stood there and blocked. Without scoring a new over began. With only two overs to go Noel faced the bowling. Frankly it was all up to him for Vince was unreliable with the bat. Noel simply had to stay in and win the necessary runs. A fine drive to leg saw 2. Then he lashed at a wild ball and in finding a gap in the field got a 4. Six more runs to win. Next he obtained a single. But on the over changing, at the start of the last he was not facing the bowler. Slim was. He did his best not to look flustered. A fast ball whizzed past him untouched. Then quite fortuitously Slim snicked the ball to fine leg just out of reach of the Monksbury wicketkeeper. That left four more runs to win with four balls remaining. Noel was seething with concentration. He was determined to make good after his rash call that had precipitated the dismissal of Jeremy. He played the first delivery carefully back to the bowler. As he did with the next. Two balls to go. And Noel needed a boundary if victory was to be claimed. The bowler tried a googly. Noel saw it coming and watched the ball onto his bat. Swinging this with venom the ball shot along the ground to an unguarded section of the boundary for 4. To a great shout from the onlookers Heathside had gained a glorious triumph in the nick of time by a single run.

The following Saturday those of us who had attended dancing sessions with the girls from St Benedict's were invited over for their School Dance. All of us in the cricket team were included. Jeremy, almost inevitably, was our star dancer along with Noel, Harry and Claude. Not surprisingly these four attracted the prettiest of the girls. Regardless, I fancied Diana. She was a brunette and had a Spanish look about her. Her principal attraction apart from a winning smile was her sense of humour.

When the chunky Harry cheekily suggested to the Headmistress that despite never having practised it we should have a go at the tango, Miss Dussek answered primly, 'I rather think not.' Diana whispered in my ear, 'she would not approve of dancing belly to belly.'

I laughed and when the time came for another foxtrot gathered up courage to hold her close while we sauntered round the floor with me just about avoiding two left feet and treading on Diana's toes. As I gained confidence I remarked how happy I was that she was my partner. When she smiled coquettishly I blushed on knowing I was now pressing against her.

Endeavouring to act more manly than my twelve years, I said, 'are you as happy as I am?'

'Yes indeed,' she replied sweetly, 'but I am not sure I should be feeling your feeling.'

Aware that she had sensed my erection and now confused, with a red face I stepped back.

The day after the dance there was no disguising that many of us were elated. Buoyed with enthusiasm, we accomplished the two and a half mile crocodile walk to Matins at church in Doveridge in record time. Harry and Slim were in jubilant form and clamoured that we might all go down to the river to fill in the fifteen minutes before the service began. Recognising that he had the opportunity for a drag on a cigarette Woodbine was agreeable to this. So we filed down the narrow path behind the churchyard to the elegant suspension footbridge bearing a plaque stating it had been built in 1839. This was the gateway to a winding path meandering through water meadows festooned with buttercups and leading on to the pleasant red brick market town of Uttoxeter two miles distant. It was popular with walkers who would tip-toe daintily across, conscious of the bridge's antiquity. Typical would be a village retiree with faithful dog in tow, intent on downing a pint or two in one of the many pubs in town. On the way he would greet an occasional townsman doing the same thing in reverse to visit one of Doveridge's three village inns and doubtless sample the beer from the cottage brewery.

That day Harry and Slim chose to play a game of Poohsticks. I was close by with around a dozen others. Monopolising the bridge we watched this spectacle for four sessions by which time the score was 2-2. Stamping out his cigarette, the incorrigible Woodbine then announced it was time to leave. 'One more time,' yelled Slim as he and Harry threw down their last stick and we dashed from one side to the other. No tip-toeing here! At that very moment there was a deafening crack as the century old Victorian bridge snapped asunder and the whole school was plunged into the river Dove. For some reason I found myself with water up to my knees. But I was unhurt and looked around wondering whether after all we would be attending church in the hope that we would not be. Most of us were standing up too but those who had lost their footing were struggling. Jeremy was the first to assist aided by Claude. Mercifully there were no fatalities. Had this occurred a week later when the river was in spate, the outcome might have been something else. As it was, the local farmer's wife heard the crash. Along with her strong young son she came running over. Finding the slight Tip and Owen thoroughly breathless, bruised, and bewildered in trying to escape the river on the far bank, they carted them off to the farm where both were regaled with tea which the farmer's wife laced with rum. Once they had recovered from their ordeal, her husband drove the two of them back to school in his Hillman. When the rest of us knew of this, were we envious!

With Gaffer and Kathleen arriving in their Vauxhall Wyvern just before the service was due, they were horrified to witness Woodbine taking charge of fifty or more thoroughly wet and bedraggled boys. Three of the smallest were bundled into the Vauxhall before Woodbine marshalled the rest of us into four sections and marched us home. Once back at school we were directed to the kitchen where hot drinks were forthcoming. Doris, my favourite among the kitchen staff, listened attentively as I breathlessly recounted the adventure.

'Well, I never,' she replied once she was finally able to get a word in, 'when I was at school if anyone even went near that bridge we were given the leather. It was out of bounds, it was considered so fragile. You could all have drowned. You don't know how lucky you are.'

Next week we had Sports Day. Claude, both an agile runner and jumper, was awarded the 'Victor Ludorum'. For the second year in a row Father made me proud in winning the Egg and Spoon race for the Mums and Dads. Equally happily, Noel and I teamed up again and carried off the prize for the three-legged race. Once adversaries, we were now pals.

That summer the sunshine continued unabated. One afternoon in a friendly cricket match at home, Noel and I hid in a cherry tree and guzzled cherries while gazing at the pony in the adjoining field in amazement at his coltish behaviour and the length of his member. For some strange reason this was evident without any sign of provocation. We giggled and were awed. We beat our closest rivals by five wickets. Life was good. But change was on the way.

A month later and four days before the end of term I was called unexpectedly to the Headmaster's study. He sat me down and said, 'Nigel, I am sorry to say I have bad news for you. You must be brave for it is hard to bear.'

My mind was in a whirl. What could have happened? Had our house been bombed?

He continued. 'Yesterday evening in the rush hour there was a train accident at St John's on the line from London's Charing Cross to Chislehurst. Your father was on that train. Seventeen people died and I am afraid that your father was one.'

I was appalled and burst into floods of tears.

The Head held my hand. 'It is terrible, I know. But it happened all so quickly he will not have known anything about it. He died outright. He will not have suffered.'

How he would have known I have no idea. Perhaps he made that up to soften the blow. He went on, 'your mother and Aunt Sibyl will be here tomorrow to take you home so that you can be present at his funeral. I am sure you will want this.'

I was inconsolable. Tea was brought with two lumps of sugar and two Marie biscuits. I could not eat them but managed half a cup of the tea.

'I have made a bed up for you in our rooms,' Gaffer said. 'Go and rest there. Here now is a small pill. It will help you sleep.' And with that he escorted me to his private apartment.

Next day Mother and Aunt Sibyl duly arrived. Nurse Ethel had packed my case and gathered together all my things. I was not up to saying goodbye to my friends. But to my surprise, one by one each of them came to me to say their farewells. Fortunately each was brief.

Tip was particularly touching. Putting his hand in mine, he looked me straight in the eyes and spoke feelingly and softly. 'I am so very sorry. I have always liked you. Now we share something we both wish we didn't. I am going to miss you as my partner in the slips. But one day I have a feeling we will meet again. Until then… good-bye.'

While my eyes watered and my lips puckered, Tip kept his cool. He had put the matter into perspective, I suppose. After all, that summer we had both made thirteen catches.

The other members of our side were equally kind. What none of them then knew any more than I did was that this would be the last time I would see any of them for many years to come. Barely conscious of the yawning gap ahead, I was whisked away the very day before the cricket team was to celebrate its vintage season. As I was stepping into the car to join Mother and Aunt Sibyl, it was then that Giuseppe appeared unexpectedly to thrust his silver cross into my hand. This kindliness made me even sadder and throughout the journey home I was utterly bereft, weeping for the most part silently. That celebration was to have been the crowning point of a glorious summer term. And now I was deprived of it.

Although Father was covered by a Top Hat insurance policy this turned out to be tiny. Mother felt she had no option but to sell up our pleasant mock Tudor house in the Camden Park Road and move to a small terraced property in nearby Lower Camden. This nestled below the tall embankment supporting the main line from Charing Cross to Hastings. At least Mother would be able to go to the same church and continue as a newly joined member of the Golf Club. To help make ends meet she became a librarian in the village at what we called the Free Library.

My life changed irredeemably. I was never to return to Heathside. There simply was not the money to do so. The fees would have been beyond her means. Next term I was sent to the local grammar school. Boarding school education was at an end. I had to start anew and grow up faster than perhaps I would have otherwise. First thing in the mornings I became a paper boy working the seventy-five minute run of Lower Camden and Lubbock Road. Childhood was over. With boyhood half-way through, I sensed that the amazing esprit de corps of our cricket team would never be repeated. I was now on my own. Ahead the outlook appeared bleak.

CHAPTER 2: TEENAGE YEARS

The move to Lower Camden did not prove unduly traumatic. The noise from the trains was nothing like as feared. Certainly the garden lost the sun in the latter part of the day, especially in autumn and winter. But then we were not likely to be out there. As for getting to school, I chose to cycle rather than spend money unnecessarily on the bus. In any case this would have required a fifteen minute walk to and from the bus stop morning and evening. Instead, pedalling up the hill on our old road was less daunting even though it was unadopted so prone to potholes. But, what the hell, I soon became used to it.

Those initial golf lessons from Gabbitas stood me in good stead. Mother I both joined the local Golf Club. Here I made friends with the bunch of lads who were also newly taking up the game. Although I was not the best of them I could hold my own. My handicap came down to six and in the summer of 1952 I travelled by train to Formby in Lancashire for a few days practice before playing in the British Boys Championship. That first morning, on scanning the draw-sheet for the knockout competition due to commence the following Monday I saw the names of Broughton and Fairest. They must be Jeremy and Harry I thought since the initials tallied. Sure enough on the second day I spotted them on an adjoining fairway. Summoning up the courage to say Hello I went across.

'Nigel,' they both chorused, 'after you have finished come over for a bite.' Harry added, 'the Lancashire hotpot is unbelievably tasty.' Jeremy smiled, 'and make sure you do too. Don't miss out. In any case there is such a lot we must catch up on.'

Indeed there was. Jeremy had enjoyed public school at Repton, become deputy head and was captain of cricket. He remained as likeable as he ever was and had become even better looking. His golf had gone from strength to strength and his handicap was now three. According to Harry he had caught the eye of the selectors so was in the running to play for England against Scotland in the forthcoming international later in the week. Harry could give him a game but was not quite as good. However both had overtaken me in proficiency. Harry had been at Repton as well and like Jeremy was a school prefect. Playing off five, he thought this was just too high to warrant selection unless he performed wonders in the trials the next day. Still curly headed, he enjoyed a sunny countenance, had a sense of fun and appeared happy to be Jeremy's right hand man which I rather think he probably always had been.

'Nigel,' said Jeremy, 'you must enter the trials too. And if you do I shall ask the chief selector old Larry Henderson if you may play with us in a threeball.'

Jeremy was as good as his word and I was in his three the next morning. No matter that I came third. My score was still respectable at just under 80. More importantly, Jeremy scored a 73 and was selected, while Harry off 76 was invited to be a reserve.

I was simply delighted to be at Formby and in finding my two former companions were so little changed and so welcoming. Coming down to earth I lost heavily in the first round to a scratch player who went on to be captain of golf at Oxford. A curious incident happened at the first hole when I sliced onto the railway line just moments before a single carriage train for Liverpool approached from Southport. It would be unthinkable today but the driver then stopped, descended onto the tracks, lifted up my brand new ball and popped it into his pocket. I was beside myself with dismay for naively I was full of hope he would throw it back.

Harry got through to the third round but then crashed out to an American. Jeremy, though, reached the semifinal only to be edged out of it at the 19th by his opponent sinking a chip for a birdie. Faced with an awkward putt of seven yards for the half, as his caddie I studied the line with him. We both agreed that despite a double break it appeared left lip. He struck it well. It dipped to the right, swung back and kissed the left edge before slewing off and stopping six inches to the right. Gracefully he doffed his cap and shook hands with the friendliest of smiles as if it was the last thing that mattered regardless of how he must have actually felt. The crowd applauded warmly. Pat Ward Thomas, the golf correspondent for the Manchester Guardian and Country Life and the most lyrical writer on golf since Bernard Darwin, was even heard to murmur that was the best putt he had ever seen not to go in. And from such an illustrious authority there could be no higher praise than that.

The week soon passed. With schooldays now at an end for Jeremy and Harry, both had been accepted for voluntary service in Borneo and Sarawak before enlisting in National Service due in September 1953, the very time that I too expected to join up. As they were kindly seeing me off at the station for the journey home, we exchanged phone numbers and addresses. While it had been a great few days I was a little wistful on wondering if and when we might ever meet again. One just could not tell.

Then quite unexpectedly two weeks later Jeremy telephoned me.

'Nigel, this may interest you. Do you remember my father worked for the Earl of Ruabon as his land agent? Well, he still does.'

He continued. 'In his younger days Ruabon was an officer in the Welsh Guards. He has long retained some connection with his regiment and is extremely keen to see the armed forces recruit efficiently "with round pegs in round holes". He and two of his cronies in the House of Lords, Lord Ipswich and the Earl of Kendal, have managed to catch the ear of the Chief of Staff. They suggested that, as the September intake for National Service is likely to contain recent as well as future university students, a special system that month should be tried out.

'It is too late to introduce this in the current year but apparently it is going to happen next year. That September intake will commence their basic training at Catterick without having been appointed to a regiment or corps, or whatever. For eight weeks they will be in a pool supervised by top Guards trained NCOs from Caterham. Then each recruit will have the opportunity to apply for whatever unit he wishes. After a further four weeks everyone will be told where they are going. The theory is that the talents of each person will be used to the best effect. Look, Harry and I have an idea. Let all of us from Heathside's cricket team of '47 do whatever is necessary to ensure we aim to arrive at Catterick in that first week of September. Or as near as possible to it. After all, we all got along famously. So it would be fun to see whether this bond still holds good. Give it a try, Nigel.'

We chatted on for a few minutes. Jeremy was preparing himself for Voluntary Service Overseas, purchasing appropriate clothing and even learning a couple of dozen words of the local dialect. I wished Harry and him well and made a note to follow up his suggestion next Easter with the Army Recruitment Board but doubting that it would make the slightest bit of difference to me as a grammar school boy. Remember, what would be would be.

The following July I duly received my call up papers. These stated I should report to Catterick in the first week of September. Having been accepted that May for university in October 1955, I recalled the conversation with

Jeremy. Momentarily I pondered whether I was to be one of the experimental squad but I had no idea. As far as I was knew the matter was in the lap of the gods. When the day dawned that I reached Catterick as a raw recruit, I was allotted Barrack Room 14 in 7 Training Regiment. Wondering if I would recognise anyone there, I did not have to wait long on. For in came Owen. Choosing the bed opposite me he rubbed his glasses before turning round to say, 'my goodness, you must be Nigel Collyer?'

He was quickly followed by Bart Warner who immediately plonked himself down next to Owen. He had developed into a raffish character. No longer the least bit gauche, he was well-groomed, full of confidence, physically mature and worldly. Innocence lay in the past.

'Bart, you will never guess who is opposite,' ribbed Owen. 'It is your old friend from Barley Farm and Heathside days, Nigel Collyer.'

Bart looked utterly astonished before allowing himself a 'Well, I'll be damned if you are not totally right.' And with no hesitation he came over to give me the warmest of handshakes and a hearty clap on the shoulder.

A few minutes later Noel Telling came in. Well-muscled, with clear eyes and a firm jaw, he was lean and handsome in a masculine way. He had matured but was still the same Noel. The bed next to me was vacant so I piped up, 'you must be Noel Telling. This bed is free.'

He looked me in the eye and gently smiling answered, 'My goodness, I'd know that voice anywhere. You have to be the same Nigel you were that summer when we guzzled cherries.'

As I nodded, Owen looked up and said to us both, 'you know I think we are all here on the advice of Jeremy Broughton. He must be around somewhere too.'

Next to appear was Theo Manners, taking the vacant position the other side of Noel. Still the cheeky chappie with no airs and graces, very much "his own man", he remained boyish. Exuding good humour he welcomed me as his partner of old when we both made thirteen catches in the slips. I recalled his surmise that one day we would meet again. How right he was.

'Fantastic,' said Noel, 'five of us here from that team of '47.'

The following day in the canteen we spotted Jeremy, Harry, Mark, and Claude. They had all arrived in the intake a fortnight ahead of us.

'Happy days,' said Noel, 'you lot can show us the ropes. We only seem to be missing Slim and Vince.'

'Spider Man Vince is on the course two weeks ahead of us,' offered Claude with a cheery confidence, 'but he seems a bit distant and condescending so not as amused to see us as we were to see him. As for Slim, expect to see him in a couple of weeks. And of course not slim at all judging by his picture in the paper after being caught in a raid on a Sheffield nightclub.'

'Trust Claude to know all the gossip,' said Jeremy adding with a grin, 'by the way did you make money at the dogs the other day when you were Bart's guest? Not a sport I go for.'

Claude thought of ignoring him before gesticulating. 'Some,' he acknowledged, leaving the question entirely open as to how much he had lost too.

A day later all the inmates from our barrack room were detailed to visit the medical hut in order to receive the required injections. Shouting out names from a roster when it was our turn to be called was a lance-corporal. Tall, spotty and clearly bored, to amuse himself and us too I suppose, he contrived to get everyone's names wrong. As was to be expected I was "Cauliflower". Gifford was "Get Off". Manners stumped him until he dreamt up "Menswear". Almost as imaginatively, to a repressed giggle Telling was "Thrilling".

'Guess what he is going to call you,' said Noel to Bart. 'It won't be Warner, that's for sure.'

Bart gave him an old-fashioned look. 'Maybe not what you think. Try Winner.'

'Winner winner, chicken dinner,' needled Noel. Then conscious he would have the last word he added, 'I rather think not'.

No prizes for guessing who was correct. Noel of course. For when the name Warner came to be bastardized we all cheered. No need to say anything further. But in racing terms that had been an absolute banker.

With Slim duly arriving two weeks later, within the week contact was made. Slim had indeed matured, was full of chatter and bluster and ready to dispense swear words in the manner of a trooper. But like Bart he was approachable and friendly enough.

At week four we all got together at Sandes' Soldiers Home for a Saturday night out. Even Vince joined us. Not that he ever showed up again. The object was to drink a few beers and relax in watching the TV show of "What's My Line?" – a game designed to entertain the family whereby a contestant mimed what he did for an occupation and the panel had to work out what that was. The stars were the irascible Gilbert Harding, the fascinating Barbara Kelly, the equally charismatic Lady Isobel Barnett and the personable Bernard Braden.

More particularly, our aim was to reminisce in catching up on what each of us had been up to in the previous five years after saying goodbye to Heathside. In my case of course the gap was six years. Apart from Jeremy and Harry I really had no notion how the others had fared.

Only two of us had gone on to the same school, namely Jeremy and Harry at Repton. Harry, never one to hold back, explained Jeremy's prowess and that he had been captain of cricket, while Jeremy told how the exuberant Harry had excelled at scoring boundaries. Claude had been to Rossall. For three years he had kept wicket for the school and in his last year was captain. He seemed unfazed and still retained the languid casualness he had displayed at Heathside. Moreover, he gave the impression that life should not be taken too seriously.

Noel had gone to Rugby and won his colours as an English schoolboy international at rugby. He had also been captain of boxing and of fencing. Indeed, he looked the part of a fine athlete being fresh-faced and clearly as fit as a fiddle. Blessed with manly good looks he rivalled Jeremy if not quite measuring up to his elegance or his height.

As for Mark, who I had never really known well, he had gone to St Peter's York and been head boy. Apparently his cricket had not progressed but he had developed into a good pianist and music was now his principal relaxation along with tennis. With his broad forehead, he looked even more intelligent than ever while retaining his modesty and thoughtfulness for others. I sensed he was destined for an academic career and with his obvious kindness and consideration would do well.

Vince had been to Bedford and with his long legs and light frame developed into a cross-country runner. He claimed to have once beaten Bruce Tulloh at the Hayes Meeting. Bruce, as is well known, later became famous as a bare-foot long distance runner, the idol of the popular press, and was a household name before Sebastian Coe came on the scene. I was also one of three hundred schoolboys competing in the Hayes Meeting but that day did not come across either.

Theo went to the Leys near Cambridge. Remaining small and well-coordinated, he claimed his ambition always was to work with horses. Since the age of fifteen he had wanted to be a jockey and in his last two summer holidays had obtained early morning ride-out experience with one of Newmarket's lesser trainers. Clearly he was dedicated. He had also distinguished himself with the local Newmarket cricket team, both with his batting and his singing in the bath tub afterwards. A well balanced chap I thought and thoroughly nice too, a real character who had overcome the loss of his Dad. In a phrase, he was a "one-off".

Owen had been to a staunch Methodist school at Matlock where he studied Latin and Greek. His eyesight was still causing problems. Notwithstanding, his passion had become gardening where his Latin would come in useful in understanding the background of plants. He was no longer slight for he had filled out and was taut. Were he not to be wearing glasses he would have looked, if not exactly brawny, almost athletic. Somehow I doubted he would want the tedium and hassle of taking over his father's department stores and would not feel happy as a company man. Modest he might be but also scholarly and ambitious.

Bart had left Heathside to go to Lowestoft. Only after drinking four pints would he divulge what had happened. Then without self-pity or revulsion he was forthright. Once a shy boy now he was a hi-de-hi boy. Words escaped his lips in a torrent as if pursued by a demon.

'A year ago the school was closed down by the authorities due to a scandal over the behaviour of two of the priests, Father Denis and Father Myron. Both were housemasters. In our first year, and when barely fourteen, each newcomer to his house was initiated by them into unseemly acts. But not until a rehearsal had first taken place in the house prefects' club room. I succumbed to this with dread but damn well pocketed the florin that was offered afterwards.'

'Would these shenanigans have made a sailor blush?' enquired Claude teasingly.

'Probably most sailors, Claude. Let me tell you the head of our house, Howe, sought out one of us juniors once or twice a week on the excuse that practice makes perfect. The youngster had to adhere to a set pattern known as the Brown Cow formula which went like this.

"How Howe?"

Then after the explanation the junior had to ask, "Now Howe?"

"Yes indeed."

Then as matters progressed the junior would say "Howe Now", to which Howe would respond "Brown Cow" as the ordeal was concluded.'

Eyebrows were raised and glasses readily topped up before Bart insisted on continuing.

'A right bastard he was too and within the year he was had up for shoplifting.'
'Where?' asked Claude feigning interest.
'In Lowestoft's Woolworths.'
'Poor taste,' drawled Claude to a mild guffaw from his fellow listeners.
'Exactly.'
'He should have tried Austin Reed or Aquascutum.'
'Nice idea, Claude, but there was not one of either. Just a family draper's run by a beady-eyed man called Harris,' intoned Bart before continuing. 'As you can well imagine our house had become a den of iniquity. But then so had the whole school. At sixteen and anxious to forget, I sought solace in a shop girl who worked at the bakery in our village. She is now expecting a child though whether I am the father I would not know. At any rate Father is bailing out the girl's parents. Lowestoft was such a downright fucking disaster that in my last year I went to a "crammer". Had I stayed on I bloody well would not have followed the example set by Howe. Quite frankly I am now praying for an overseas posting. The last thing I want is to be part and parcel of the carry-on that is sure to take place at home.'
Slim too had an unhappy tale to tell. His school had a drug problem. He had been caught up in this and was one of five who were expelled. This had been reported in the national newspapers although the names of the culprits were withheld. It did the school no good at all. It was not closed down like Lowestoft but the governors replaced the headmaster with a stalwart figure who had once been a famous rugby player for Scotland. Slim, too, had gone on to a "crammer" and had passed the necessary 'A' levels. But life was not the same, with his workaholic down to earth father distinctly unamused.
Recognising that our time together at Catterick would be all too short, Jeremy had exercised his initiative to ascertain from our officer in charge that within a few months many postings in Kenya would be up for grabs. The Mau Mau terrorist attacks were increasing and the Government was determined to stamp these out. So after we had completed our initial eight weeks basic training, Jeremy suggested that if any of us wanted to keep in touch this might best be achieved if we applied for a position in Kenya, no matter for which branch of the military we were selected.
Vince made it clear that the past was indeed the past and as far as he was concerned that was where it should remain. Without actually saying as much

he saw little to be gained by linking up with chaps to whom he had said good-bye several years earlier. As it transpired he was the first to complete his training and surprise, surprise, enlisted with the Royal Military Police who accepted him gladly in the knowledge that his father was such a very senior police officer. I never knew if he chose to go to Kenya. But that is where he was posted.

Jeremy, Harry and Claude all joined the infantry in the full knowledge that their forthcoming assignment was indeed to go to Kenya. Noel chose the Royal Engineers and was seconded to the Kings Own Yorkshire Light Infantry, also in Kenya. Slim went for the Catering Corps. However he was posted to Cyprus. Bart volunteered for the infantry and somehow wangled himself into the Kenya Regiment. I joined the Royal Signals and was invited to choose where in the world I wanted to go. I was neither a natural soldier nor even a signalman. But after partnering our Colonel at golf in a match against the Royal Army Ordnance Corp at Sunningdale and holing the winning putt – a tricky one with a left-hand borrow of five feet – he overlooked my deficiencies and granted my request. So Kenya it was.

Theo adopted a different approach. Appreciating that the pay of a subaltern was less than that of a corporal, he chose to go through the ranks. As he already knew what he wanted to do in life, if convention beckoned another course he did not feel bound to follow. In fact his fate was to be Kenya too. What none of us knew was that for some of us life would soon change considerably. One thing was certain. We would all mature.

CHAPTER 3: NATIONAL SERVICE

In some ways Theo had the last laugh. Outpointing his peers with ease for he was as bright as he was sunny, he was promoted to Sergeant in the Royal Army Transport Corps where his pay was vastly greater than what it would have been had he been commissioned. I was delighted when I found that like me he was stationed in Nairobi's Buller Camp. I ran across him not infrequently when out on manoeuvres and, again, when we junior officers were invited into the Sergeants Mess where these wily men did their level best to get us drunk. Theo was foremost in exercising the art of persuasion and joining in the fun. As for Owen, he was accepted by the Royal Army Educational Corps where he too was posted to Kenya based at our Mess. Along with Slim, the other odd man out was Mark. He was sent to West Africa. So for some years I did not see him.

I suppose the only fly in the ointment was Vince. Although he was member of the Buller Camp Mess he chose not to be that sociable. Not exactly unfriendly, he was just distant. As a military policeman and now six foot three, he considered himself apart from the rest of us and spent as much time as he could, squeezed into his red Bond mini-car, cruising around the less salubrious sectors of the city. His purpose was to apprehend soldiers who misbehaved and frequented clubs that were strictly out of bounds to them. Spider Man seemed to be in his element and I wondered if he intended to make a career of the army.

Jeremy, Harry and Claude were all serving upcountry in the Aberdares. Jeremy was with the Duke of Wellington's as was Claude. Harry, no longer Jeremy's sidekick, was with the Kings Own Yorkshire Light Infantry along with Noel, now their junior resident engineer. How Bart got into Bart the Kenya Regiment I never found out. But he appeared to have a roving commission. Sometimes he was upcountry; at others he toured the Kikuyu homelands between Nairobi and the Rift Valley so was seldom far away. I longed to be upcountry too but the one position for a young Signals National Service officer with the King's African Rifles had been taken by a fellow who had arrived in Kenya a month ahead of me. However, being in Nairobi meant I was able to maintain contact with all five old Heathside boys when from time to time each descended on Buller Camp for a long weekend as respite from the forest.

It was on one of these occasions when Jeremy was with me and we had fought ourselves into exhaustion over a game of squash that we hatched a plan. This was to aim for a few days leave on the coast with the other ex-Heathside boys. As our squadron had a small Royal Signals detachment in Mombasa this would provide an excuse for me to visit and then sneak off for a few days leave. Jeremy agreed to be in touch with Harry, Noel and Claude to coordinate the dates. I said I would try to persuade Theo and Bart to come along too but I was not going to bother with Vince for I knew he would want nothing to do with this. Instead I told Jeremy he seemed determined to be dead set on achieving a medal of some sort, probably for devotion to duty and instilling discipline in the miscreants who were tempted to visit the city's nightclubs that were off limits. Justifying his conduct he professed that he was trying to prevent active soldiers from acquiring venereal disease and reporting sick. I did invite Owen but I suspected rightly he was up to his neck in running a series of courses for the African askaris. So, much as he would have liked to join in, he could not get away. Once Owen decided to do something, or in this case had to, he was totally dedicated.

However, when I approached Theo he was all for it. With the agreement of my commanding officer I fixed for him to come to Mombasa and instruct our detachment in the art of vehicle maintenance. This would be valuable as we had a small fleet of ancient Land Rovers which were virtually all clapped out. He would then stay on when we were to fly to Zanzibar – Jeremy's idea – and take a boat to Pen Island. Word from upcountry was that the local girls were more than hospitable. Moreover, they were said to fancy the British soldiery.

While Bart made his own way to Mombasa, the four from the Aberdares motored to Nairobi from where they took the overnight train. This ran through a spectacular game park where giraffe, wildebeest, gazelle and zebra roamed seemingly free from concern. These were thoroughly used to the train. Only young gazelle took fright and scampered away to what they considered a safe distance. I met Jeremy, Harry, Noel and Claude at Mombasa station and whisked them straight off to Nyali Beach Camp where we were joined by little Theo and Bart. We swam, played football and quoits, and linked up with Derek Mulholland who was the officer in charge of the Forces Radio in Kenya.

He interviewed them and recorded their comments. Jeremy in particular was eloquent. But then so was Harry. Neither Noel nor Claude seemed that concerned. They were there on holiday and jabbering into a microphone was not their idea of fun right then. I knew Derek slightly for I was once on a quiz show where I failed lamentably. On one particular subject I could only answer one of three questions and even then I got this wrong. I felt foolish. But what really rankled was that the padre against whom I was pitted had three questions to all of which I knew the answer. Fortunately not many heard this disastrous programme. At least if they did, no one tackled me later on my abject performance. However Derek must have remembered for tactfully he did not bother to interview me. I was not put out. In any case he was charm itself and dispensed cold lagers from an enormous ice box. He and his wife Melissa will have frequented Nyali often for both were exotically sun tanned, almost dangerously so. If ever anyone had a cushy job it was Derek.

That evening I introduced our intrepid six to the Nelson restaurant in town where we dined on lobster thermidor and supped white wine. As we were leaving Jeremy received a signal on his radio. He learned the unwelcome news that he was to double back to base early next day. A massive exercise against the Mau Mau was imminent and a fellow officer had been shot and severely wounded. So Jeremy was required to take over his duties. A plane would collect him next morning at 1100 hours and fly him to Nanyuki. It was tough luck. We had the best breakfast that our detachment could rustle up before driving off to the airport. There we said our goodbyes, mindful that Jeremy who had organised the whole trip was now denied the fun of being with us. Stoically he awaited the arrival of his flight while the rest of us embarked for Zanzibar. With our carefully contrived plan thwarted, we were now down to six.

The idea was to spend one day in Zanzibar staying in Stone House. We toured the island, saw clove plantations aplenty imparting their strong aroma, and in the evening witnessed the Sultan being chauffeur driven in his highly polished scarlet custom-made Austin limousine. This was his regular routine when gravely he waved to his people. Sporting a turban and a trim silver grey beard he looked avuncular and well deserving of the onlookers respect. That evening in the hotel, as we were dining a man approached our table and introduced himself as Monty Woollacombe. Originally from Southport he was a doctor at the local hospital. Due to participate in a regatta the next morning, he wanted one of us to crew for him. The ever optimistic Harry volunteered and the two duly won the race commandingly. Apparently Monty lived for his yachting. He was divorced and had found Zanzibar a fitting place to unwind, help the afflicted, and have fun the best way he knew how.

Naturally the doctor was delighted at Harry's assistance. So over lunch at the Yacht Club when we were celebrating their victory, he suggested that he arrange for his friend Ali to take us on his dhow to Pen Island that afternoon. 'You will find this far preferable to the ramshackle old ferry which runs later and docks at an out of the way little port after sundown. As the island is only a few miles offshore, even by dhow it can be reached comfortably inside an hour and a half.'

Jeremy had ascertained from his colleagues in the battalion there were some huts where visitors were welcome and we were duly booked in. Hearing this Monty assured us there was a simple restaurant right next to where we would be staying which served local food he was convinced we would find tasty enough.

'Nothing delicate. Mainly fish and vegetables. But they also produce a decent curried rabbit and there are sure to be countless cans of beer. You will almost certainly be offered gazelle or kudu too. I only went once. That was a long time ago. But I continue to hear good report.'

Then he added, 'the ladies of the island will look after you. They have a fine reputation for beauty and generosity. By the way it is not known here as Pen Island but as Penis Land. You will have fun. You do realise it is a naturist resort, don't you?'

Judging by our surprise quite clearly none of us had the slightest idea. The concept seemed fraught with the unexpected and I for one wondered how we would cope.

'Do you think Jeremy knew this?' piped up Bart.

'No, not at all,' replied Claude. 'I reckon our fellow officers will have been having fun at his expense. Believe it or not, I was also kept in the dark. I think they sense Jeremy is just too good to be true and could not wait to hear his tales on his return. They will be heartily miffed now that he cannot be part of the joke. Maybe they had it in for me as well.'

'Fantastic,' said Bart paying attention. Ever the extrovert these days as opposed to his diffidence as a nipper he added, 'I can't wait. How about everyone else?'

'Why the hell not!' said Noel. 'Let's go for it. But only under an oath of secrecy. Got it?'

Harry agreed. 'Absolutely. No tales out of school. And no photographs!'

'I'm game,' added Theo. 'Let's live a bit. Live for Life.'

'Quite right,' said Claude warming to the idea. 'You look doubtful Nigel. Is this OK with you?'

'Oh yes,' I hastened to say. 'I have got to lose my virginity one day. Let that be Plan A.'

The others laughed.

'Monty,' said Bart rubbing his hands, 'where is the nearest chemist?'

'No problem, Bart. I guess you will want to return to the hotel to collect your kit even though that will be largely superfluous. A hundred yards before you get there, on the left hand side is Mwangi's. You cannot miss it. He will have what you lads need. Be sure to be back here by quarter past three when Ali wants to set sail.'

'Am I the only one not yet to lose my virginity?' I enquired of the others.

'Had you worked in Newmarket,' said Theo, 'you would have lost it in the first fortnight. Those stable lads – the girls I mean – know a thing or two and are happy to share their expertise.' Ill prepared to pander to his good looks, in any case Theo knew well how to protect his backside and woe betide anyone who thought otherwise for like Noel he was handy with his fists.

Noel confessed that on a rugby tour of Italy the entire team had had it away. Harry admitted he had happily succumbed to a belle from Chelsea after a debs' ball at Grosvenor House. Claude had been there too and likewise did not miss out, spending the night with a girl in her parents' flat in Dolphin Square. As for Bart we all knew his saga. So, yes, I was the ingénue to borrow a phrase.

Ali turned out to be an Arab with a hawk-like nose, a face the colour of leather, and teeth stained red due to his habit of chewing betel. He had been a mariner all his life and was wise to the ways of the sea. He pointed out the coral reef and two shipwrecks, all three of which were a haven for gloriously multi-coloured fish. He spoke English rather well and agreed to collect us forty-eight hours later.

Sensing we needed advice he volunteered, 'you must be careful of the sun. Use your sun cream lavishly especially on those parts of your body that do not normally come into contact with it.' Grinning salaciously from his red-stained lips, he spat – a normal practice for those who chewed betel

– before adding, 'I don't want to see you all suffering from the sun and totally exhausted one way or another when I come to collect you.' He gave a little chortle.

As we reached the shore he pulled up a few yards from the sands and pointed out the track to the huts and the small restaurant located two hundred yards away. We leapt off with our back packs held aloft. No other Europeans were to be seen. The beach appeared empty apart from some local fishermen attending to their nets and obviously unfussed by us. So much I thought for a naturist resort wondering if I would be able to overcome any innate shyness if indeed this were to be the case. Slowly and somewhat lackadaisically one of the fishermen troubled to look up, smiled, and came over to greet us. His English was surprisingly fluent and he appeared friendly enough.

'Hey fellows, welcome to Pen Island. Tonight Bwana Fabio is laying on a sing-song especially for you guys. So I trust you are all in good voice. I am Charlie. I shall be there too with a pal. We will bring our drums. Another mate, Saleh, has a guitar. And, boy, can he sing! We'll have quite a party. You do know, don't you, this is also known as Penis Land,' he added, chuckling.

In return Bart laughed. 'Yes, we have heard that. I expect we will find out more shortly.' As for me I wondered just what.

Fabio was an Italian of uncertain age. Since he owned the restaurant and huts in its immediate vicinity, he was regarded as the big man and a source of employment and entertainment. His wife was a large local lady who answered to the name of Monica. She laughed a lot, walked with a waddle, and was responsible for the cooking. Fabio was glamorous in an oddly handsome way. Not exactly seedy he was weather-beaten and his strong wavy grey hair would not have looked out of place on a film star. He had distanced himself from the western world and was mightily content with his beachcomber life administering to the needs of his few visitors as a genial host, and making sure the local girls were in useful employment while pandering to whatever his guests fancied. I suppose a puritan would have considered him a pimp. But that was the last thing on my mind.

In his melodious Italian accent Fabio welcomed us warmly. 'It is my pleasure to see you young men have the time of your life. Feel free to do whatever you want. And remember, no clothes are required at any time other than at meals when I think you will be more comfortable wearing something should you spill anything hot. In any case the ladies of the island will find it very strange if you do not conform. They expect to admire you in your birthday suits. I take it you all have plenty of Durex with you. Please choose whatever huts you like. But you will have to share. Each one has two double beds protected by a mosquito net and a thick palliasse raised well above the earth floor. So no need for you fellows to share a double bed since that will fall to one of our lovely ladies. A tank on the roof of every hut holds enough water for probably four showers as long as you are not too extravagant. This comes from a fresh water lake close by so is not saline. Oh! And the bar is open twenty four hours a day. If no one is on hand to serve you, just write down on the pad what you have taken and we will settle up when you leave. All clear?'

We tossed for who would share with whom. Harry and Claude paired up as did Noel and Theo. So, left with the irrepressible Bart, I began wondering what I would learn.

We freshened up and headed for the bar where we found three young Italians who were chatting to Fabio. They were immediately most friendly towards us and introduced themselves as Orlando, Mario and Luigi. It transpired they were staying in some other huts of Fabio's two minutes away and were on their second or third visit, having arrived a day earlier. They worked for a Genoese shipping company in Mombasa and had come to regard the island as their special hide-out. Here they reckoned they could be entertained by the local girls without fear of disease so highly prevalent with the ladies of the night in the port. To assist their holiday go with a swing and to curry favour with our host they had brought a case of Italian white wine with them, as they recognised the impracticality for Fabio to obtain this in Stone House. Happy to share in this booty they generously provided, we decided at once they were a breath of fresh air and fell in line with the party spirit.

It was not long before three young ladies sidled up to the bar. They knew the Italians and gave them each a big kiss and a hug. Turning to Noel they smiled and said that they would be joined shortly by other girls who were just longing to meet us. Then they embraced each of us with Noel first in line doubtless due to the attraction of his blue eyes, strong arms and sturdy smooth physique. Clearly, distinction at rugby could pay off. Within the half hour half a dozen other young ladies arrived. Word had got around about us six soldiers. Charlie had wasted little time. My goodness, we were in for a treat. Each was young, sunny and nubile, and able to converse in pidgin English in between giggles. Coyly if unerringly they accepted a drink on opting for the local rum. When Charlie and his fellow musicians entered with a cheery greeting we knew the promised party would soon be under way.

By now Monica was grilling fish and attending to what looked like sauté potatoes simmering in a large dish with pimentos and onions. Fabio was handing out beer cans as fast as he could while two bottles of wine stood in ice buckets to indicate nobody need hold back. Enhanced by the flickering fire hurricane lamps gave out eerie illuminations. Soon everyone was chatting as though they had known each other for weeks. Having entered as strangers we were already behaving as friends. I was in seventh heaven as Charlie's troupe beguiled us with his pal Saleh as guitarist leading the African chant. Probably in his mid-twenties, his Sudanese face could look lugubrious in repose. But it lit up when he sang in his crinkly, crunchy, crackly timbre. Somehow this reminded me of Kathleen Evans's crinkly, crunchy, crackly treacle toffee which she had dispensed at Barley Farm that memorable Halloween when I was barely six. We clapped hands to the beat and when not doing this held the hand of the girl next to us. Mine was called Sadie. The other girls had European names too.

As the evening progressed Charlie asked for a short break, citing the need for liquid refreshment. Fabio promptly obliged then produced his tape recorder to play bewitching Italian arias. Now Orlando was to launch forth magically. Good looking with Roman features and blessed with dark curly hair, he electrified the bar with sensuous tenor tones. We listened enraptured. Back to Saleh who, cross-legged, appeared surprisingly solemn before strumming his guitar. Looking around and singing softly to a catchy tune reminiscent of Hoagy Carmichael he murmured as he made eye contact with the boys,

> *'Nevah Solicit for your Sister; Believe me that just is not Nice*
> *Unless you are Sure to Secure… one Helluva Slice of her Price.'*

Then to a different rhythm he branched out and eyeing the ladies employed his sultriest tone. Saleh mimicked wickedness. In his case not at all difficult.

> *'I cannot afford her Mother or even her younger Brother,*
> *So Check around with this aim in mind and jolly well Find me Another.'*

Mario stared at Luigi and blasted him, 'You frigging nincompoop. You should not have taught him that. See how you have lowered the tone. Arias one minute. Now this!'

Luigi, looking guilty if unrepentant, just shrugged his shoulders as we soldier boys stifled a smirk and chortled. Perhaps Luigi did have something to hide. Sitting next to Claude I dug him in the ribs. I suppose that as a fair haired six-footer he was the most glamorous of our sextet. At any rate on his other side was the most striking of all the girls. Out of the blue he turned and questioned me, 'where the devil's Bart? He's been gone some time.'

'Probably relieving himself. It is not as though he is exactly abstemious,' I replied.

'I bet the blighter is in the sea having a skinny dip with that floozie Lisette,' retorted Claude.

I gave him a sideways look. 'Who is playing policeman now that Spider Man is not around? More likely, he is having it away while we are here so that I cannot gawp and later comment.'

'Nigel, I think there is no need at all for you to leer and learn. But be aware that when you and Sadie are at it later whatever you do will be noisy. You might even wake him up.'

'Thanks a lot Claude. Much bloody well appreciated. But the last thing Bart will want to do is watch me. In any case with any luck he will have crashed out and be away with the fairies.'

As the evening drew to a close, Theo enquired who was up for a moonlit skinny dip. I declined not wishing to miss out on the opportunity that beckoned with Sadie. More to the point I was concerned my ardour might cool. As we both took our leave we saw Theo and Noel heading towards the ocean with two of the Italians, the blonde eye-catching Luigi and the taller Mario. In no time all four were discarding their clothes with carefree abandon. Watching them with amusement were their lady escorts happily lending encouragement while they brazenly played leap-frog and frolicked in a sea now sweetly caressing the sands.

Once we reached the hut I knew immediately that Bart was there for Sadie and I could hear groaning. No midnight swim for him then. Lisette, dark and glistening, was straddling his thighs while he lay on his back and pumped away. 'Nearly there,' he called out as we entered.

Stealthily Sadie and I crept to our bed while they climaxed followed by heavy breathing and a deep and certain instant slumber. We embraced tenderly before she took the initiative. Soon we were rocking gently, forgetful of Claude's advice that we would be noisy. Even had we been, Bart and Lisette would not have heard a thing. With business done rather quicker than I would have liked, we too fell asleep.

51

Next morning I awoke to hear Bart thumping away and could just discern him in the rear entry position while Lisette lay on her front and he fondled her breasts. 'Another thirty-six hours of this,' I thought, 'and even Bart will be knackered.'

On trying to go back to sleep, after a little while I recognised that was not going to happen. Then Sadie awoke. Gently she clasped me in her arms. So we resumed where we had left off in the early hours. And this time I lasted longer, happily heedless whether we were quiet or not. Having climaxed and now exhausted I heard Bart whispering, 'Bravo, bet you feel better now.' With me blissfully unaware the blighter had been watching the entire performance. First time around he had indeed been oblivious.

'Thanks. You may be a right bastard but you are so damned right,' I replied. Leaping up still naked and grabbing a towel I urged Sadie to run with me to the shore where, elated, we fell into the water laughing and splashing and feeling marvellous.

Monica conjured up fried eggs for breakfast to accompany the Fray Bentos tinned meat. Every one of us looked a little bleary. At Bart's request not one of us was willing to recount the adventures of the night. The sun was now up and the morning temperature perfect for sun bathing. So we seized a towel and lay on the beach. As naturists do.

Bart stretched out on his back. Soon he was well away in the land of nod. I sat up with my hands behind my back gazing on the ocean and reflecting on the pleasures of the night while the others were in assorted poses as we listened to Fabio's music machine playing discreetly. Two by two, the girls from last night sauntered along the beach scarcely veiling their intention to check on our manhoods. Not surprisingly it was the sleeping Bart that grabbed their attention. The girls stopped briefly, drew breath and giggled. Not only was he the most mature of us six, he possessed the most enormous member. Even in recline, below a chest and belly matted in soft dark down this was truly formidable. Recovering their composure the girls chatted in dulcet tones anxious not to disturb him. Clearly their aim was to switch partners and if possible to sample Bart's body in the next twenty-four hours. No assignations were made but we sort of gleaned an impression which girl might be next to entertain us. With Jacob arguably giving best to Esau so to speak, the smooth Noel, aware that he was not quite the centre of attention and mildly puzzled because of it, rose to see what all the fuss had been about.

Gazing on Bart who by now had woken up he was taken aback.

'Blimey Bart, where did that come from?' he quipped. 'When we were six and measured ourselves, weren't we all much the same? Have you now recorded a world first in obtaining a penis transplant?'

'Bugger off,' responded Bart. 'It grew some when I was around fifteen. It just happened. No medication. No nothing. No point in being jealous either. No one has yet complained.'

'What do you mean, it grew some? Gruesome, certainly! And my guess is it must have grew some more since. You are welcome to it. Don't you feel embarrassed in front of your tailor when ordering a new suit even if it is from the mighty Montague Burton?'

Bart did not deign to reply to Noel's barb, knowing well his best suit had indeed come from Leeds and the very tailor in question. But then so had the liveried uniforms that the Queen Mother's household wore. Unconcerned he just shook his head and looked out to sea.

Joining us to see the fun were the three Italians who we had met the previous night. All three stopped to look. Orlando smiled while the elegant Mario merely shrugged his shoulders. The blonde sensual Luigi, however, stared longer than was polite and then took another long good look before joining his companions and stripping off to recline – all three seemingly intent on regaining their share of attention from the ladies. I detected Luigi's lascivious gaze did not go unnoticed and figured that even a blind man could have sensed the rising tension. Soon approaching us along the beach strolled Saleh of the guitar and crinkly crunchy voice, accompanied by his mate Charlie and their fellow drummer.

'You are a lazy lot,' called out Charlie. 'How about a game of football? We three will team up with Mario, Orlando and Luigi and take on you soldier boys. Are you up for it?'

Bart, about to doze off again, heard the commotion and sleepily rubbed his eyes. 'Hmm, why not,' he mumbled.

'Look alert, Bart,' called out Noel. 'You better be the goalie. You have not got the energy to run around like a blue-arsed fly.'

'Well, fellows,' he continued, 'what say we play for fifteen minutes, have a break, change ends, then have another fifteen?'

'Deal done,' said Mario smartly. 'We are on. OK Charlie?'

Charlie beamed and put a thumb up.

Our team scored first thanks to a nifty piece of footwork from Theo. Then Noel banged in a second goal. Perhaps this made us careless for before half-time the athletic Luigi reduced our lead to 2-1. Next thing we knew was that Saleh had scored from a corner by Mario to equalise. Bart was beside himself pouring out oaths to make even a sailor blush.

A moment later he called out, 'Stop, fellows. A laddie fishing out there on the rocks has lost his balance and is thrashing around in the sea. I think he needs help. He looks in trouble.'

Claude now abandoned his cultivated lackadaisical demeanour. Acutely aware that the rocks might be a haven for the sharp spines of sea urchins, nimbly he donned his green and silver swim shorts then shot off along the sands before hurling himself into the waters and swimming towards the floundering youngster. Saleh followed in hot pursuit naked as the day he was born, for he was quick to realise that it was Fabio's eleven year-old Tino who was in difficulties. In the nick of time before he finally went under, Claude reached the boy – slippery, limp and scarcely wriggling. Passing him to Saleh, he lifted Tino onto his giant shoulders and waded back to the shore to be greeted by our fellow footballers. Moments later the lad could well have drowned. As it was he had swallowed more of the ocean than was good for him. Miserable and weak, he began retching. Theo took charge and performed the necessary antics to ensure he was breathing normally. Once it was apparent that Tino was going to recover, Noel wrapped him in his towel, cradled him, and with Harry's help lifted him back to Fabio's premises. By this time I had run back and forewarned Fabio and Monica of the near disaster, assuring them both that all was going to be well.

With Tino being attended to satisfactorily by his mother, Fabio confided that he had warned the boy ceaselessly not to go fishing from that point for the currents were fickle and more fierce than one would imagine. His gratitude knew no bounds. Cans of beer were proffered direct from the cold chest. Although it was barely noon, sausages were placed on his makeshift barbecue to which onions were added. Meanwhile Monica rustled up home-made bread rolls to make hot dogs lashed with mustard. Football was forgotten as was Fabio's advice that clothing was expected at mealtimes. So for the moment were the anticipated assignations with the local ladies.

Orlando reached for his guitar and commenced to sing. There was magic in the air with silence almost reverential. Had anyone dropped a pin one would have been aware of the culprit. Suddenly I noticed Noel bridle. He was looking at Luigi who was staring at Theo.

'Stop ogling little Theo as if he was a prime cutlet at the butcher's,' he commanded.

Mario interrupted and in his soft lilting voice said, 'Luigi, I have told you before, stick to girls. Boys will only get you into trouble.'

Luigi ignored this and in his strong Genoese accent assailed Noel, 'What is so precious about your room-mate? You seem to be be…' Deliberately he had put the emphasis on the word "precious". But before he could finish taunting him Noel was enraged and promptly floored him with a right hook. Luigi could not have known he had been captain of boxing at Rugby.

'Steady on boys,' called out Fabio. 'Take it easy. You are all on holiday. Enjoy yourselves. But not in this way. Now shake hands and you, Luigi, apologise to Noel for any innuendo.'

Luigi looked stunned at this rebuke. He gathered his composure and complied but with rather less gallantry than might have been expected from a fulsome Latin temperament. With Harry thanking Fabio for this intervention, I explained to him quietly that when Theo was ten he had lost his father in an accident at their timber yard. As a result his school peers had been protective of him and perhaps that attitude lingered on. In any case it was obvious Noel and Theo enjoyed a special relationship and in my view this had always been so. Further conjecture seemed pointless. I considered it best to be grateful to Fabio and ignore Luigi. Harry must have thought the same for now he took the initiative, 'Look fellows, let's forget this and have a game of cricket. If you guys don't know how it is played, we will show you.'

Anxious for peace to be restored Orlando agreed immediately. He struck me as the leader of the three Italians for the other two immediately chorused approval. In little time they had entered into the spirit of things with Orlando practising what he thought to be the correct movements for a fast delivery, and Mario going forward to imaginary balls. Saleh joined them. So to equalise matters we tossed lots to see which one of us would transfer to their side. Claude, arguably our most adept player, was the odd man out and joined the others as captain. With the ice now broken, camaraderie was resumed.

Harry captained our team and although winning the toss sportingly invited Claude's side to bat first. Within ten minutes he began to wonder if he had done the right thing for Saleh and Luigi both proved adept at watching the ball and belting it. Saleh departed first to a fierce ball from Noel while Luigi, after a mighty connection, was caught by a gleeful Theo on the edge of the sea. But all credit to him as he avoided smirking. Luigi looking furious swore loudly in Italian and walked off sulkily. Claude now showed he had lost little of his skill and was as stylish as ever, running up forty in a few minutes. When they were all out for a hundred-and-ten inside the eight overs on which we had agreed, we knew we had a huge task on our hands and that national pride was at risk. Fabio had been watching and brought out cold lagers. To all intents and purposes, excepting Luigi who was still sparking, the spat had been forgotten. Happily fortified, with four balls to spare our team overtook them with a cracking boundary from Noel. Just as well for we had lost three wickets and doom was beckoning.

With the sun still high, more lager was called for. As we imbibed gratefully four figures could be discerned in the distance, each one leading a pony. Theo jumped up. 'Let's try a spot of riding if we can gain the cooperation of that crowd over there.'

'Why not indeed,' said Orlando and Harry almost in unison.

'Fine,' said Noel. Then ever practical he added, 'I think we should abandon nudity and put on our swim trunks. You don't want funny fleas gnawing at your vitals.' With Bart the first to agree, we strolled along the sands waving in a friendly manner. Saleh accompanied us. He knew the chaps and chatted amiably with them to see if they would loan their steeds for a paltry amount. Claude and Harry produced the ready in an instant. Theo now showed his affinity for horses. He selected one who looked the most promising, spoke to it in gentle tones and mounted it with barely a lift up from its owner. He walked it slowly all the while addressing it softly. Only when he was satisfied the horse was calm and acquiescent, did he trot for a while before quietly breaking into a canter.

Returning to us he volunteered to assist any who were minded to follow him. Harry, Bart and Luigi took up the challenge. Theo accompanied Harry and Bart while Saleh did the honours for Luigi so that each in turn could become accustomed to their mount. Ultimately we all had a go, spending some minutes aboard before deciding that we were safer on two legs rather than four. Then at Saleh's suggestion, Theo accepted the challenge of one of the locals for a pony race along the beach while we cheered them on. No prize for guessing who won – Theo in a style not one of us could ever have contemplated.

Noel professed he was impressed. 'Tip,' he said, 'you are a natural.'
'No one has called me Tip for at least six years,' was the guileless reply.
'Never mind, when I have made my millions, if you are still in the horse business I want you to ride for me. Just think of it, "Tip Manners", what a great name for a jump jockey. You might even become famous.'
'Good on you, mate, I will bear it in mind if I am down and out. Don't forget', he quipped, 'you have got to make your millions first. Horses cost a load of money.'
I looked at Claude and together we caught the eye of Harry and Bart. I ventured forth, 'who among us lot is going to make it big? I don't think I have it in me.' Claude was the first to proffer an opinion. 'I rather think Jeremy although sadly he is not with us. But you know probably better than me that Noel here has a steely inner core. I have a feeling he could surprise us all. You can see he has ambition. He is not just a loud mouth.'
With nothing further to add, we adjourned to Fabio's and made a bee line for the ice cold lager. Thanking politely, the owners of those ponies downed their glasses glad they had cooperated with Saleh from the outset.
Bart then spoke up. He looked mischievous. 'Why don't we have a three-legged race and see if Noel and Nigel can still perform well enough to show us how it's done?'
Support came from Harry and Theo. 'We will take them on,' said Harry. 'That leaves Claude and you to make the rival third party', he pointed to Bart.
'Well, I could have done a lot worse. I could have got Luigi and he might have bowled me over.'
Orlando looked daggers for a moment before collapsing into laughter.
'Mario and I will take you on. Luigi can have Saleh as his third leg. By the way, are we to be in the buff or wearing our modest swimwear?'
Even Fabio guffawed at this.
'Luigi and Saleh can forfeit their trunks. Everyone else, please wear modest attire,' he intoned as if this was to be the most serious contest that Pen Island had ever seen.
Deciding it was high time I made a contribution, I blurted out, 'Done.'
Luigi and Saleh were well tuned on the lager by this time, so much so that the dubious Luigi readily agreed before Saleh had any opportunity to demur.
As you can imagine the race was little short of a fiasco. Everyone fell over at least twice except for Noel and me. Then once we had rediscovered our

rhythm of old we flayed the opposition. As for Luigi and Saleh, they found themselves by chance in a number of compromising positions. The ladies who were watching were convulsed. Saleh was far from amused and when he had final disentangled himself from Luigi announced that never, ever, would he take part in a three-legged race ever again. And certainly not with a hairy-arse like Luigi!

Ever the diplomat Fabio called out, 'gentlemen, time for Prosecco. You have deserved it.'

The evening was soon to draw in. All the girls were in evidence and as chatty as could be. Monica had promised a rabbit curry. I was delighted for I remembered Monty saying this was the local speciality. Charlie joined us with his little troupe so that our drinking was accompanied by laughter, singing and dancing. It was the friendliest few hours ever. What is more, the rabbit curry with its side dishes fully lived up to the billing that Monty had given.

Noel was watchful for he doubted whether the evening would pass without some untoward incident. Deciding that he could not trust Luigi not to cause mischief, he had a quiet word with Bart who nodded his head and in a sotto voce tone replied, 'Been there. Done that. OK, I'll give way.' Now with Bart's permission Noel approached Fabio asking that Lisette forgo Bart and take up with Luigi. Fabio raised his eyebrows. Noel intimated that he did not wish to see Luigi pursue Theo again.

'He wants him off his back. Literally.' Then he added, 'if that were to happen I fear a fracas. And such a thing could turn nasty after all the booze that has been sunk.'

Fabio told him not to worry. Tonight was Ladies Choice and he would see to it that Lisette gave the benefit of her experience to Luigi.

'He is not a one-trip pony, you know. We remember him from last year. He can go with girls. And he does. But as that may be his second option I take your point.'

Whether Fabio orchestrated matters or whether the girls just took charge and got their way, the evening was a huge success. Next morning at breakfast the informal reports were all uniformly excellent. Before we left for the shoreline to greet Ali and his dhow that had come to collect us, we called upon the Italian trio to bid our farewells and promise to look them up if and when we next came to Mombasa. Luigi, unabashed, was quite fulsome towards Theo. Giving him a butter-wouldn't-melt-in-my-mouth look he said, 'come to

Mombasa any time you like. But let me know first. My motorbike requires tuning. Subtle tinkering I think.'

Theo had looked at him deadpan not in the least swayed by his lascivious look or Genoese lilt.

'Subtle tinkering? Sorry mate. Not my scene. Possibly these other guys may return to the coast but not me. I am required upcountry. Still I am sure Sergeant James in Nigel's squad will find you a young black mechanic who will know a trick or two and gladly attend to every one of your needs. I guess you will be more than happy with that. Just ask him.' Adding a quick 'Cheerio' Theo took himself off. Forgoing even a brief backward glance he vaulted into the dhow, thankful to be shot of the persistent Luigi once and for all.

Back at Buller Camp the next day Owen sought me out before lunch. Discreetly I brought him up to date with what had gone on at Pen Island carefully glossing over the intimate personal details. After grimacing on paying attention to what he had missed he said, 'you are not going to believe this but Vince has been suspended.'

'Why on earth? He is so flipping officious,' I countered.

'It is like this. It seems that Vince, while ostensibly keeping our soldier boys away from those questionable nightclubs in Muthaiga Road which are in effect brothels, has been receiving back-handers from the owner of three of them, that Canadian Pole, Jet Jaworski. Apparently Vince has been somewhat selective, for several senior NCOs from upcountry have gained admittance on account of the fact they had the wherewithal to spend freely. It is only those of the rank of corporal or below who have been thwarted and arrested.

'Jet has had the patronage of and protection from Joshua Mzuri, a senior man in the Cabinet and a sort of friendly uncle to that rising young political star, the trade unionist Tom Mboya, a future leader in the making if ever there was one even though he is not a Kikuyu but a Luo. Shortly he is bound for Ruskin College in Oxford. But enough of that. What do you think of Mzuri for a mission boy's name – Joshua Good? Not bad is it. Jet divorced his Canadian wife on the grounds of her adultery. She got mixed up with that film crowd making "The Snows of Kilimanjaro". You know – Gregory Peck, Susan Hayward and Ava Gardner, along with the innumerable technicians, stand-ins and hangers on.

'As for Jet, he is now married to Joshua's young sister Helena even though she is a good twenty years younger. He used to make nature films on Kenya and was good at that. But they did not make the money he craved. Then like so many he got seduced by Africa. You can find him three or four times a week in the Golf Club at Royal Nairobi downing whisky and playing the fruit machines. Incredibly he is a winner. But if I were you I would steer well clear of him for he is dangerous company.'

'You have been well briefed,' I said before adding, 'where is Vince now?'

'Under house arrest here while the Colonel and the Brig endeavour to come to an agreement on what to do next. That sandy-haired Presbyterian Scot, Colonel 'Stovie' Donaldson, cannot stand Vince and is keen for him to face a court martial. I have always thought of him as a Scottish bully – something of a freckle-faced braggart devoid of deep substance. On the other hand old Bertie Burridge plays the gentleman he strives to be. He does not want any of this to come to light, for he feels it will reflect poorly upon the discipline under his command and might even prevent him gaining the promotion to Major General that he so desperately seeks. The Brigadier is quite a toady, you know, behind all that smarmy cheeriness and "hail fellow well met" attitude.'

'Tell me, how did Vince get rumbled?'

'It's quite complicated actually,' said Owen. 'At the end of the week it was customary for Vince to be invited into Jet's inner circle, given a drink and offered cash either to spend on charity or to frivol on the Njoro Races. This was because he had turned a blind eye to prospective customers who could fatten the coffers of Jet's clubs. As a stout Methodist, he had always chosen the former. Moreover, he seemed to feel that this was both perfectly fair and a reasonable option that would not upset anyone. However, while you were away on the coast last weekend he was given £50. This was twice the normal backhander. He was told that on Saturday he should put it on number 4 in the fourth race. This was an animal named Shaft of Light. Surprise, surprise! Up it came at 11/2 making him £325 better off. The next occasion when Jet invited him in for a quiet drink, Joshua Mzuri was there too. Apparently the conversation went something like this with Joshua seizing the initiative. 'Vince, when your tour of duty is over we have a job for you. This is to train our Nairobi police force in certain aspects. We can make it very well worth your while even though the published scales for the job seem a bit miserly. That is because there are a number of side benefits. I presume I do not have to spell them out explicitly.'

'OK,' I intervened, 'but who grassed on him?'

'It was one of his own team in the military police, an African sergeant. A corporal in the Kings African Rifles had been granted admittance. He happens to be the youngest brother of Helena, Jet's current wife. Now up until then anyone below the rank of sergeant had either been warned off or arrested. The African sergeant was jealous of Vince. In any case the two did not get on. And when word got out that Vince had won a small fortune, the sergeant went to his Regimental Sergeant Major and blew the gaff. He thought that in doing so he would be well in line for promotion as a result. The RSM then went to the Adjutant who in turn reported the issue to 'Stovie'. So there we have it. A nice how-do-you-do, don't you think!'

'What is Vince doing now?' I questioned.

'Actually he is helping me in acting as a film projectionist. We regularly show films to the camp's askaris. We have dozens of training films as well as ones that are educational. So apart from being in the dark, he is literally lying low. Having set himself up above the rest of us he has now got his come-uppance. In the process, interestingly enough he is almost companionable and no longer stuffy and patronising like he can be.'

'Do you think he will fall for the bait that Mzuri has set?'

'I very much doubt it. He knows he has been foolish and is highly unlikely to trust any African ever again. On his part it was a complete lapse of judgement.'

A few days later I found myself having a cup of coffee with Vince and tackled him on what had prompted him to assist Jet.

'Blandishments,' he replied somewhat meekly. 'Look, I and my small team could never totally stop British servicemen and local askaris from visiting his premises. All we could do was to act as a deterrent. So when Jet asked me confidentially which charities I would like to see gain some measure from his clubs' activities I saw an opportunity for good to come out of evil, even if modestly. Between them, in a few weeks three charities obtained some £300. Not a lot I know, but at least it was something. And it was much appreciated, especially as they were never aware of the source.

'My big mistake was firstly to allow Helena's young brother entry and then to accept the £50 and act on the inducement of a hot tip at the races. I realise now this was a trap and that were I ever to agree to work for Mzuri I could never be my own man. Instead I would be in danger of becoming putty in the hands of the authorities.'

'What are you going to do now?' I enquired.

'The Adjutant says the Brigadier is trying to get me posted to Aden for the remainder of my three year stint. You may not know that I signed up for three years instead of the usual two. If I am lucky this will be the outcome. The alternative is too frightful to contemplate. Father would never forgive me if I am cashiered. Then any career in the police would be doomed once I am demobbed. That may yet be the case of course. It depends on who writes my personal report. I think what I will do in Aden if there is ample spare time and I am something of an outcast is to study law. Practising as a lawyer should be more profitable than opting for the police or joining a security firm, both of which have been in the back of my mind.'

I listened carefully, recognising that he must have been desperately upset to have unburdened himself on me. Clearly he was mortified that he had let himself down and, frankly, been a bastard who was caught out. I recognised I was a soft touch so wished him well adding my lips would be sealed. That appeared to calm him for he thanked me and shook me by the hand. Having been humiliated, for the moment he was humble.

Within the week Vince heard he was to be transferred to Aden. The Brigadier had painted a rosy picture of him and Vince looked to be set for redemption in a post that would doubtless challenge him. That business with Jet and Joshua Mzuri was hushed up and never fully came to light. As for the African sergeant who ratted on him, he was sent upcountry to Nanyuki on the promise of a promotion rather more quickly than if he stayed in Nairobi. So Jet was rid of him, while the practice of even National Service officers and NCOs occasionally visiting his establishments quietly continued providing that they were in mufti.

Vince's fellow officers were not sorry to see him go. But as they had never been judgemental prior to a decision as to what to do with him, a discreet farewell party was arranged at which Bart was invited thanks to the intervention of Owen. However it did not prove possible for Theo to be included. When he learned of this he just laughed and claimed he would not have wanted to attend in any case. The Brigadier had said he would be present but at the last minute claimed to have a more pressing task. This rather confirmed my suspicions that he was two-faced. Colonel 'Stovie' Donaldson however did look in. He had assumed the Brigadier would be there and considered it politic to show loyalty to him as his superior in presenting a united front. Now clearly put out, he was formally polite to

Vince. He wished him well but warmth was lacking. Absolutely nothing was said concerning his departure or how it had been engineered. Instead 'Stovie' hoped he had been able to sell his Bond Minicar well, adding he was sure to find Aden both refreshing and challenging.

'Make sure you are careful when swimming in the sea. Sharks are known to frequent the coast and two years ago the wife of the Commanding Officer was caught by one and killed.' True though it was, that was about as far as he could go to be courteous.

I arranged for Sergeant James to see him off at Mombasa so that he did not feel too badly about his sudden exit. He left with a hard-hearted determination never to be caught out again or to be so stupid. On his behalf I wondered if and how his time in Aden would work out. I let Jeremy, Claude, Noel and Harry know of the outcome by radio. The general view was that he had been extremely lucky and this was due more to Bertie Burridge's ambition than anything else. Bertie had played the old boy network with smooth ingenuity to rid himself of impending trouble sensing that from now on Vince would fall into line and not be a maverick.

Staying with us at Buller Camp was the wounded officer whose accident had necessitated the recall of Jeremy to his company upcountry. Rupert Lyall was an interesting man. He regaled us with stories of the Mau Mau, and the appalling atrocities these rebels were inflicting on the villagers as and when they were reluctant to support the insurrection they were endeavouring to foment. Many a time young village men were forced into initiation rites that sought to degrade them in public for they consisted of disgusting sexual acts. The consequence was that, frightened and intimidated, they were impelled to become part of a brotherhood.

In due course our proscribed period in Kenya drew to a close. My old schoolmates from upcountry were to spend their final weekend at the Camp, both for a debriefing and one happy party before we sailed for home in a troopship from Mombasa. While Rupert had left two months earlier, Claude, Jeremy, Harry and Noel were all present and we ensured that Bart too took part in the festivities. At once we detected an air of excitement for it had transpired that Jeremy had been nominated for the Military Cross on account of exceptional bravery in raids on Mau Mau hide-outs and in armed forays. Jeremy preferred to dodge questions saying that what he had done was nothing out of the ordinary. Claude knew better. But as Jeremy's oldest friend he chose to be discreet and let the matter come out in the open as and when the medal was pinned on him and the citation became public. This time, rather predictably both Bertie Burridge and 'Stovie' were present at the farewell party. With no dirty washing on display, so to speak, as there had been in the case of Vince, Bertie was never one to miss out on some fun. But primarily he wished to be looked upon as an affable Brigadier who inspired morale. He just longed to win promotion to Major General, a step he felt might be within his grasp. Actually he never did. And I have to say I was not surprised.

CHAPTER 4: BACK HOME

The voyage back to Liverpool lasted four weeks. We passed the time playing deck quoits, bridge, sunbathing, and chatting about our plans for the future. Bart who was also with us had other things on his mind. He could not forget the ecstasy of fornicating with Lisette. Having looked around at the talent available he chose to link up with Tricia, the tall slim lady who had run our telephone exchange and had split from her husband. I think he chose well. I knew her and liked her. What is more, without thrusting herself forward in the course of thirty days this attractive lady showed herself willingly amenable.

While I was playing bridge with Claude, Jeremy and Noel, Harry too was on the prowl. Seeking to emulate Bart in spending the afternoons in bed with an unattached female he was fully up to the challenge. He must have found at least three willing partners during the voyage. Harry was reasonably proficient at bridge but in crossing the equator, bypassing Somalia and travelling the length of the Red Sea, he had other things on his mind.

These were palmy days of no great consequence. We stopped at Port Fuad and Port Said on the Suez Canal, had our photographs taken aboard camels and were amused by the antics of the Egyptian "gully gully" men up to their tricks in trying to sell us things none of us needed or even remotely desired.

Occasionally after lunch Theo would join us as we discussed our plans for the future. He was aiming for an apprenticeship at Derby with Rolls Royce. Noel was off to Cambridge to study engineering. Jeremy was also choosing Cambridge but to study Land Management. Harry was opting for law at Oxford on his father's advice while Claude decided to forgo university. He had been offered a position with a firm of stockbrokers in Liverpool which his Dad recommended. The reason was simple. He did not want his son to cause embarrassment by making a mess of things in the firm where he was senior partner. Bart thought he would go into the hotel business, while I was set on becoming a journalist and learning my trade initially with the provincial press. I was not clever enough to be awarded a scholarship and the money for a university education simply did not exist. Mother explained this as well as she could. I understood and regretfully had to forgo the place I had been allotted. In any case I sensed that a career as a journalist might be full of variety and fun. As for Owen he was told in no uncertain manner that he was destined for the family business and that the best training for him would be with a similar small chain of department stores which operated elsewhere and so were not competitors. In other words, Owen's father thought similarly to Claude's.

On our final night at sea we sat down and determined that if at all possible we ought to meet up the next year with our old colleagues from that Heathside cricket team. The tricky thing was to decide where and when. It was Jeremy who cracked the ice.

He volunteered, 'maybe I can provide the rendezvous. Our mentor and guide, the old Earl of Ruabon, has long said that when I attain twenty-one he would like to throw a party for Claude and me, not that he would be present for more than the first hour. As you may know Claude who is his great nephew is two days older than me. The Earl has an orangery at Somersal Herbert that would make a splendid location. What with our house and Claude's we ought to be able to accommodate everyone who needs it. In addition if necessary we can also use our local inn the Dog and Duck as well. They have half a dozen letting rooms or so which, although not grand, should surely be adequate. What is more the date may well suit for it is 25 July when any of us at university will by then be on vacation.'

With this suggestion warmly welcomed, Jeremy continued, 'I'll see if I can get in touch with Slim and Mark. Vince may be a problem. It will depend if he has completed his three year turn of duty. Either way it will be a close run thing even though I doubt his final days will be spent in Aden. But it would be good to see him should he make it… also to find out whether and how he has changed, don't you think!' We exchanged addresses and phone numbers before promising to keep in touch and update everyone as and when these altered.

Several months later we received an invitation to attend Jeremy and Claude's joint twenty-first birthday party in Derbyshire at the premises of the Earl of Ruabon. And every one of us made it. His orangery, stylish and imposing, was enhanced by half a dozen paintings. Three were old masters and a further three late nineteenth century impressionists. In fact on asking where the loos were I was told to turn right by the Rembrandt. Well, of course.

The girls who I did not know were stunning, even svelte. All were clearly well at ease with each other as well as most of our old cricket team. But being the only southerner I felt an outsider. The big surprise was to see how Gaffer's daughters Myfanwy and Cressida had developed. Myfanwy was spectacled with straight hair and regular features not unlike that ever popular Cretan born chanteuse Nana Mouskouri. In contrast Cressida had blonde curly hair. Vivacious and carefree she was a tomboy but still wonderfully feminine. Less surprising was to see how many girls, attracted by Jeremy's upright demeanour and clear eyes, were keen to be seen in the company of the gallant holder of the Military Cross.

The evening was unforgettable. The Earl spared no expense. After welcoming us he gave the shortest of speeches and referred to our cricketing exploits at Heathside in that summer of '47 as a vintage year. 'Rather like the quality in 1947 in Bordeaux and Oporto. Just marvellous! It is also unusual for Bordeaux and Portugal to share a great year. However tonight you will be drinking both claret and port from '47.' One sensed he was licking his lips at the thought.

Ruabon had always liked his great nephew. Yet he looked upon Jeremy as the grandson that sadly he had never had for his own son had been killed in the war and his sole daughter had given him grief by never marrying. She was a thoroughly nice lady but apparently not of the marrying kind.

Tommy Kinsman and his band regaled us with the popular dance tunes of the age as well as before the war. He had made his name at London's Ritz hotel in the early thirties before beguiling a discerning clientele in Bond Street's most exclusive restaurant. His forte was the clarinet and saxophone. But by this time he was content merely to lead the band in strict tempo dance music, notably that evening from the musical Top Hat. His entourage was known as the "Deb's Delight Band" due to his willingness to play in private houses. Curiously he never courted publicity so is no longer a well-remembered household name.

Tommy Cooper agog with his fez gave us his madcap performance as a conjurer whose tricks do not work and had us all helpless with his zany laugh –'just like that'; and a steel band beguiled us when Tommy Kinsman and his quintet needed a respite. The champagne was Louis Roederer, Zind Humbrecht supplied an Alsace riesling and the claret was the 1947 Chateau Beychevelle. As for the port that was Graham's '47. The Earl had been as good as his word. Buxton provided the sparkling water which I recall was very much required.

I could not help admiring Claude. His girlfriend of the moment was a shipping heiress by name of Gemma Gough-Wilcox. She had an eye for the boys. For some of us, even though obviously very taken with Claude she was the star of the show. Her family owned the Wallasey Line whose boats had long plied the sugar route between the West Indies, Honduras and Cuba. Now they were branching out into cruise liners. Claude thought they might be a little ahead of their time as apparently they were finding it difficult to make these profitable.

Much as I appreciated the exquisite food and libations I found it particularly heartening to catch up with those of the team who I had not run across in Kenya, namely Mark and Slim.

Mark was interesting on West Africa. While he took the poverty in his stride for that had been fully expected as was the incessant corruption, it was the warring factions between the tribes that disturbed him along with certain aggressive attitudes of Islam depending upon where one was. He was ambivalent concerning Nigeria's future despite the optimism that huge oil reserves were within grasp and was worried for the Christian community which he regarded as threatened. He recognised that the British government had to undertake the most strenuous efforts to make peace with the more gentle of the Muslim leaders. Furthermore he wondered what would be the effect of Moral Rearmament on Islam and indeed the country, now that such an awe inspiring leader as Chief Awolowo had espoused it and was prepared to be the figurehead in full page advertisements in Britain's major national newspapers. These advocated four tenets in terms of the absolute: honesty, purity, unselfishness and love.

Many leaders had been impressed by MRA including curiously the king of Morocco. But Mark admitted, 'frankly I am a shade confused. In studying theology at Oxford I confess I am uncertain whether MRA offers the ultimate solution. What I can appreciate is that it provides a moral code for the idealistic in the unsophisticated grain belts of Canada and the USA. But I doubt whether this is sufficiently robust to save the world from power hungry politicians and to combat the threat of hatred of the West from certain sects of Islam.

'What really has shaken me to the core is that my friend Richard, the young Nigerian veterinary surgeon with whom I played tennis at the Lagos Club, was assassinated within weeks of returning to his Ibo homeland in Biafra. Radical Muslims were held to be responsible. I met Richard when he was writing up his thesis for the Nigerian government. He was a Roman Catholic and just such a lovely chap. A graduate of Glasgow University, he told me in his jocular high-pitched squeaky voice how friends had begged him to remain in Britain and pursue a career in the West Country. They longed for him to get wedded to one of his fellow students, a delightful young lady vet, for it was to the West Country that she was determined to return. He was very fond of her and together they would have made a great team. But he had declined, placing duty before affection. Most probably in Richard's case his fondness for the lady in question was the beginning of love, yet selflessly he said his obligations were not to himself but to his country. It is tragic. His dedication and talent have gone entirely to waste. No nation let alone Nigeria can afford to see that happen. There are only so many – I mean so few – who have the ability even to attempt such a profession.'

Listening to this was Myfanwy, the elder daughter of Gaffer. She hung on his every word and I sensed she was smitten. I recalled that as a girl she had thought that one day she might go to Africa either as a missionary or as the wife of one. She had now developed into a clever girl and was at Oxford reading PPE – Politics, Philosophy and Economics. What I did not realise right then was that Mark was soon to go to Nigeria as a missionary and with Myfanwy as his young bride. Somehow he had wanted to repay his brief friendship with Richard. As it was, a couple of years turned out to be enough. Nigeria was not heaven on earth. When the band struck up I thought it time to leave them and sidled over to Slim.

'What have you been up to since we last saw each other at Catterick?' I asked.

He recounted his days with the Army Catering Corps in Cyprus and told how fortunate he was to have studied under Toshy, an amazing chef who could not only cater to hungry soldiers but also pander to the fads of a difficult commanding officer at important Mess functions.

'The army was singularly lucky to have Toshy, a character larger than life with a fund of tales unfit for repetition. He had been in the merchant navy but somewhere along the way there had been a falling out. I never asked him why and Toshy chose not to divulge. In any case I guess his own story would have gone and on. Anyhow whatever happened will have been hushed up – either embezzlement or a sex matter with matelots if hearsay is to be believed. But he never hassled me and was a fine tutor with a sense of humour. So who cares?'

'Did that drugs episode at school ever bug you?' I was brazen enough to enquire. 'No, not at all. I put it behind me and have since been determined never to travel down that path again – in my mind far too dangerous and for what? I think I have discovered myself now. I can be a successful chef and I have sufficient interest to develop my skills and become a business proprietor in due course too. Father's milk bars have seen him and the family good. Whether they will survive and be seed corn for me I don't yet know. I think I can do better. One problem is that not all his sites have a high property value. We shall have to see.'

I was encouraged by Slim who in the short term was working with his father for I had feared that he could possibly fall by the wayside. He now looked good. Although he remained naturally tubby he said he tried to contain his weight by going for a daily run. Moreover, he had heard that soon a gym was going to open in Sheffield and when this occurred he would join at the outset. It looked as though Slim's dark days were behind him.

Next I sought out Owen. He was serving a traineeship with Semleys, a department store in York and with two more in Harrogate and Leeds. Like Claude's father, his own father Joe had fixed this believing that any mistakes Owen might make in his youth at the beginning of his career were far better undertaken away from home. Semleys apparently were a shade more upmarket than Giffords. But that was scarcely surprising for they operated in areas where there was more money about.

Owen was forthcoming. He was lucid. 'The boss is an absolute charmer called Francis Whyte. He possesses the most perfect white hair and is always immaculately groomed. Knocking on seventy he is gentle, cultivated and extremely shrewd. He is also very good at motivating others. His elder son Freddy is a driving force and pleasant enough. However he has a ruthless streak and can be distinctly offhand. Like me, the younger son Bernard has been a trainee. We rub along nicely enough but are cast in different moulds. Although we have a bit of fun together I doubt if we can ever become really good friends. But old Francis has gone out of his way to ensure that from time to time we have had joint assignments, and on completion has never been other than kindly in his assessments. One can't possibly do other than admire him. He is such a splendid upright fellow. I just accept him at face value.'

Noel admitted to loving Cambridge where he was renowned for his ownership of an early 1930s Alvis. He was upbeat.

'I have been very fortunate and elected to one of the smart dining clubs where there is a noticeable following of the Turf. I have also become a member of the Hawks Club due to my rugby. Perhaps more importantly, I am really enjoying engineering.'

Jeremy's demeanour was the same as ever – friendly and open, calm and confident.

'I am a member of the same dining club as Noel but am not as passionate on the Turf as he is. In my first year I won my Blue for golf. The Varsity match at Royal St George's Sandwich went well. My partner and I got a half in the foursomes and I won my singles. So it was with some foreboding I approached the captain later to say I would no longer be continuing with golf since I had decided to focus on my studies in the Michaelmas and Lent terms and play cricket in the summer. The captain was a medical student from Southport. Although disappointed he accepted the situation with good grace. Like Noel, I too am a Hawk. Crossing fingers I have a chance of a Blue at cricket with golf now on the sidelines. More to the point I am enjoying my course on Land Management with its emphasis on accountancy. So, yes, Cambridge is great. I am thrilled to be here.'

Harry was another loving university. He seemed in his element at Oxford's Christchurch College on studying law and playing golf for the University Divots, their second team. He suggested that if ever I could get away he would willingly give me a game at Huntercombe, halfway between Henley-on-Thames and Wallingford. A popular chap, he was elected to the Bullingdon Club where he rubbed shoulders with the well-connected and those who one day aspired to go in to politics.

Never one to be lost for words, Theo explained he was taking his apprenticeship with Rolls Royce seriously but finding time to ride out occasionally with the young trainer, Nicholas Broadbent, whose horses tended to frequent the smaller racecourses of Uttoxeter, Thirsk, Hexham and Catterick Bridge. I found him chatting to Cressida, Myfanwy's younger sister. Clearly they were hitting it off. And understandably; for I was shortly to learn they already knew each other since she was in to horses and working for the very same trainer as Theo visited at weekends whenever he could.

Bart was direct and to the point. 'I am not keen to follow Dad into the greyhound business and have commenced training as a hotelier where I am working with British Transport Hotels at the Royal Station Hotel in York. It is something I have to do to get my foot on the ladder.

It is a cracking good training. But they only pay peanuts. You may not know it but they are the largest group in the country owning four and five star hotels.'

'Are you learning anything about wine?' I asked.

'Very much so. BTH have their cellars below St Pancras station and along with the Savoy Hotel group there are probably none better. They have been good enough to send me to Germany for a week to be with Deinhards who have some of the finest Moselles and Palatinate wines that money can buy.'

'What will be your next step?'

Bart looked at me and shrugged his shoulders. 'I have a number of ideas but won't burden you with them until all becomes much clearer.' Bart was both mature and level-headed.

As for our co-host Claude, he had started to learn the ropes as a stockbroker with Henriques Lovell. Since he still retained the laid-back attitude of his army days on the beach at Pen Island I wondered if he would ever rise to that degree of enthusiasm that could compel a client to invest. But because he was such a pleasant fellow I decided that his restrained manner might well be a better way to influence a doubter than shouting the odds.

Vince duly made the party after arriving quietly and a little late. Not unreasonably he was circumspect since he was unaware if his misdeeds in Nairobi had ever leaked out. They probably had but no one thought it wise to dwell on them or indeed to raise the issue. All were coolly polite and did their best to put him at his ease once he had intimated he had embarked on a course at Guildford Law School. If Vince appeared somewhat withdrawn, even a closed book, I suspected this was because he had distanced himself from those childhood days and saw little to be gained in trying to recapture them.

On the other hand I felt very privileged to have been invited. After all I had left Heathside a year earlier than the others. Had I not entered for the Boys Championship at Formby in 1952 and then run across Jeremy and Harry on that magical golf course I supposed I would never have regained contact with our vintage team of '47. Such is fate!

Next morning, on saying goodbye we exchanged contact details. I caught the train from Derby to St Pancras in a state of melancholy. Most of my former team mates had gone on to fine schools and seemed to know where they were going. Slim, Bart, and now Vince had their plans. By contrast I could only envisage my future as a lowly paid hack for a provincial newspaper. I felt the odd man out and began to wonder if this was my lot. And if this were to be the case I could not foresee any easy way out.

Imbued with a nagging feeling that our paths might seldom if ever again cross, discomfited I fell asleep.

CHAPTER 5: WORKING FOR A LIVING

In the event, working for the Kent Essential at Maidstone was seldom boring. The editor, Steve Cruickshank, took an interest in how I was doing and appointed me to a whole variety of assignments. These ranged from County Court offences, to planning applications, to Kent cricket, to county golf, to film and book reviews and even the occasional society wedding.

'I want you to show some imagination,' he said. 'Jazz it up a bit. Don't be too formal. Look behind the scenes and ascertain the story that others will miss if they just devote themselves to reportage.'

I liked Steve. This was sound advice. He was a good egg and took the trouble to give me a rounded education as a journalist. I had been there five years when one morning there landed on my desk a press release for a book entitled "Emergency in Happy Valley". From the title I guessed it referred to Kenya and when I saw that the author was Rupert Lyall the name rang a little bell. This must be the chap in Jeremy's battalion who had been wounded so giving rise to Jeremy's recall and preventing him from experiencing our extraordinary few days in Zanzibar and Pen Island. I wasted not a moment, sat down and skipped through it with growing appreciation.

His tale evoked the dark time of the Mau Mau uprising in Kenya, described the insouciant days of the Happy Valley that preceded this and then the very circumspect atmosphere pervading the farms of the white settlers once they were continually under threat. It also dealt without fear or favour with the bestial and inhuman atrocities that accompanied Mau Mau oath-taking. These involved drinking human blood, extracting the eyeballs of the decapitated and then sucking the liquid from them, placing the meat of a ram or ewe in a female orifice and then being forced to lick it or eat it regardless whether it was a penis, testicles or something else. The more advanced the oath the more appalling were the actions demanded of those compelled to adhere. Intercourse with a live ewe or with a prostitute might also be required before the elders were satisfied that a young man was sufficiently indoctrinated to carry out a command so heinous as killing a parent.

I wrote a guarded but favourable review and telephoned the publisher asking for the opportunity to get in touch with Rupert on explaining we had met in Buller Camp some years earlier. After asking me a few questions to satisfy himself I was "bona fide", he gave me Rupert's number. Rupert was thoroughly cordial. He said he remembered me and suggested we meet on Saturday for lunch at a country inn called the Holly Tree prior to a local Derby between his village cricket team and their age old rivals.

Instantly we recognised each other. Rupert appeared to have recovered fully from his injury but confessed that although he was able to manage golf he had decided long ago never to run for a train. He had qualified as a chartered surveyor and was working for Frenshams, the Kentish brewery that owned the inn. They had only recently merged with a smaller company, Dixon Powell, with whom they had long been friendly. Rupert's mother had been a Dixon so he was treated as one of the family. There was a lot of rationalisation planned which Rupert confided was sure to keep him busy for years provided there was sufficient capital to activate this. As we downed a bottle of hock he was fascinated to hear of our escapades at Pen Island. Rupert had had an inkling that this was a naturist resort for he had been privy to the joke aimed at Jeremy. But when we initially met at Buller Camp I had resolutely refused to spill the beans as to what had occurred. After all we had agreed to keep our fun and naughty goings-on under wraps. The cricket was highly entertaining and I paid attention, determined to compose a light-hearted sketch for the Essential that would help fill up the Wednesday edition for often this was a tad short on content. I also wrote a flattering review of the Holly Tree that I considered well deserved.

A week later, quite unexpectedly Rupert phoned up to invite me round to the brewery. Once there he took me into the office of the Managing Director, Ben Goddard, where over coffee Ben explained how much he had enjoyed my two sketches.

'Tell me,' he asked, 'would the Kent Essential be prepared to run a series of articles publicising the group's pubs and hotels? I do not expect any of this for free but am prepared to do a deal for a modest sum. You know this could be ongoing, for in Phase One we have more than a score of the company's one hundred and ninety hostelries earmarked for a radical facelift. At Frenshams we have witnessed with horror and fascination how a major London brewing concern has gone headlong for modernisation. In the process they have laid waste to some fine Victorian pubs when replacing their opulent interiors with plastic and ersatz furnishings. Combined with their sweet chemical beer, achieved apparently after copious market research,

in our view the result will be disastrous. That is the way it is looking now.'
I surmised he was referring to Watneys.

He drew breath and continued, 'neither Frenshams nor Dixons, for we are retaining the two names, are going to make the same mistake. We shall be focusing on atmosphere with all the latest bar equipment discreetly under the counter and well hidden.'

Feeling reasonably optimistic he would play ball I said I would discuss this with my editor.

As I was about to depart Rupert enquired if I saw anything of Jeremy. I replied, 'not really. But I have his contact number and that of Claude who served with him in the Duke of Wellington's and indeed the other five from the cricket team who had taken part in that frolic on Pen Island.' I related how Jeremy had studied Land Management, enjoyed a scintillating career at Cambridge and was now working with Beale Thompson, a leading country estates company in the north of England. Reckoning that Rupert and he would find a lot in common, we left it that if ever Jeremy came south I would be in touch with a view to arranging that we all link up. I was fairly sure this would not come amiss.

That evening I phoned Jeremy to let him know of Rupert's book and how he and I had met up. He was more than willing to renew this acquaintance and said that in a few weeks he was due to be south on business and would gladly make time to see both Rupert and me.

Rupert arranged for us to meet at the Savoy for drinks before we headed off to a family run French restaurant opposite Leicester Square tube station called Chez Solange. This was renowned amongst other things for its amazing French onion soup. To my surprise Ben Goddard was there too. Clearly this was not to be just a recall of the old days. There had to be a business rationale too. Over dinner this became transparent when he asked for and obtained my promise that all conversation from now on would be off the record.

Ben was frank. 'At Frenshams we have found our joint potential with Dixon Powell is a bigger challenge than first thought. So the changes we need are likely to cost rather more than originally envisaged. Our shares are quoted on the stock market but they seldom move for control is tightly held by the founding families. However the Board, although minded to go to the market to raise cash, is reluctant to do so for they fear loss of control. There is also no great wish to place ourselves in the hands of merchant bankers. What we would prefer, if one can be found, is a wealthy private investor happy to be at the forefront of a renaissance of our two hundred year old business.

Goddard continued, 'Jeremy, it has occurred to me that in handling the affairs of wealthy private clients you might well know of certain parties who would appreciate a substantial presence in the preference shares of a sound provincial brewery and view this as a smart investment. Could I be right?'

Jeremy replied he knew of two or three wealthy landowners who might well be glad to diversify their holdings. He would mention this prospect to them in confidence and be happy to revert.

Goddard took up the cudgels again.

'The other matter that might involve you personally is a strategic overview of the best way to go forward in promoting our major properties so that they produce an enhanced return on the investment we are proposing.'

Goddard elaborated. 'In Rupert we have a qualified surveyor who will ensure that any building we seek to improve is capable of being achieved economically. I am sure you will well understand that many of our inns require considerable upgrading whether they are in towns, villages or even the remote countryside. Those five years of war took quite a toll on our estate. Such an undertaking as is now necessary will be an ongoing exercise. In the process we will almost certainly jettison a number of properties by offering them for sale either as a tied house or as a free house. If the latter, we should still retain a decent share of their trade as their patrons will be familiar with our products. Would you be interested in conducting such an overview? I ask this as we feel that a fresh pair of eyes allied to an alert brain will be of immense value to us. You will approach this with an uncluttered mind – something that we in the company cannot claim to have. There is a company operating in the south-east who we know reasonably well. This is Surridges. In the past we have used them to market these surplus properties and possibly they could fulfil this role again.'

Jeremy thanked him for the invitation and smiled. 'Your invitation could not be better timed. My boss and I have been in London this week thrashing out the final details of a takeover that we have worked on for the last nine months. This will appear in the trade press next week for we have just bought Surridges. They are in the same line of business as us but are smaller. In addition to their commercial activities in the retail and licensed trades, they have recently taken to advising major landowners on how best to take advantage of their estates. In doing so they have adopted a low profile. At one there is a go-cart track and at another an ice rink. At a third there is a riding school. At a fourth, a new golf course designed by the Charles Lawrie partnership is being brought to fruition. In the north I have recently been working with a chain of wine bars on just such a remit as you propose. You might think this an ideal preparation. What is more Beale Thompson have asked me to take charge of Surridges now that the chairman and MD are retiring. So I shall be moving south within the next few weeks. If you grant me this assignment it will be my top priority.'

'That is good news. I could not be more delighted,' countered Goddard who now turned to me. 'Nigel, if you have any contacts with Country Life or The Field, and in due course are able to get an article or two accepted, we would show our gratitude in the traditional way. Something to bear in mind!'

Addressing Rupert he said, 'thanks for convening this meeting. I think we can look forward to some real progress in the not too distant future.' What none of us knew at the time was that this task entrusted to Jeremy was ultimately to be so very rewarding for him.

Back home in Somersal Herbert he discussed Frenshams proposal with his father regarding the strategic overview and whether he thought the Earl of Ruabon would be interested in investing. Having checked Frenshams financial record with Extel, he had found it to be very steady with profitability growing around 4% to 6% compound for the last ten years and debt at a containable amount. On the face of it, therefore, preference shares seemed sound enough and non-speculative.

'The Earl lives well below his income and has no extravagant tastes or vices,' acknowledged his father. 'Yet he is no gambler and a cast iron investment in preference shares in a well-considered country brewery not far from London might suit him nicely. Let me put it to him.'

Born in 1890, the Earl was seventy and in good fettle. He listened carefully then said he rather liked the idea. So the following week the three of them travelled south to meet the Frenshams Board. Jeremy's father acted as the Earl's adviser while Jeremy was present to evaluate the company's prospects if he was minded to invest. In the event the outcome was positive and Frenshams offered a return of 5.75% on a seven figure amount with which the Earl was fully satisfied. So the deal went ahead.

Before Jeremy left for the south he had asked Bart and Slim and Bart to a meeting and explained he expected to be in Surridges London office for at least three years. In fact he was uncertain at this stage if he would ever return north should all go well. He put it to the two of them that regardless of his duties with Surridges they should form a consultancy, Broughton, Marston & Warner. Bart and Slim both showed interest and liked the idea of the word play on the BMW motor car.

'Bart and you too, Slim, have often said you would like to be your own boss. Bart, your training in the hotel world is as good as any, if not better. Slim, you have been engaged both in army catering and now, these last few years, in feeding hungry steelworkers. You know what the soldier and the working man wants to eat and you have been able to formulate and work to a budget. Your Dad's milk bars must surely have only limited appeal even though one day they will become yours. Meantime, why not branch out? I am absolutely sure you can go places. I have a job for both of you which should help to kick off the partnership. If you agree I shall only be involved were Surridges to negotiate the contract and then with my Surridges hat on.

'What I should like you two to examine is how best to develop their hotels and how they should change their attitude and practice towards food in all their establishments. I think probably a fifth of them don't even offer food at all other than a ham or cheese roll, and possibly nuts and crisps. In future there has to be far more emphasis on eating out in pubs if they are to make the kind of returns that they should. Merely selling beer, spirits and simple table wine is not making the best of their assets. What is more, the Chancellor always sees alcohol as an easy target for raising revenue. And that impinges on margins. Bart, I suspect that a large number of the group's hotels require a complete makeover or should be the subject of disposal. I shall be looking to see if they cannot be converted to flats or demolished altogether in favour of brand new residential or office accommodation. But where the hotels serve a valid purpose your professional opinion will be more than welcome. I can see them competing with the best of their pubs for investment.'

And that is how BMW came into being with Jeremy adopting a low profile whatever the circumstances. The advice of the consultancy was welcomed by the Frenshams Board who confirmed their relationship with Surridges under Jeremy's direction.

A tripartite plan was drawn up to offload around a dozen underperforming pubs annually for the next four years: to upgrade six each year with the assistance of the proceeds and the Earl's investment and to review the hotels with the aim of reducing these by half and classifying the others according to conference, city, or resort. In towns which were way beyond their heyday and the economic returns if any were unsatisfactory they would be seeking a sale for site redevelopment. Station hotels and roadside inns with accommodation were also candidates for the chop. Bart's advice was seen as a welcome breath of fresh air for where Jeremy identified properties as possessing hidden potential his proposals to reinvigorate them were constructive. Slim came forward with a whole set of menus according to the revised objectives of each and every type of property. As for strengthening their interest in wine, Bart's advice was pragmatic.

'May I suggest you use an independent specialist to buy your house wines direct from growers. Focus on France. Consider not only Bordeaux but also the Beaujolais and Languedoc. Additionally, try working with at least two merchants to build a list that would be in line with what a good London club might offer at under £10 a bottle. The Loire valley too can offer very good value.'

Jeremy was attracted by the common sense approach of both Slim and Bart. Reflecting on this he considered the consultancy had a fair chance of success.

As it was he stayed on in the south with Surridges but Bart and Slim returned north to pursue such other opportunities as their training could unearth. Reluctantly due to the normal run of day to day activities, contact between us Heathside cricketers drifted for there was no annual get-together. Each was getting on with his life as best he could. Then one morning in 1961 a notice in the Telegraph and Times announced the death of the Gaffer, Gwyn Evans, with details of his memorial service to be held in the private chapel of the Earl of Ruabon at Somersal Herbert in six weeks time. Claude took the initiative and phoned round where he could or sent a letter where he was unable to get a reply. He suggested this would be the ideal time not only to show respect to Kathleen and the family but to congregate for a reunion. The response was unanimous. All said they would try to be there.

I informed Steve Cruickshank of the Kent Essential that I wished to attend and enquired whether an article on an outstanding prep school headmaster was of the slightest interest. Steve thought for a moment, frowned momentarily, then in typical positive fashion replied that the newly launched weekly coloured supplement would be the appropriate platform.

'Yes, Nigel, go and have a go. Somewhere around 1,500 words might fill the bill. We could start on a series of obituaries if the feedback is encouraging and the subject is outstanding in his or her own way particularly if you can unearth some connection with Kent. That is all important. Furthermore it would indicate our broad pursuit of excellence no matter in what field. The sort of thing the supplement will not be featuring is local football and complaints about buses or the railways. I leave that to our much respected competition.' He laughed, conscious of his sarcasm.

I had not seen Harry for well over a year and phoned him at his chambers in the Middle Temple. Was he going up to Somersal Herbert? He could not have been friendlier and suggested we meet for dinner at the Cheshire Cheese just off Fleet Street where he would be happy to entertain me. Here he explained how he was living the high life and consorting with wealthy young ladies who, after attending finishing school, "came out" as debutantes.

Harry was jovial and frank. 'Until 1958 the debutantes at Queen Charlotte's Ball used to be received by the Queen. Then this presentation ceased on the grounds that it was no longer politically acceptable. But the partying still continued and eligible young men were much sought after. Although a Yorkshireman, I have been lucky enough to be one of these. You may not know but the small clique of hostesses has a code for grading us chaps. NSIT stands for "Not Safe In Taxis". APQ denotes "Avoid. Probably Queer". OTM signifies "On The Make". Other acronyms are passed round like hot cakes between these ambitious mothers such as SPOH, "Safe Pair Of Hands" and GHM, "Good Husband Material" for all are anxious to find a suitable husband for their lovely girls. In this way they hope to weed out the dross and those who will do little for their daughters other than bed them or fleece them.'

'What are you graded? Have you any idea?' I ventured.

'Well, I cannot be sure. But apparently one can get away with one NSIT although if you are reported three times then you are dropped. The top mark is OOU.'

'What does that stand for?'

"One Of Us," replied Harry. 'I am not sure I have ever attained that. Perhaps if I happened to be a property lawyer or a specialist dealing with trusts that would go down better.'

As we chatted away I asked how he intended to travel up to Gaffer's service.

'By car for it is some time since I went to Sheffield and I do need to see my folk. Father has been receiving takeover bids for his steel business and is minded to negotiate with a view to selling. I simply must catch up on what is going on.'

Harry indicated he now owned an elegant if unusual Armstrong Siddeley Sapphire saloon and kindly he offered to take me with him. 'I may stay on for a few days. So if I do can you come back by train?'

'No problem,' I answered.

'By the way, can you come down to Sussex on Saturday week for a game of golf? Although I am a country member at Rye I am keen to play the new course at Camber Sands of which I hear good report. However they seem set on fourballs. So is there an interesting couple that as my guests you would like to invite to make up the four?'

I suggested Steve Cruickshank, my boss at the Kent Essential, and Rupert Lyall of Frenshams. 'Great,' said Harry, 'sounds fun. Go ahead.'

Both Steve and Rupert happily agreed. Finishing our game at half-past-three we wondered if we were still in time for lunch. On ordering a drink we sat down whereupon a little old lady called Dottie approached us. She looked the epitome of an old retainer. Apparently she had served at Littlestone Golf Club for something like forty years before deciding to take up this post at Camber where she now lived.

'Is there anything I can get you gents?' she enquired solicitously on handing us the menu.

With Harry in the lead we all ordered lamb cutlets with redcurrant jelly.

'Well, gents, I shall have to see. Hot food goes off at half-past three, you know.' And with that she sauntered off to the kitchen in her slippers. A minute later she reappeared.

'Sorry, gents, hot food is now off. So no lamb cutlets. But food of a sort is still available.'

Hoping for a belated concession we ordered soup and a warm bacon roll.

Back to the kitchen Dottie padded before announcing to mild relief this would be all right.

In due course she reappeared again with the bacon rolls and two menacing sauce bottles.

'Is everything OK for you gents?' she asked once the bacon rolls had been consumed.

'Yes,' was the reply hastily followed by, 'but what happened to the hot soup?'

'Bugger,' said Dottie standing resolutely. 'Forgot. Too late, gents, to sort that now.'

Recognising that his hospitality had not gone quite as well as Harry had envisaged we all downed a kummel and a coffee before retreating to the car park. Here we met Dottie clambering into her aged Morris Minor. As she did so the chef appeared with a bag crying, 'Dottie love, don't forget your lamb cutlets. Here are four beauties.'

Clearly oblivious of any concern, Dottie duly popped them on the seat beside her.

'Gracious,' said Harry to me after we had bid goodbye to Steve and Rupert, 'this is weird. Looks like a case of Alzheimers plus. I think in future I shall stick to Rye no matter that the second shots at the short holes are likely to be so fiendish they border on the infernal.'

A month later Harry collected me from Charing Cross station in his graceful limousine to commence the long drive north to the memorial service. On the way I asked him what precisely he was up to as a barrister and whether he was specialising. He explained he was in a dilemma for he was becoming increasingly involved in the defence of criminals.

'It is not something I ever planned. It has just come about. I was handed a brief when senior Counsel in our chambers fell ill and everyone else was too busy to take it aboard. This is all very well,' he continued, 'but the mothers of those ravishing debutantes whose balls I am invited to are far from impressed. They imagine I am hobnobbing with the most undesirable section in all society. Already one or two have declared me "persona non grata".

'What has been your most high profile case to date?'

'A major one defending Ronnie Kray in a murder case.'

'That gangster who with his twin brother and known as "The Kings" rules the East End?'

'The very same,' he replied.

'What happened and did you get Ronnie off?'

'I did indeed for it was a case of mistaken identity. Just the once Ronnie was blameless. His brother Reggie was the culprit. And even then there was no premeditation to murder.'

'Tell me more,' I ventured.

'A bookmaker in Bethnal Green called Jack Smithers was robbed one Saturday evening of £23,000 – a big sum and the result of a betting coup which went awry. Scarlet Daisy was gambled upon heavily to win the 4 'o'clock at Sandown coming in from 12/1 to 7/4. She went down by a neck to The Tailor, whose victory at 20/1 shocked the punters. The Daisy's Australian jockey Brandon Mitchell was the subject of heavy abuse and critical comment in the papers the next day. Those in the know thought he had been well paid to see his horse lose. Anyhow the bookies made a fortune instead of being taken to the cleaners. Very few punters had bothered to consider The Tailor.

'Reggie Kray was furious. He had lost £1,000 and was determined to see this back. With three of his firm they called upon Jack before he shut up shop. When Reggie demanded to recover his money, or else there would be trouble, Jack would have no truck. Reggie threw a tantrum, struck him on the head with a mallet and the four of them walked off with the entire swag let alone Reggie's thousand pound wager. What they did not know was that Jack had an eggshell skull. That blow was only meant to incapacitate him – not to cause his death.

'When the evening newspapers relayed the story that Monday for it was the morning cleaner who discovered poor Jack, Reggie sought an alibi. Knowing that nobody would believe he could possibly be in consort with him, he went to his arch enemy the gangster Solomon Doull. While the two saw each other frequently in clubland, they were ever watchful and wary for each had their own area where they liked to think they reigned supreme. However for £3,000 Solly agreed to give him an alibi. That sum was spent on a new Jaguar. Solly of course was laughing and now would not split on Reggie. A sort of honour among thieves!

'The Met were quick to place the blame on Ronnie although it was Reggie and his three colleagues who had been seen making a getaway. Yet Reggie had his alibi. So not unnaturally the investigating superintendent Arthur Walker-Harris assumed it was Ronnie, widely regarded as the more violent twin, who had been Jack's visitor.'

'What had Ronnie been up to that evening?' I asked.

'Something that he did not wish to be aired in public.'

'Namely?' I prodded.

'He was introducing to his mother Violet his new boyfriend, a twenty- two year old Moroccan called Ibrahim. He had been on holiday in Tangiers. Seduced by his olive skin and male good looks he had picked him up in a gay bar. The Moroccan made a change from an Italian or Greek who for some time had been Ronnie's preferred choice. While Violet accepted Ronnie's homosexuality both his elder brother and father absolutely did not. Reggie may well have been inveigled into it once as well. But my guess is he definitely prefers girls. The point is that Ronnie did not wish his sexuality to become public knowledge. So his very genuine alibi had to be tailored somewhat. Fortunately Violet's two neighbours were there, May and Iris. They were able to vouch for the fact Ronnie had indeed spent an hour or more at his mother's at the time of the attack on Jack. Naturally no mention was made of Ibrahim.

'The head of the Met was livid at the failure to succeed in a conviction and Walker-Harris was side-tracked to a post overseeing immigration at Harwich. As for Ronnie he swore to get even with Solly. He considered he should never have been in the dock. Solly is still around now but you can bet your bottom dollar he is continually watching his back.'

'How long did the Moroccan last?'

'Not very long at all. Ibrahim was unreliable and a petty thief. He was shipped back to Tangiers within a few weeks and replaced by a svelte Sicilian with a penchant for pink shirts and glitzy jewellery. Curiously, Ronnie never thought his affairs with young men compromised his macho image. While those in gangland were well aware of the fact and behind his back would refer to him as a fat poofter, he was adamant this should never leak out beyond his very tight circle. So please treat this as strictly confidential. Even though it is sure to be known to the tabloid newspapers no one will dare publish it.'

On reaching Somersal Herbert we booked in at The Dog and Duck. Most of us stayed there since the parents of Jeremy and Claude were putting up old friends of their own vintage who had long known Gwyn and Kathleen. To my surprise, although it was the local rector who took the service it was Mark who gave the address. After Corpus Christi at Oxford Mark had gone on to theological college at Durham and been ordained. It was then he spent two years in Nigeria as a missionary, something he had resolved to do once he learned of his friend Richard's death at the hands of terrorists. On his return he had become the padre at Lichfield Cathedral School, coaching cricket and keeping up with his piano skills.

What I had not fully appreciated was that some time earlier he had married Myfanwy so was Gwyn's son-in-law. Myfanwy's childhood dream had indeed come true. No doubt with her help Mark had done his homework thoroughly. He ran through Gaffer's academic background.

'You may recall he excelled at Modern Languages. Indeed he did for he gained a first class degree at Cambridge before going on to study in Heidelberg. Here he earned good pocket money on playing the accordion in a nightclub popular with students. He also developed his artistic talents. He did not experiment much with paint for he preferred pencil and charcoal and was remarkably skilful at drawing the human body. At Cambridge his talent with the accordion won him much admiration and contributed to his participation as an active Thespian with the Footlights. You will recall his incredible impersonation of a witch's cackle at that Halloween when we young ones were at Barley Farm all those years ago.'

'Absolutely,' I said to myself. That was something I would never forget. I also recalled how magically he played "Goosey Goosey" on his accordion, a wonderful little tune that was recorded by both Jack Hylton and that highly accomplished accordionist Horst Wende. At our Christmas pantomime Woodbine delighted in hamming this up. Behind a lighted screen we could see his well-padded shadow waddling on impersonating the Goose Step, the Nazi manner of marching that appeared ludicrous. We would hoot with laughter totally ignorant that not that far away Jews were being herded onto railway trucks bound for concentration camp and the gas chamber. Six and a half million continental Jews were to suffer such an unspeakable fate at the hands of the Nazis to include the best part of one million from Hungary.

Apparently Gaffer's first job had been at a prep school in Tunbridge Wells. So he did have some connection with Kent which I was happy to stress to Steve when I relayed my report. A keen Christian, he had attended Summer Camp between the Wars where he consorted with the Duke of York, Prince Albert, before he became George VI. A picture gallery was on display among which was a striking photograph showing the two together in casual shirt and shorts clearly happy with each other's company. Mark was both scholarly and entertaining.

With Gaffer having retired two years earlier in 1959, the reception was not held at Heathside. Instead the Earl had invited us into his orangery where champagne and canapés were served. Two hundred people must have been there paying their respects and recalling anecdotes about such a remarkable man. Jeremy had organised a dinner at The Dog and Duck so I restricted myself to a couple of glasses. As it was agreed that members of the team of '47 should catch up with each other later at the inn, we circulated quietly chatting to those of the teaching staff whom we recollected along with parents of our old friends. In my case I also sought out the Earl. Now seventy-one he had not noticeably aged and seemed more than happy with his investment in Frenshams.

With the duty calls out of the way I looked forward in anticipation to the reunion in the pub. Perhaps those misgivings I had suffered when returning from the joint twenty-first of Claude and Jeremy, on possibly being cold shouldered by my ex-cricketing colleagues, would not be borne out. I just hoped so for I realised that one cannot have enough friends in this world. If I were to ever break away from being a simple journalist, I knew I should have to work at this.

CHAPTER 6: THE FEEDBACK

That evening the team of '47 filled the snug bar in The Dog and Duck bent on playing catch up. Any misgivings that I may have had vanished soon enough. The atmosphere was tremendous. The friendliness and interest in our achievements and plans was genuine. At the outset, rather to my surprise both Myfanwy and Cressida looked in for a drink but along with Mark understandably excused themselves so as to support their mother Kathleen. After bidding them farewell Jeremy suggested we go through the batting order to hear how we are all doing. That was nodded through in an instant. With Mark now absent Theo was the first to speak having opened with Mark at number two.

'Guys don't laugh. But I have won an award from Rolls Royce for being apprentice of the year. This has earned me the proud sum of £300. However in some respects promotion seems very much a matter of luck depending on which aspect of their complex businesses you are in. I will stay a little longer but might well look outside the company in the next year or two. Meanwhile, I enjoy riding for Nicholas Broadbent at the weekends over fences and hurdles. At nine and a half stone I am too big ever to be a flat jockey.'

His most important news he kept to the end. 'I am going to try my luck at proposing to the bubbly, blonde and pretty Cressida. We have been going out together for quite some time and have an interest in common through horses and racing. She is a gutsy girl, I can tell you. Very talented too. Need I say more? Watch this space,' he added with a twinkle in his brown eyes.

Jeremy's tale induced a touch of envy in some of his listeners no matter that he was modest in playing down his success. After his time with Surridges and still working for their owners Beale Thompson, he spearheaded the next acquisition of this thrusting concern.

'I am now responsible for integrating Rawlings Clifford into the Beale Thompson organisation. They have long been prominent in the east of Yorkshire, Durham and Northumberland. So for the time being I am based at York. While I have been lucky enough to be elected a member of the golf club at Ganton, it does not do me as much good as I would like for Saturday is a working day. Unusual recent assignments have included advising on how two large boarding schools could best make the use of their grounds and facilities during the holidays, and devising attractions for a couple of racecourses when they are not staging races. Otherwise I contribute to the management of a few landed estates.'

Harry was equally forthright. 'I appear to have become involved in defending members of London's criminal underworld when they are caught out. The most high profile case was when Ronnie Kray was accused of a murder that was more likely an unintended homicide occasioned by his twin brother Reggie during the course of a robbery. The Met mistook one for the other and were not overly meticulous in verifying the facts. Ronnie has twice asked me to be his guest at one of the regrettably notorious pubs in the East End where he and Reggie hang out. Fortunately both times I have had a legitimate excuse not to accept. In any case I don't want to get too involved. If I did it would be sure to backfire.'

He went on to sidestep his amorous dealings with gorgeous and frequently spoiled debutantes and said he had been elected to the MCC. He now went to see first class cricket at least twice a year. In addition to being a country member of the golf club at Rye, as often as he could he knocked a golf ball around Wentworth. All in all, he was having a high old time and relishing living in Pimlico.

'I thought you were a member of Huntercombe,' I interrupted.

'True, I was. But I was unlikely to find a potential client there. Most of the members are either doctors, dentists, judges or Generals. It is not quite the case at Wentworth.'

Bart intervened, 'what makes you think there was no criminal among the Huntercombe members?'

'They would not have got past the vetting process instigated by Lord Nuffield who owned the whole caboodle,' was the smart reply.

'Wouldn't you have done just as well in joining Sunningdale?' I ventured tongue in cheek.

'Possibly, but among the captains of industry and notable sporting characters they possess a sprinkling of famous actors and film stars. Were they to be in need of Counsel I don't think I have yet acquired sufficient gravitas for them.'

Noel tried to hide his smiles, while Jeremy let it all pass as though Harry had never intended the slightest innuendo to deride the well-to-do membership of Wentworth.

Claude had a very different tale to tell.

'Many of Liverpool's traditional businesses are no longer quite the force they were, typically the shipping industry which is facing tough times. There is still a lot of inherited money and the stock exchange, although small, is reasonably active. Nevertheless every year another family broker seems to shut up shop. It is all very tricky. I am choosing to focus on mining shares. This means that in order to be on top of the job, site visits are very much required. No other Liverpool firm indulges in this. But our firm's senior partner is adamant this has to be a worthwhile exercise where new discoveries are considered to have far-reaching potential. Recently I have been to the Congo, Tanganyika, both Northern and Southern Rhodesia, and South Africa.'

'No,' he replied to a question when asked if he had been back to Pen Island. 'No minerals there so I am told. But I would not mind! No time either to discuss politics in Africa right now. That is a cauldron forever on the bubble. However if you want a speculation, the Mallinson diamond mine in Tanganyika shares the same geology as the Williamson mine whose shares have never been quoted. These days it is managed by De Beers. They and the Tanganyikan government have an equal share. Alas, their grades are not as high as they were. But under the late Dr John Williamson's eagle eye this enterprise was remarkably profitable. No diamond mine has ever been bigger. Mallinson is likely to go public next year. While not the same size, it still covers ninety acres and the characteristics of their stones are similar to that of the Williamson kimberlite. I am hugely optimistic.'

Next to say his piece was Owen who used to feature at number six. 'I have problems,' he announced. 'But I do not think this is quite the forum for them to be aired. Maybe Jeremy and you, Harry, can spare some time tomorrow morning after breakfast. I will be grateful if Slim can be around too perhaps a little later on. For the moment I am still with Giffords. That is all I want to say right now.' The three he called upon said they would be happy to listen and comment as appropriate the next day.

Noel came next. He explained that he had qualified in engineering having specialised in motor mechanics. 'I foresee a far better future for earth moving equipment and agricultural machinery than for luxury cars like Rolls Royce. Selling these would bore me to tears. So I am now in the process of extricating myself from the family firm. This will allow my elder brother Russell to work unfettered with Father. Russell does not share my ambition so that is probably a good idea. More to the point I am in talks with a Canadian company and two others so when we next meet I should have more to say.'

My story was more modest. 'I am now in my sixth year with the Kent Essential but am toying with the idea of setting myself up in public relations. If successful that ought to bring in a lot more cash than the role of a humble reporter. It is high time I stepped out and stopped working solely to make a run of the mill living. I need to do something more worthwhile with my life, show some entrepreneurial spirit and create something.'

Jeremy intervened, 'Quite right, Nigel. Give it a go. I am sure you will find plenty of support from your old friends here if you take the plunge. Count on me for one.'

Noel added, 'I believe I can help as well once I have got my show on the road for I shall then be in need of a lot of back up.'

I smiled in return. 'Any help will be gratefully received. Many thanks for your kind words.'

Rather like Owen, Noel and me, Bart was at a crossroads in life. He had done well to help sort out Frenshams. More recently after a barren spell in the north he had completed an assignment in Le Touquet for Gary Hawkridge, a wide boy turned boxing promoter who owned two nightclubs in Essex.

'A year ago Gary added to his portfolio a hotel and a casino. Both overlook Le Touquet's two fine golf courses. My job was to train the French manager. In the process I enjoyed the company of a French girl called Mathilde who was hoping to become a sommelier. I am not sure who trained who in what but one thing I can say is it was not just bedroom French she taught me! However, what I really ought to be doing now is to run a hotel in either the Home Counties or London. I shall have much more credibility in the profession once I have got that under my belt. Right now I am with an agency seconded to London's Stafford Hotel.'

Sotto voce Harry whispered to me Bart had a lot under his belt.

'Don't interrupt,' I replied.

Bart, who had heard, gave Harry a dirty look and continued, 'You know, on one occasion the two Kray brothers were guests of Gary. They behaved well enough according to their lights but I found Ronnie in particular very strange. At some slightest thing, however trivial, he would get upset then flare up. So briefly the atmosphere would be electric. You could almost smell the danger in the air. As far as I was concerned they could not leave quickly enough.'

Jeremy motioned to Slim. The consultancy he had enjoyed with Bart and Jeremy had not failed so much as lapsed and he had yet to find his feet in the north.

'I have now joined Bart and on his recommendation am working as sous-chef at the Stafford not far from the Ritz. This is so discreet that there is not even a brass plaque to indicate it is a hotel. Patronised by politicians and captains of industry there is no passing trade. My lips are sealed as to who frequents the place. But as you know I am a northerner at heart. So I am pondering whether to return once again to a land where I feel that little bit more at ease. On the other hand very possibly I too need to gain further experience in London. Either way, with things somewhat up in the air, like Bart I am ready to move on.'

Vince said he had now qualified as a solicitor and joined a practice operating out of Ilford. 'Most of my clients are from India and Sri Lanka and one way or another are keeping me very busy. One of them treads on eggshells. And he is far from the only one. If they get into serious trouble, I may have to call upon you, Harry.'

He refused to elaborate more but one got the impression that several could well be distinctly dubious and that Vince's practice just might not have the utmost approval of his father.

Next morning Owen was in quiet enclave with just Jeremy and Harry. Not an extrovert or a romantic, he was a realist who was conscious of his strengths and weaknesses.

'I am back working with Father at Giffords after my training with Semleys. As you know they own department stores in the prosperous towns of Leeds, York and Harrogate. For some years we have had a joint buying company with Semleys in order to attract a better discount from suppliers than either of us could attain on our own. This is Holderness. It has worked well and we have shared the warehouse on a 50-50 basis. Now Semleys is offering to buy us out. Not just Holderness but Giffords as a whole.'

Harry intervened. 'Am I right in thinking that the chairman of Semleys is Francis Whyte?'

'Indeed. He is an old charmer. I like him a lot and would do almost anything for him. But his elder son Freddy is a ruthless sort whom I don't really trust. The younger son Bernard I could work with. However I doubt the chemistry is right for me to be a partner with the Whyte brothers as and when old Francis retires. I think these two might gang up and step all over me. Even if we split the shareholding 50-50 between us I would feel threatened for I suspect that although they have three stores to our four they would be seeking a majority holding as their sites are probably more valuable than ours. In addition to Sheffield and Derby we have two more. They are in Chesterfield and Doncaster. Other than our flagship in Sheffield, these other three locations do not have the purchasing powers of those Semley sites. '

With Jeremy nodding his head in agreement, Harry returned to the Whytes.

'Owen do you know their background?' he asked.

'Actually I don't but Father surely will.'

'Well, I can tell you that my father's brother Uncle Gideon once acted for them in a lawsuit when a neighbouring property owner was thoroughly objectionable. The Whytes are Jewish refugees from Czechoslovakia who were born Weiss. In the 1930s they read the tea leaves correctly and came to Britain, rightly fearing that Hitler would endeavour to create an empire and turn against the Jews in any country he sought to subjugate. Old Francis could not be more charming. But he is very patient and far sighted too. You can be as sure as night follows day he will have been planning this coup for many years and just biding his time until your father is contemplating retirement.'

'Thanks Harry, I hear you well.' Owen looked circumspect.

Jeremy now spoke. 'I know the Semley stores. They occupy prime sites. If your father will only do a deal on a 50-50 basis, you must make sure that the Whyte family do not retain the three freeholds. If they do, income will be syphoned off to provide them with handsome dividends. That could threaten the profitability of the joint business quite substantially. Giffords might want to do the same even though the merger is in effect a takeover by Semleys. By the way, what percentage of Giffords shares do you, your mother and sister hold? And what is the state of your father's health?'

'Dealing with the second question first, Father had a heart attack last year and has had a quadruple bypass. It is difficult to say how much longer he will want to involve himself in the business even though it is very much his baby. He inherited only the Sheffield store. The others he has built up himself. And he is very much a "hands on" proprietor. As for the share split, father retains 50 %, Mother has 10% while my sister and I have 20% apiece.'

Jeremy looked Owen in the eye. 'What do you really want to do?'

'I am not clairvoyant but I sense that family run department stores may be nearing the end of their time. The John Lewis partnership is growing fast as are Marks & Spencer. Tesco is also a threat for Father doubts that they will stick merely to food. I believe Chiesmans of Lewisham is finding it tough going even though they have around a dozen well established department stores in the south-east. Their share price is scarcely wonderful. It could be that we at Giffords should sell. If we do I think I would like out. What I have in mind is setting up a garden centre and working for myself.'

'Very interesting,' said Jeremy. 'That is something to which I have been giving quite a bit of thought. But a garden centre on its own will have a seasonal trade. To encourage footfall throughout the year it makes sense to have a restaurant, a retail shop and a play area, possibly with roller skating or that new craze of skateboarding. You might want to have a USP too. A unique selling point that strikes me as offering potential is to focus on the old varieties of English apple that seem to be under threat from imports from Canada, Tasmania and France. I can think of more than half a dozen that are delicious and sadly now are virtually ignored. Think of Allington Pippin, Egremont Russet and Laxton Superb. I could go on. And if you like the idea of catering we will see if Slim is still around. I don't think he was in any hurry to get away. The key thing will be to select the right site and if that works out then to develop others along similar lines.'

Harry piped up. 'Here in Yorkshire we have a number of racecourses. These are readily accessible by trunk road. What say you, Jeremy, to garden centres adjacent to racecourses where umpteen days a year there will be thousands in attendance?'

'Indeed. I have thought much the same. In the London area there simply is not the space available. I explored this notion in Folkestone. Alas it came to nothing. But here in the north quite often it is a different matter. Think of York, Wetherby, Beverley, and Ripon. Also Doncaster and even Pontefract. Catterick Bridge is another possibility. It is near the A1. How does this concept appeal to you, Owen?'

'I like it a lot. Jeremy, now that you are up here in York, would this fit in with your plans at Rawlings Clifford?'

'Very well I would say. Let's talk to Slim to see whether he would want the catering franchise once you have your first garden centre up and running.'

Slim was summoned and was all for it. 'Were I to return north and take over Dad's business, in Sheffield I have only two milk bars which are worth converting to restaurants. Once I have seen to those I shall have time on my hands. If you can acquire sites near racecourses then I foresee the venture taking off. I might even be tempted to undertake catering at racecourses. Presently Eshelby & Percival has a stranglehold on those in the north. They are good but a bit 'old hat' and far from cheap. I think one can do better and would be happy to have a crack.'

Harry laughed. 'You are right,' he said. 'Trust you to see the big picture. You must have learned something in that BMW consultancy with Jeremy and Bart. In fact you might want to resurrect it to get the restaurant facilities right. That is where Jeremy can help too.'

Jeremy returned to the dominant issue. 'Owen, discuss with your father the sale of Giffords and tell him you want to cut and run as you cannot see a happy working relationship with Freddy and Bernard. He will understand I am sure. Sell him on the concept of garden centres in strategic locations. Let me find you your first site. Give me a couple of months. No more. I think you could be arriving in this market at a very interesting state of its development. It is virtually in its infancy.'

As we were about to depart Noel came up to me. His manner could not have been friendlier and he reiterated the sentiments he had expressed earlier. 'Nigel, if you go ahead and set up in public relations, please get in touch with me when you are ready to start. I am going to have need of someone like you once I have secured the agencies that I have my eye on. I know we can work well together.'

His generosity and sincerity were evident. I thanked him and promised to let him know of my plan. Noel was not in any way patronising. He understood that he wanted to work with people he knew and liked and could trust. Moreover, he possessed the demeanour of a man who was born to succeed. Whereas I suffered a measure of self-doubt, this deficiency was totally absent in Noel's make up.

Harry had decided to stay on for a day or two. So alone in the train on journey to London I thought long and hard. Noel was sure to pursue his ambition and in my view be a success. Owen, clearly stimulated by the support he was receiving, had also had a brief word with me as we said goodbye and indicated he too hoped I would set up a PR consultancy. Were I to do so, he said he was sure to use my services. Bart was supportive as well for he was determined to win a role running a London hotel. And when that day came he emphasised it would need careful handling by way of promotion. Much encouraged by all this I resolved to chat to my boss Steve at the Essential and ask if I could become a freelance reporter rather than continue on his books as a member of salaried staff.

Steve listened carefully and did not turn me down out of hand. In fact he was positive.

'I think we can work something out, Nigel. We could either pay you a retainer or a fee for every article that you produce and which we publish. I will discuss it with the Chairman and let you know. I don't envisage too much of a problem.'

Conscious of so much good will from members of a team I knew so many years ago, as well as from Steve, I set up a consultancy called Nigel Collyer Associates which I then abbreviated to NCA. It was time to break out, be a man and not a mouse.

In the first week at my new desk I received a phone call from Owen.

'I have had a difficult time with Father,' he explained. 'He seemed certain that I could work with the Whyte family and was most put out when I told him I wanted to branch out on my own and develop garden centres. He just would not accept that Freddie, in particular, would not behave other than in the same gentlemanly manner as his old friend Francis. But I was adamant. He did his best to explain to me how legal safeguards could be introduced so that all could proceed smoothly. But, you know, with the best will in the world these might not be worth the paper they are printed on. Father became quite upset and I feared he might even have a heart attack. But Mother sided with me and eventually he calmed down, thank goodness. The sale of Giffords went through with Francis and Father both well satisfied in the end. However as you can imagine it was a stressful time.

'Nigel, I shall be in touch again. It may be sooner than you think. But I promise I shall give you plenty of warning when I am after your services.'

I returned south heartened for it appeared that my fellow team members from that vintage year were budding entrepreneurs and would be glad to put business my way if I followed their example. What was equally clear was that they were prepared to make use of each other's expertise. I sensed that the teamwork of those prep school years was wonderfully alive and well. Extraordinary I thought. But that is how it seems. What is more, long may it last!

CHAPTER 7: SETTING UP BUSINESS

It was three months later that I heard from Noel. He was off to Canada to try and secure the agency for agricultural machinery and earth moving equipment where one particular firm was proving such a success with both in the mid-west. But first he intended calling in on John Deere at their US headquarters having had pleasant conversations with their representatives in their London office. In the event it transpired that John Deere was satisfied with distribution arrangements in the UK and in any case the company was working flat out to satisfy their home market.

By contrast in Canada's Medicine Hat the reception Noel encountered was altogether more promising. The well-established agricultural machinery firm of Toogood Buchanan had branched out into earthmoving equipment in order to take advantage of the potash mines which were being brought to fruition in neighbouring Saskatchewan. Both a Toogood and a Buchanan were running the show. They were each second generation in the business and Noel found the two of them extremely go-ahead. The original Buchanan had hailed from Glasgow where the family firm had specialised in the manufacture of components for bridge building. He had quit when the halcyon days of exporting heavy metal sections to the Empire were clearly fading in favour of the enormous potential in supplying machinery for the grain belt along the 51st parallel. Selling what was still a prosperous business before it inevitably retracted, old Alistair Buchanan had linked up with Seymour Toogood, an American of Irish extraction. The partnership worked brilliantly and the sons of each, Bob and Peter, possessed the same fortunate chemistry as their fathers. It was the happiest of stories.

Noel spent a week with them both around Medicine Hat and in Saskatchewan to acquaint himself thoroughly with their range of equipment. With its distinctive livery in royal blue and deep yellow as background to prominent red maple leaves, their machines certainly cut a dash. In no way could they be taken for Caterpillar, JCB, John Deere or Claas. Bob Buchanan was as enthusiastic as he was fair. He explained the differences between their prime products and the competition and was anxious that Noel only started with their winners. They were not yet represented in Britain. However, both he and Peter Toogood were immensely supportive of Noel's plans for distribution.

On his return Noel explained how he was borrowing money to set up three distribution centres to handle the Good Doctor range as the Toogood Buchanan machines were known. He confided that in stocking both agricultural and construction machinery he aimed to ride the waves when one or the other was perhaps not doing as well as expected.

'Nigel, would you be prepared to advise me how to market our products to two such different industries bearing in mind two precepts I admire and wish to borrow from that fashionable photographer Cecil Beaton. In his view the world's second worst crime is boredom.'

'And the first?'

'Well, that is simply to be a bore. We have to make sure we do not fall into either trap. I would like you to focus on how we inform, educate and entertain.'

We chatted a while before agreeing on a joint plan of action. Noel was so positive I was encouraged to believe we might be able to work well together if our initial efforts proved to be successful.

The concept with which we came up was that, firstly, we would run a series of articles in the relevant trade journals to explain the virtues and objectives of each and every machine that would be imported. After this softening up period a number of farmers up and down the country would be invited to state what they required from the range of agricultural machines that Noel would have available. Three months would elapse before the formal presentation which was to include a short film, dramatic and possibly romantic but in no way jokey or juvenile. Then at lunch the farmers would be sat at tables of eight with two representatives from Noel's company who would listen avidly to their responses to learn whether they were content with the extras on offer. A similar programme was drawn up for the earthmoving equipment. Building contractors as well as local government planners, engineers and so called experts would be invited too. In the meantime articles in the appropriate trade magazines would introduce each item of equipment one by one. Every guest would be supplied with a hardback ring-bound dossier to form a permanent aide-memoire. As for terms, the option was open to lease or purchase.

One nice touch was that on departure every guest was to be presented with a calendar and a specially commissioned Lesney Matchbox toy in the form of one of the Good Doctor range. The calendars were designed to outdo the popularity of Pirelli's whose underclad ladies adopted all sorts of unusual postures. At any rate these Canadian ones were stunning, risqué certainly but not lacking in good taste, and far too good for a customer not to display in his office. No chance therefore either of boredom or of being a bore!

By January 1962 Noel had assembled a good team around him. He had the confidence and personality to attract capable people of ambition who would be able to work well on their own. Foremost was Theo who he had persuaded to come and be his technical director. He liked him, trusted him, valued his opinion even when it differed from his, and in his heart of hearts understood he needed him if he was not simply going to be a one-man band employing yes men. Clearly Theo had developed into an outstanding engineer. I concluded that Rolls Royce must have been sad to see him go. But they will have appreciated that a lot of their bright students seek pastures new once they are qualified. Equally clearly, Theo was positive about anything which he decided to undertake. Noel admired this attitude and believed their combined chemistry would reap rich rewards. He exuded confidence.

Within the year, on my advice and thanks to Slim's contributions – now that he was back in the north – a Good Doctor cookbook was produced containing homely Canadian recipes. For most British housewives this struck new ground. It advocated waffles with maple syrup, new and exciting salads, ranch house meat loaves, turkey chilli, stuffed peppers, the harvest pot-au-feu, clam chowder military style, crab quiche, and imaginative home baking to include zucchini bread, fudgy brownies, chip cookies and banana oat muffins. One unusual feature was the recommendation of cuts of meat not normally associated with British butchers. Slim went on television and in the 'Good Doctor' programme promoted the simple economical style of Canadian cooking. The series ran for ten weeks. The public liked it for the recipes worked and were relatively easy to make. In the process Slim came to be regarded as something of a celebrity. Noel was quietly amused. In fact Slim never looked back.

The Good Doctor range of agricultural equipment rapidly achieved success, almost as quickly as it became a household term thanks to television and the accurate and delightful Matchbox toys that were now captivating children. However it was in earthmoving equipment that Noel foresaw the biggest potential. He asked Jeremy for his thoughts on how to break into this.

Jeremy pointed out that land development was going to be the big thing for decades to come.

'Link up with the best and most progressive firm of builders you can find. I shall help you. Together we will ascertain where planning permission is most likely. I will deal with the landowners. At Beale Thompson we have an architect who specialises not in the houses themselves, but in the design of urban estates that conform to the typical aspirations of local planners. He could be very useful to any firm of builders. The company I like is Bassett Tompkins. They are enterprising, technologically advanced and not frightened of developing on terrain which can be a bit hilly, provoke problems, and entail a lot of earthmoving.'

Noel immediately established a rapport with the Bassett people. He then tackled Mortimer Wyse, another up and coming concern and one who specialised in low cost houses of immediate appeal. He was surprised to find an open door almost wherever he went.

The next target was to approach the fledgling companies who had begun to search for potash of which the north-east of Yorkshire had plenty. He already knew the big landowner in that area was the Talbot family. Through Jeremy he obtained an introduction to Sir Eldred Talbot. Together they hit it off from the start and in no time Sir Eldred had invited Noel to his box at the Yorkshire county cricket ground. With the two finding a common interest, it was soon apparent to Noel that Sir Eldred was more than keen to see the deposits of potash on his land exploited rather than just lying there for future generations, since in no way did he disguise his lack of confidence in politicians.

'Frankly, one can never be too sure. A Socialist government might easily confiscate all the mineral assets beneath the surface saying this was for the good of the community at large. My family would then be left high and dry and have to put up with all the massive inconvenience associated with mining, whose operators would doubtless not have their interests at heart in any way at all. Just remember how Manny Shinwell behaved to the Fitzwilliam family at Wentworth House not so very far from here. Utterly disgraceful! And prime minister Attlee who had the opportunity to forestall this did absolutely nothing. He did not wish to be seen conniving with celebrities even where they had a close connection with America's Kennedy family.'

Sir Eldred was in full flight. 'One or two companies have been snooping around. Two of these are vast international concerns. You say your Good Doctor machines were initially developed with potash in Saskatchewan in mind. Noel, go and talk to these predators. I shall be behind you if they show any spark at all. I cannot think other than that you are sure to meet with success.'

Sir Eldred was not only perceptive, he was right. Within the year operations commenced on the Talbot property at the Burrell mine. By now Noel was very much "persona grata" with the family. He was happy to mix business with pleasure for the elder Talbot daughter Evie was quite simply a stunner. She had been to a leading girls school, was able to converse freely on a whole range of subjects and was now acquiring a reputation as a landscape gardener which she found a happy medium for her artistic talents. Eldred and his wife Belinda were quickly aware that the two were mutually attracted and were supportive, going out of their way to see that when at all practicable they had the opportunity to meet. They recognised that Noel was not only handsome but well educated, purposeful and ambitious and would make a suitable son-in-law. Moreover they liked him.

So it was no surprise to be told of the good news that Noel and Evie had become engaged. Jeremy was asked to be best man and other than Vince all our team from '47 were invited to an afternoon wedding in the summer of 1963 at a medieval church outside the charming town of Malton. Two hundred and fifty guests packed the aisles to capacity. The reception was held in a marquee within the grounds of Talbot Hall. Champagne flowed throughout and after speeches, wedding cake and canapés, the happy couple departed in the latest most recherché Rolls Royce for a secret rendezvous before flying off the next day to the West Indies for their honeymoon.

As I had not seen Claude for some time, with glass in hand I took the opportunity to ask him how it was that Jeremy had been awarded the Military Cross.

'Jeremy will not tell you the full story,' confided Claude, 'and I am not sure I know it either for it had to be hushed up. Not because of Jeremy. But because a regular NCO was involved. So there has been a discreet veil drawn over the whole proceedings.'

Harry was listening by now as were Owen, Theo and Bart. 'Tell me more,' I persisted.

'You will recall that Jeremy was whisked away and never made it to Pen Island. The exercise he had to lead was to break up a local Mau Mau cell whose headquarters was deep in the forest. Jeremy and his section were tracking them and had to rely on word of mouth as to its whereabouts from the local Kikuyu who were terrified out of their wits. One of the objectives was to rescue a British soldier who had gone missing. The regiment did not know if he was dead or captured. I cannot tell you who he was, nor his rank, for what happened was unique and reflects little credit on the regiment. Not that Jeremy was in any way to blame since this fellow had disappeared a day or two before Jeremy had returned from Mombasa. For simplicity's sake let's call him Corporal Wells or Patrick. But that is not his name. However, the gist of the story is as follows although the actual events will doubtless have been even more hair-raising.

'After overcoming a series of outlying guards subtly and silently, when Jeremy and his team alighted on the cell they were slap bang in the middle of a Mau Mau oathing ceremony where the initiates were being overseen by armed elders. What then confronted our soldiers was the sight of poor Patrick naked and being compelled to comply with the Mau Mau oaths which were so disgusting I am not going to attempt to describe them. The elders were caught entirely by surprise and disempowered. Three of the principals were shot in the knees so as to disable them. Not one was killed but all were taken prisoner. Wells was freed and the other initiates arrested along with the organisers. The problem now was how to get him back to base. The guy was in a dreadful state. But somehow Jeremy and his team succeeded.

'Wells never really recovered. He was taken immediately to what passed for a sanatorium where he suffered hallucinations. From there he was motored to hospital in Nanyuki and in due course was taken to Nairobi from where he was invalided home and discharged. His nerves were shot to pieces. The army thought it best to steer clear of a court martial and not to publicise this horrific event. In Jeremy's citation there is much left unsaid.

'Just take it at that. Never question Jeremy. He won't divulge anything for he wishes to forget the whole episode. It is a pity but there we are. And it is fully understandable.'

In thanking Claude we all agreed to keep Mum.

Next I enquired of Theo how he was doing. In typical fashion he was forthcoming.

'Life is very good. I am working well with Noel and am engaged to Cressida who has now moved into a training establishment that Natty Hurst used to occupy. This is outside Malton on land belonging to the Talbot family. Natty has retired.'

'Really?' intervened Owen. 'Natty was a good friend of Francis Whyte, another Czech. 'These two came over to Britain before the War to escape the threat of the Nazis. Natty was born Hirsch and changed his name by deed poll on arrival here. When Francis was cosying up to Giffords on behalf of Semleys he used to invite Dad and me to the races at York where he had a box. And we met Natty a number of times for he trained some of Francis's horses.'

'Small world,' I heard myself say.

'Are you still riding at the races, Theo?'

'Yes, indeed, but only at weekends. And now seldom at Uttoxeter for Nicholas Broadbent, since we have seven race courses here in Yorkshire. In the main this is where Cressida sends her horses and where I am slowly gaining a small reputation.'

'Your turn next to get married,' I teased.

'No huge hurry. We shall live together first. But stick around. You will be on the wedding list. And you too Claude, Owen and Bart.'

As we came to leave I saw Jeremy. On his arm was a lovely girl to whom I had been introduced earlier. She was Fiona Southerness, the daughter of General Sir Ramsay Southerness. I was sure Jeremy had had the pick of the Yorkshire girls so I was in no way surprised to see him in the company of such a delectable creature. I guessed that no matter how reticent he had been over his award of the Military Cross, the General will have known the full story and will have kept his counsel too.

As ever, Jeremy was his usual charming and intelligent self. 'I have been talking to Noel,' he said. 'Nigel, he tells me you are finding a flair for Public Relations. I feel the time may have arrived when you can move on from the prosaic name of NCA. Try and find another one, one that will invite questions or signify something understandable.'

'That is very thoughtful of you,' I countered, 'for it has been exercising me too. Let me put on my thinking cap. Meantime I am open to suggestions. Have you a better idea?' I enquired.

He smiled but no response was forthcoming. Jeremy was reticent. He did not wish to put himself forward on any matter which was not his metier. I was not disappointed, merely respectful. Better, I accepted, to voice an opinion on a subject one arguably knew a little about even when one could fathom that there was something not exactly quite right. His judgement was not in question. He had hit upon an issue that was most likely an Achilles heel and which required further consideration. But that had to come from me.

Several weeks later when Noel was back from honeymoon he phoned me and asked if I would get on the next train to York. He had a lot he wanted to discuss with me.

We met in his new offices where a smart young lady brought us coffee served from a silver pot set on a silver tray. 'Nigel, quietly I am very pleased that Evie wishes to pursue her interests in landscape gardening. Do you know that she has begun to work for Owen at the new garden centre he is creating near York racecourse?'

'I am delighted,' I said. 'Owen and I had discussed how the entrance to this should be marked and I suggested a rockery with a range of plants that come out at different times. Additionally he is building the most splendid rockery as a key feature outside the restaurant. May I presume that Evie is involved in that too?'

'Absolutely! Now I am getting on rather well with Sidney Bassett and he has become a good customer for me. However he has a blind spot. He believes his houses are so superior to those of his competitors, he leaves it to the new owner to choose his own flooring and to develop a garden if he has the interest and the money. As a result some of the properties that he has built do not do justice to those of their neighbours. He puts in a drive and that's that. I tell him that he must do more than just take the money and run and get on to the next project. But he does not quite see it that way.

'Look, I'll make sure you are not out of pocket but can you come up with a plan to enable him to see that he ought to be offering the total package to include landscaping? If I badger him too much he will be irritated and think I am after feathering my nest, especially if I introduce Evie into the equation which I would like to do. But of course if she were to win his confidence this will be a huge boost for Owen's venture too.'

'I am sure I can. But tell me does he use a PR outfit at present?'

'Yes, but merely for brochures depicting the various designs of his houses.'

'I think I may have an idea,' I said. 'In the same way that I have counselled Owen, in my view the entrance to a Bassett Tompkins estate ought to be the first thing to attract a buyer. One way would be to design stone walls with carefully chosen shrubs and floribunda and a large notice in stone giving the name of the estate. This would brand his product. If Sidney accepts this premise then he may also accept a package that details at least half a dozen basic garden designs according to the size of plot. Do you think that Evie would be able to come up with something like that? These could then be individually tailored to suit the terrain and the purchaser's whim. I could bring in Evie as an associate. She would not therefore be seen as having anything to do with Tellings, especially if she were to trade under her maiden name of Talbot.'

'Nigel, I shall talk to her. I like the concept, particularly the idea of creating a brand image for the entrance. Let's see what she can come up with that would fit the bill and still permit furniture vans and other types of large vehicle uninterrupted access.'

'By the way, Noel,' I continued, 'Jeremy approached me after your wedding. He thinks I should change the name of my consultancy from NCA to something more imaginative. I have been giving this some thought. One name I favour is the seat of the Duke of Devonshire, namely Chatsworth. Didn't we once visit it when we were at Barley Farm? It has a certain splendour as well as a handy "double-entendre". How do you like it? I have not mentioned this yet to anyone else.'

Noel laughed. 'Yes, I do. Try it out on Jeremy too to gauge his reaction. I think he was only thinking of your best interests when he broached the subject in the first place. If he is supportive, go for it and register it smartly.'

'How do you suggest that I get in touch with Sidney? Would he be agreeable to a cold call? Quite honestly I rather think not as he seems to be so averse to landscaping.'

Noel thought for a moment. 'I have an idea. The Wetherby races are on in eight weeks time. If you and Evie can get together before then and come up with something to appeal to the old curmudgeon, and Sidney and you two are among my guests there, then how would that suit? Theo and Cressida will be there and Theo is living up to his nickname of Tip too. He has a remarkable eye for a horse. Look, come to dinner tonight and stay over. Float the idea with Evie and see what she has to say. I remember that when I went to Canada at virtually every new housing estate – and they were springing up all over the place – a scenic entrance was regarded as vital.'

'Lovely. Thanks. If Evie relishes the challenge I shall contact a friend who can wing me pictures of what is being achieved both in Canada and in California. That will be a start and may provide food for thought.'

As expected, Evie was supportive of the proposal and keen to see what was already being achieved over there that she could adapt where necessary. By the time the races at Wetherby approached she had finalised a dossier. This looked magnificent and incorporated the best of what she had favoured the other side of the Atlantic.

Sidney turned out to be anything but a curmudgeon. He was an approachable northerner who struck me as well balanced if of firm opinions. Somehow the subject came up of branding his estates. He listened carefully and was not one to dismiss anything at all. With the feature race of the day at 3 'o' clock we both chose a horse called Dynamic Tom and sauntered down to the bookies for a change to placing a bet on the Tote. We had spotted the animal on CCTV as it was led round the paddock and both approved especially as Tip was with us justifying his "nom de plume" and giving it his blessing. It had been 7/1 but was now available at 13/2 in just a couple of places. Elsewhere it had come down to 6/1 and then was soon at 5/1. Clearly there was late support for it. We both scrambled on at 13/2 in the nick of time. Dynamic Tom started slowly. Then after taking the first two jumps with a rather deliberate circumspection he found his rhythm and began to move up the field all the time jumping better and better. Level with the favourite at the final fence he stayed on well on the run-in and won by half a length.

As we celebrated back in the box that Noel had hired, Sidney turned to me and said, 'I have been thinking about what you said earlier. At the express wish of my partner Harold Tompkins we are to launch a small range of upmarket houses under the Tompkins banner rather than Bassett. It makes sense to try out your ideas on these don't you think? And as for Evie Talbot's dossier I liked it a lot. I shall bring this to the attention of Harold.'

The conversation soon drifted. We had another drink and backed another winner, this time very much on the advice of Tip. The day had been fruitful for by the end of the year Giffords Garden Centre was under contract as the prime supplier of garden materials for all the Bassett Tompkins houses and not just those marketed under the name Tompkins. To no one's surprise Sidney had seen the sense in offering purchasers gardens made to measure even for the less expensive houses. Any future relationship with both Sidney and Harold now looked assured. As for the beneficiaries, as well as me these looked to be Noel and Evie, Owen, and most probably Tip should Sidney contract the racing bug. And that is not beyond the bounds of possibilities I thought. As for Harold, who knows?

CHAPTER 8: THE LONDON SCENE

When I returned to London Jeremy phoned to say that while the Earl of Ruabon had been well pleased with his investment in Frenshams he was now minded to move on and invest in a hotel in London. The Frenshams Board was not too unhappy about this since the company was doing well and they thought that the Earl's holding should not be difficult to place. Jeremy had been asked to recommend a suitable location in London for the Earl to consider, no matter that he was now based back in York. He spoke succinctly and sensibly.

'I am minded to suggest either the area around Covent Garden, or South Kensington, or perhaps even a little further west near the Hammersmith Bridge. There are good arguments for all three places. Covent Garden deserves to be radically upgraded once the Flower Market relocates which I understand is on the cards. The Opera House is already there as is the Drury Lane theatre. The market superstructure is a graceful landmark. It could have an exciting future. South Kensington is fashionable and unlikely to lose its appeal. It is only a short walk away from museums and not that far from Harrods so might be a safe option. Hammersmith is at the start of the motorway that we will be seeing from London eventually through to Bristol and South Wales. Big business is moving into the area just to the west and there is a distinct shortage of hotels unless you go further out towards Heathrow where large international hotels are likely to be attracted. Nigel, these are the options as I see it but I should appreciate your views. Could you find time to furnish me with a brief report. Meantime, I have asked Surridges to examine this too and find if any hotel is on the market and capable of being renovated to the standard of an upmarket discreet bijou residence.'

I was flattered and not a little surprised for I sensed that any contribution I might make should come after the acquisition of a site rather than before. I got in touch with Bart, and told him of the Earl's aspirations. I asked him to have his ear to the ground at the Stafford where he was acting as Assistant Manager, to ascertain what might be coming onto the market for I was well aware that those fellows in the hotel industry networked like mad. I suspected they could be privy to information even before the professionals like Surridges.

After a few days Bart came back to me. 'Nigel, I have looked at all three areas which Jeremy has suggested. At Hammersmith I have drawn a blank. There are indeed several successful pubs alongside the Thames but in the main these are closely tied to Fullers or Youngs. Right now I see no opportunity for a hotel that would appeal to the Earl. On the other hand Covent Garden is interesting for a small hotel in Shelton Street near the Cambridge theatre might well fit the bill. The old lady who owns it wants to retire. Although it has no obvious appeal it is within walking distance of Shaftesbury Avenue and Soho, which as you know is the homeland for theatres and continental restaurants and three major hospitals.

'Rather better in my view, I have also found a small hotel in Thurloe Square a couple of hundred yards from South Kensington tube station. Two gays own it and have fallen out. One is intent on relocating to the Highlands. The other wants to move to Brighton and run a bar with a tall young fisherman from Mombasa. Something of a turnaround! The hotel's façade is attractive in the extreme and its orientation, unlike its owners, appears right.'

So at Bart's suggestion I decided to investigate the area.

Nearby was a little Polish restaurant called Daquise offering good healthy peasant food akin to that country's home cooking. For example, their cabbage soup served in a large tureen and light years away from a watery concoction reminiscent of a foul school lunch must have comprised all kinds of ingredients to include slivers of pork, cuts of sausage, potatoes, cabbage and sauerkraut spiced with caraway seeds. Unbelievably tasty it was a meal in itself. Quenching a thirst were decent house wines and two Polish beers – Tyskie and Zywiec. Equally to the point it was unbelievably cheap. I could only assume that the two hardworking ladies who ran it will have been on a peppercorn rent and that this may have been due to some heroic action by a Polish relative during the War which was now being repaid. Supporting this contention which may or may not be right, the walls were decorated with photographs of famous wartime personalities to include Churchill, Eisenhower, De Gaulle and the leading Poles of their day. During my visit the elderly clientele were reading newspapers – both English and Polish – secured in wooden frames such as one finds on the Continent. Also noticeably at ease were two gentlemen who were clearly habitués. One was sketching something for the other to appraise. As the motherly waitress was friendly enough I asked if she knew them.

'Oh, yes,' she answered, 'they are from the Royal College of Art. The elderly gentleman is Polish, a scholar and the senior professor. We see him quite often with other gentlemen well reputed within their own milieu.' I rather enjoyed her choice of expression.

Just then a renowned goldsmith entered. I had met him at Frenshams when he was undertaking a commission to produce a magnificent rosebowl to commemorate the company's dual centenary. He was the bearded and charismatic Gerald Benney. As he was advancing towards the couple from the RCA, he spotted me and generously came across for a chat. Gregarious as ever, he asked what I was up to these days. I explained I had set up a PR company called Chatsworth and was nosing around on behalf of a client to see what hidden facets there might be to an investment in a hotel in one or two areas including this one.

'If your friends take over a hotel near here they will be on to a gold mine,' said Gerald encouragingly. 'The teachers at the Royal College just a minute or two away have immense influence and are very sociable. A discreet hotel might very well suit them. If your pals do go ahead, the curators at other museums nearby may also be more than interested. They are required to entertain from time to time and, when they do, they do it in style. By the way I love the name Chatsworth. Let me have your card if you will, for I could well be glad of your services shortly if I land a contract of which I am hopeful.' His eyes twinkled mischievously.

I handed him one and said I would keep in touch for I knew where he had his atelier in Whitechapel. As he went on to greet his friends I realised he had opened my eyes to a style of patronage that otherwise I would never even have contemplated.

I reported to Jeremy that at present Hammersmith seemed to be a no go area but there was potential both off the Charing Cross road and at South Kensington. Perhaps he could get Surridges on to the case and value both the properties so as to compare each to the sum being sought. Then I brought Bart up to date. He liked the idea of a regular upmarket clientele and could see that off the Charing Cross road one might be able to appeal to the literary fraternity in contrast to the artists and intellectuals worth cultivating in Thurloe Square. Of the two hotels, I far preferred the one at South Kensington and in no great time that was the one the Earl chose too. The question now was whether Bart would be sufficiently enthused to take on the task of managing it. As he had yet to move on and was still at the Stafford working as a locum Assistant Manager, that seemed a pretty fair speculation.

Bart responded positively. He was happy to take over as General Manager but first would like to be involved in the renovation the hotel was bound to need. Jeremy explained this would be no problem adding, 'my new girlfriend Fiona is an architect who specialises in interiors. She has a remarkably good eye and an innate colour sense. The Earl is happy for her to be given the assignment. In fact he suggested it. He has known her father, the General, for years and has said he is pleased that we have got together. I shall give Fiona your contact details. Expect to hear from her shortly once the builders have been engaged. In the meantime I shall send you the interior drawings for the hotel as it now is, just as I have for Fiona. Do you want Slim to have a say on the kitchen? I understand it will require a complete makeover.'

Slim claimed he was honoured to be asked and in due course came forward with plans that were both appealing and practical. With these accepted and before returning north, Slim proposed a discussion on the lunchtime menus.

'That is going to be important if you are not going to have a huge gap between breakfast and dinner, in which case you will merely appeal to those staying overnight many of whom will want to try any one of the score of local restaurants available that Kensington and Knightsbridge offer in great variety. May I suggest the Ruabon offers something akin to a Club through a really good set lunch with two first courses and two mains but always with a top rate cold table in addition. This will simplify the choice for people who like to think they are busy and probably are.'

Bart needed no further persuasion. 'That sounds straightforward enough to me. Moreover this would make my life relatively simple I would like to think,' he said with a smile.

It was now my turn to make a contribution. 'Price this right. Promote it properly and you will have customers walking through the door. Let me assess what the competition is up to. You will need to consider not just Daquise, which in any case will always deserve a following.'

By now Fiona's input had been thought through carefully. With Bart nodding approval she advocated that a small private dining room be available for private parties. 'I have in mind an exquisite room with a bay and an alcove, that this will be beautifully decorated in soft apricot, gold and cream, the cornices embellished, and gilt mirrors to enhance the size. It will look stunning.'

'Concept agreed nem con', said Bart on seeing me nod vigorously too.

And so it transpired. The structural alteration was minimal. The professors at the Royal College of Arts and the museums approved of the private room wholeheartedly. On my suggestion they had been wooed by vouchers at 50% off, excluding wine, valid until the end of the month. Moreover, they had been invited to the opening party in the autumn of 1964.

The principal art tutor Professor Carel Weight was there along with Ruskin Spear, known for his intuitive portraiture that exposed the soul of his subjects. Ruskin arrived in his wheelchair and, problematic though he could be, asserted he was happy enough with the arrangements. A sprinkling of Carel Weight's pupils was present too including a young bespectacled blonde man then living in Los Angeles and ultimately due to become the most famous of all present that day. But perhaps the most positive personality that morning was the influential well coiffured and bearded art critic by name of Mervyn Levy. Somewhat out of character this small but outgoing man was almost deferential in his praise and said he hoped to be a regular visitor. Other well-known people from the art world were also present, among them John Nash, Julian Trevelyan, the surrealist and expressionist, and his wife Mary Fedden who was acquiring an enviable reputation for her flower paintings.

Much to my delight and surprise so was Gerald Benney, the goldsmith. He came over to me and chatted like a long-time friend before confiding with a wink, 'Nigel, I am just checking up on you.'

What a guy, I thought. I just hope he and I can get together. If nothing else he is the most amazing conversationalist. Clearly he was fully accepted by the artistic establishment. Equally apparent he was full of fun, more so in my view than that lot.

Seeing a rather unassuming elderly man enter the room Gerald excused himself saying, 'that is L.S. Lowry. His paintings of the industrial north where he grew up will one day be highly prized. They are the most enduring commentary on that murky if hugely profitable era for those entrepreneurial mill owners. See you later.'

I was vaguely aware of Lowry's matchstick men but not fully cognisant that he had gone beyond pop art and was considered with such esteem. The next I knew Gerald and he were engrossed in conversation with Carel Weight, a tall bespectacled man with greying curly hair encircling his balding dome and almost as withdrawn as Lowry. At least that is how it seemed to me the outsider.

By the end of the month it was apparent that the Ruabon was going to be a sure-fire success. Lunchtime became so popular that the regulars all knew they had to book to be certain of a place. The restaurant critic of the Evening Standard was highly complimentary as was Punch magazine. Not infrequently members of the Garrick Club graced it. Naturally, when he was in London the Earl never stayed anywhere else. Often old friends from his military days and members of the House of Lords were spotted as his guests; and they too chose it when they wished to be discreet and entertain in the private dining room. With such a distinguished clientele Bart considered it had indeed acquired the role of a Club thanks to the input from Fiona and Slim. I called in from time to time and always found Bart immensely solicitous. This will be the making of him, I thought. Twice I saw him in the company of Carel Weight. Though the two could not have been more different, the professor had obviously taken a liking to him. When he learned that Bart's father owned the greyhound track in Rotherham, he said how much he would like to attend one for he had always fancied painting greyhounds in action. It would be something totally new for him.

'They will make a change from the melancholia which many regard as my trademark. I have got a bit stuck on unhappy folk — typically those seeking the warmth of braziers below stubborn brick walls in south and west London and, simply, just trying to survive.' The man was being unbelievably honest and modest, even if a shade morose and rather like the characters he chose to feature.

Bart said he would be delighted to arrange an outing. Knowing that the Catford dog track would be open for business the next Wednesday, he asked if I would like to accompany them. Not having been to a greyhound track before I readily agreed.

'I'll tell you what,' said Bart, 'let me ask Harry to come along too. I don't think his new girlfriend Veronica will enjoy it so I shall suggest he comes without her. Do you think he will accept?'

Harry was all for it as he recognised that in no way would an evening at the dogs be Veronica's scene. By the time Harry and I arrived well in time for a drink before the first race, Bart was already there. Nearby was the professor sitting contentedly alongside the track on his three-legged stool, confronting his easel and sketching the layout with its gaudy advertising boards and banners. Effortlessly he was capturing the ambience.

'I shall be down there in that spot when the racing commences and taking photographs while Carel will be on his stool and continuing to absorb the images,' intimated Bart. 'I have managed to get Robert Barron to cordon off a small area around him so that he can watch and paint undisturbed. Robert is the owner of the stadium and widely known as Robber Baron for short. He hates that and always refers to himself as Bob!'

The atmosphere at the dogs was amazing. The races took place every quarter of an hour. But until two minutes before the off all seemed quiescent. Then mayhem erupted as punters weighed in to shout out huge wagers on the dog they fancied by calling its number from one to six. Never by name.

After the third race I sauntered down with Harry to see how Carel was getting along with Bart still acting as his protector. Stepping out of the crowd and joining us was a well-dressed man who appeared to recognise Harry.

'Allo Arry, how are you doin'?' he enquired with a casual if imperious confidence.

Harry looked somewhat startled before responding positively and shaking his hand. I tried to dissemble my surprise for this intruder looked a most unlikely acquaintance for Harry.

'Are you goin' to introduce me to this geezer?' the well-dressed fellow continued pointing to Carel. 'You know my hobby is to paint. I just don't seem to find the time to do much.'

In an instant Harry showed great courtesy towards him. Then unexpectedly he turned towards both Bart and me regardless that his acquaintance was showing interest only in Carel. 'Nigel, may I introduce you to Charlie Richardson.' Then to Bart he said, 'Bart, this is Charlie. Charlie is something of an amateur painter. He would like a word with the professor.'

As the three of us shook hands, Carel, who had heard these efforts at introduction, looked up. He offered a weary smile. 'Hello,' he intoned before lapsing into silence.

'The professor teaches painting,' said Bart in an endeavour to break the ice.

'Would you, Professor, be prepared to teach me?' said the well-dressed fellow.

'Well, I am extremely busy right now. Moreover, all my pupils are full time students.'

'I could make it well worth your while,' the stranger persisted.

'I would dearly love to. However it is just not possible. Why not try the Camberwell College of Art?' Carel was doing his best to be polite.

'Camberwell! That's where I was born. But I have never been in the college.'

'They have a very good painting department. Excellent in fact. Tell them you were born there. It might help. Who knows?'

Carel nodded and went back to his sketching oblivious that he had been talking to the most villainous man in south London. Ignoring the brush-off Charlie thanked him and slipped away to consider his bet on the forthcoming race.

'Harry, who the hell is he?' said Bart and I together. 'He appears to know you well enough.' Sensing trouble Bart ushered Harry and me away from the great professor so that he could not hear. Harry looked around to check he was not overheard then replied, 'Richardson. Don't you know? He is a gangster and rival of the Kray Brothers. Charlie operates mainly in south London which the Krays regard as Indian territory, whereas the Krays hold sway in the East End. He is a very dangerous man. Never fall out with him. His reputation goes before him. He is mixed up in scrap metal while his brother Eddie dabbles in fruit machines and makes it hot for any publican who does not wish to install one. The two are in consort with Mad Frankie Fraser. Don't be fooled by his gentle wispy voice. Frankie is a nasty Army deserter. Cross him and he will yank your teeth out with pliers. They are all shockers. They only know me because I got Ronnie Kray off when he was wrongly charged with the murder of that bookie Jack Smithers. This brought my name to the attention of the underworld. Rumour has it that if either of the Richardsons steps sufficiently out of line to be apprehended they will approach me to defend them. But I tell you I am not going to go looking for their business. Quite honestly I see no need to go down that road.'

It was unlike Harry to be diffident but one could understand why. While he was earning a handsome living and growing reputation in criminal defence, he had no great wish to push his luck too far and become immersed in an unknowingly precarious and sordid world.

Once Carel felt he had obtained enough of the local ambience to work on his picture back in his studio, he murmured that he had got enough to work on. So at Bart's instigation we four adjourned to the dining room overlooking the tracks where Bob Barron introduced himself and produced a magnum of Bollinger. As he poured the champagne he graciously thanked us for coming and said that if Carel was happy with the results of the evening he would dearly like the opportunity of purchasing his painting. When he had left us to ourselves Carel murmured, 'I could always produce two pictures I suppose and offer him one.' What I did not realise at the time was that he intended to give Bart the original for the Ruabon.

As the weeks went by the relationship between the tutors at the RCA and the Ruabon deepened and Bart felt bold enough to suggest that their pupils hold a summer exhibition at the hotel. Carel agreed and he and his good friends Ruskin Spear, Julian Trevelyan, Mary Fedden, John Nash and Edward Bawden all said they too would like to produce a work to complement their star pupils. A reception was held and I was entrusted with the task of organising this and told to liaise with Marilyn Parr, a pupil of Carel. She proved highly efficient, not bossy and very pleasant. She advised on which pictures should be hung where and assisted with the guest list and the relevant addresses. That was marvellous for it was beyond my purview. Among Bart's friends naturally Harry was invited. And this time he was only too happy to bring Veronica with him accompanied by her father, an avid art collector.

I knew of him but had not met him before. He was Kyros and of Greek extraction. His wife was part Austrian and part Hungarian. She came from a wealthy family whose fortune had been largely confiscated during the war. Kyros was a property developer, a big man, with a trim goatee beard, irritatingly self-assured, and as shrewd and far sighted as they come. He ran a company called Monument Securities where he was the majority shareholder. Other than his family and his work the three loves in his life were horse racing, bridge, and collecting art with an emphasis on works by the impressionists active in the fin-de-siècle era.

He showed real interest in the paintings on display. In particular, seemingly mesmerised he stood in front of one for a long time. It was a large landscape emblazoned in brown umber and rich green with just a touch of yellow under a pale blue cloudless sky.

'I like this,' he said, 'and would be pleased to buy it. I have noticed the price in the catalogue.'

'It is by a young man called David Hockney,' I replied. 'He now spends most of his time on the west coast of America. He is considered the star pupil of Carel Weight. Let me see if it is still available. It should be as it does not sport a red star in the corner.'

It was a surprisingly frightening price but clearly not sufficiently terrifying to put off Veronica's father. So the deal was agreed at the price stated. Harry went up to congratulate him. He was both slightly formal and very correct. The Earl of Ruabon was staying in the hotel at the time and was happy to be introduced to Kyros. He too praised him on his purchase, adding, 'I think this young artist might well become very collectable. If you have a large drawing room that will accommodate a few, they could prove a fine investment. On a slightly different scale, come and see Carel's picture of racing greyhounds hanging next door. They are so totally different to anything else that I have.'

Tactfully he refrained from mentioning this was a gift, for although it was donated to Bart he in turn had passed it onto the Earl as a memento for his kindness and support. Kyros stood still for some thirty seconds simulating admiration. Then he nodded.

'Charming and adventurous,' he pronounced diplomatically.

The Robber Baron was not forgotten either for Carel sold him what was virtually the duplicate at a tidy price on the suggestion of the wily Marilyn. I rather think that otherwise Carel may not have charged enough. Possibly only around half was my guess when I heard what the Robber actually agreed to pay.

I had enjoyed working with Marilyn and was very taken with her. It was good to know that along with her other virtues she was also shrewd and sensible. She preyed on my mind to such an extent I pinched myself and determined to get to know her better. While I was fairly sure she liked me I recognised that if our relationship was to blossom I should have to make the running.

CHAPTER 9: THE UNDERWORLD

That exhibition at the Ruabon was a success and well reported on in the art world press, notably Arts Review. For several weeks I saw little of Bart as I was busy cultivating clients for my fledgling company Chatsworth. Meanwhile the legal column in the Times indicated that Harry was far from idle. Clearly he was making a name for himself even though he was invariably defending people accused of some dastardly crime. Then one day he phoned me.

'Nigel, you would not believe it but I have been briefed by Vincent of all people. You will remember he works as a solicitor at Ilford in an arguably dodgy practice and has admitted to certain clients from India and Sri Lanka who may not exactly be above board. Well, he also acts for undesirable characters in the underworld. One of these is Charlie Richardson who we met at the Catford dogs. Apparently Charlie is to be prosecuted for receiving stolen goods. Amongst other things he deals in scrap metal. This of course could come from anywhere for these fellows trade in cash and there is seldom any serious documentary evidence. Anyhow the authorities are after him.

'I asked Vincent why he recommended me. But he said he did not. Apparently Charlie insisted on me as not a few in gangland had been impressed that I got Ronnie Kray off. Mind you, that was really due to the incompetence of the Met rather than anything to do with me. Anyhow Charlie must have noted it. And of course we ran across each other at Catford.'

I was unsure whether to congratulate him or to sympathise. 'How can I help?' I asked.

'I don't quite know right now but in the event I win the case for Charlie it might be useful to have a diplomatic write up in the appropriate papers. Of course if I lose then I may be shot of such assignments in future and the less said the better.'

I sensed that Harry was a touch ambivalent. Happy enough maybe to earn excellent money from the criminal law, he still did not wish to become too high profile. I felt his main priority at that moment was to win the hand of Veronica Vasiliou and obtain the blessing of her mother Vera and tricky father Kyros.

The case was complicated and when I attended the court at Harry's request the Crown Prosecution Service was making a meal of it. Charlie made a compelling witness. He was cheerful and confident and explained how he transacted his metals business in terms that made him appear a paragon of virtue. I was not impressed with the detective inspectors from the Met and Harry dealt with them in what I thought was summary fashion. Rather than dwell on the complexities and technicalities, let me merely say that Charlie got off even though the judge clearly did not fall for the line that he was a paragon of virtue.

I spoke to Harry afterwards to congratulate him and he suggested I call round and have a drink that evening before going back to my flat. Over a bottle of Chablis he explained while he had done a reasonably professional job he was worried about two things. Firstly, Vincent had phoned him back in his chambers both to congratulate him and say that Charlie had lodged a large donation with the Police Fund. Apparently that did not particularly surprise him. But what did astonish him as quite out of the ordinary was that Charlie had also given Vincent a voucher for £100 for Harry to spend at The Ivy restaurant as a personal thank you.

'What do you think I should do with this?' he enquired.

I prevaricated by asking what did he want to do with it. After all he was in the pay of Charlie, come what may.

'Well, the obvious thing is to take Veronica out and propose to her. And The Ivy would be wonderful. We can have a very nice evening there on £100 and splash out on champagne, a top Bordeaux, and liqueurs or cognac to finish with. It is a genuinely nice venue and we will probably be able to engage in a bit of people spotting if we take our time since it is so popular with theatre folk.'

I could not see any harm in this apart from the fact that he might be seeing rather more of Charlie in the future than he strictly desired. Not that Harry would necessarily be in the initiative. But Charlie might. And I said as much.

The evening passed off just as Harry planned. The dinner was perfect as were the wines. Harry proposed and Veronica said 'Yes' and then was thrilled when Harry produced a diamond solitaire with further diamonds on each shoulder. What really took him by surprise was that a few moments later Charlie came up with his wife Ronnie – also a Veronica – and with a photographer in tow who then snapped the four of them. Harry was taken aback. But Charlie was all smiles and as friendly as they come on explaining that the photographer was from the London Illustrated News.

'Classy weekly, Arry. None better my boy. It will look really good in next week's issue.'

Seeing that Harry looked a mite flummoxed the Maitre d'Hotel came across. 'Sir, we are very honoured to have you present tonight with your lovely fiancée. This is the happiest of coincidences for tonight we also have Paul Jefferies from the London Illustrated News. We see him regularly, for a good couple of times a month he photographs the celebrities who choose to patronise us. And this evening we have dining with us the famous theatrical couple John Clements and his enchanting wife Kay Hammond. The two of them will be featuring in next week's issue. As you may be aware they are starring in the stunning revival of the play he wrote called The Happy Marriage. This is playing in St Martins Lane and tonight marks their hundredth performance, hence a very special occasion.'

He did not address Richardson or Ronnie but nodded courteously in their direction.

Harry felt stitched up. But there was nothing he could do now. Nor could he wave an admonishing finger at the Ivy or the "Maitre D" much as he might have wanted to.

The picture of Harry and Veronica with Charlie and Ronnie was duly published. In those days the London Illustrated News graced virtually every doctor's or dentist's surgery along with the lounge of every London club and fashionable hotel to include the Ruabon.

When he saw it as was inevitable, Kyros "hit the roof". He lambasted Harry in private but not before Veronica, and subjected him to a diatribe about how long it had taken for his Austro-Hungarian wife Vera and he himself to become accepted as British citizens.

'And now this,' he rampaged, 'a picture of Veronica and you with arguably the most dangerous ruffian in London!' He was beside himself. 'It would not surprise me if you two were barred from the tables of all the London hostesses where otherwise Veronica would be more than welcome.'

Harry chose to keep quiet and adopt the policy of "the least said the soonest mended", although in his heart of hearts he doubted if anything he said was going to mollify Kyros. He realised that he had gained a reputation within his profession which, while laudable as a successful barrister, was not perhaps as honourable as he would have liked due to the company he was keeping. And it was this that was bugging Kyros and presumably Vera too.

It fell to me to take Harry on one side some time later to extrapolate on what Kyros had said and to ensure he fully understood the thoroughly unsavoury details of what the Richardson brothers were up to.

'Harry, you are living dangerously. You must know even better than me that these Richardson brothers are into torture. Those who fall out with them can be subject to whippings, being nailed to the floor with six-inch nails, possibly having their toes removed and, worst of all, given electric shocks. I have it on good authority that an electrode will be attached to nipples or genitalia – to put it politely. Afterwards the victim is good for nothing. Having 240 volts assail you is no fun. But the brothers give him £150 and a clean shirt. This is because the shirt he was wearing will be soaked in blood. The practice is known as "taking a shirt off Charlie". You may well know this already but honestly you don't want to know!

'And his brother Eddie is equally villainous. I heard that one of their mob called Nobby was entrusted with the task of acting as a "collector of pensions". By that I mean obtaining protection money from landlords and club owners. Nobby thought he could go one better. Off he went to the Catford dog track where he hoped to multiply the takings. Well, he failed to do so and blew the lot. He was questioned, bound and tortured. Afterwards as a final farewell his fellow mobsters urinated on him. I think you should give this lot a wide berth.'

Harry listened carefully before saying, 'I hear you well. As I am sure you know I am not totally unaware. But there is a problem. If you are given a brief through the normal channels it is customary that you accept it. If you have no good reason to refuse, very quickly you get ignored. One therefore has to rise above the sordid world that comes to you with a problem and expects you to obtain what they would call justice within the law. I am now involved in criminal law and that happens to be my expertise. I am not sure I actually chose it. But somehow it chose me the day I stepped in and took on that brief for our senior Counsel in Chambers when he was taken to hospital as a matter of emergency. That was how I got the job of defending Ronnie Kray.'

'OK. Understood,' I replied. 'Is Veronica happy about it for you know what her father thinks?'

'How can one put this in perspective?' asked Harry.

'Awkward. But I could write you up in an article, try to put matters in a realistic light and offer this to friends in the press.'

So at Harry's instigation I wrote a piece on him for the magazine Everyman's and the Yorkshire Evening News. The Sunday Courier got wind of this and commissioned me to write something similar. I was fairly sure this would not come to the attention of Kyros and Vera so obliged. Instead the article came to the attention of the London underworld. Dubious lawyers now knew of Harry even if they had not heard of him before. So, were their less than desirable clients to find themselves in trouble with the law, Harry's name was sure to feature as a possible lifeline.

CHAPTER 10: THE BETTING COUP

That September there was a betting coup which drew headlines not just in the sporting press but in the nationals too. The gist of it was that a trainer who had forfeited his licence and was nominally in retirement had pulled off the most almighty gamble. This was Bunny Fearnley who used to train outside Malton. Now Bunny had links to the underworld in the East End, notably with Solly Doull. The two had long planned a heist on the bookmakers. When Bunny retired he had four three-year old colts in training that in his view were the best he had ever had. He persuaded Solly to buy all four, which he did at knockdown prices so depriving the rightful owners of their real worth who were told by Bunny in plausible terms that, sadly, as they would never even make the frame let alone win races they might as well cut and run.

'You win some. You lose some,' he had explained. And that was that.

On Bunny's advice the four went to two different trainers who were new to the game. One was David Grace. The other was Dickie Birkmyre. With each pair of horses came the young apprentice jockey who had been engaged by Bunny but who was now looking for a job, since the trainer who had taken over Bunny's yard already had a full complement. So the two new trainers each took on one young aspiring jockey. The deal delighted them for not only were these colts soon seen to possess talent but so were the apprentices that Bunny had encouraged them to employ.

When the four horses reached the age of four they were considered fit to embark on a career over hurdles. By this time Bunny had long lain low. Not so, Solly. He was in regular contact with Bunny and both the trainers who by then had two other apprentices. All four of the young jockeys were ten pound claimers so their mounts were able to run with ten pounds off the published weights. When each was of the opinion that Solly's horses were ready to race, Solly contacted Bunny who talked to the two trainers. He was both firm and persuasive. One fine spring day racing was due to take place at four tracks. These were Carlisle, Fakenham, Hexham and Exeter. So the horses and jockeys were duly despatched there. None had any form for apart from having participated in minor point-to-points which were not the subject of critical approval, they were unraced. However the two trainers were each emphatic both horses had a sound temperament, were neither tense nor excitable, and what is more knew their jockeys well for only they had schooled them.

The plan was that Ossie Pick would take Holbein to Carlisle, Eddie Redvers would take Cunning Joe to Fakenham, Rufus Hodge would take The Lamplighter to Hexham, and Buck Layton would take Kandahar to Exeter. The races for which they were entered were the 1.45, the 2.50, the 3.40 and the 4.45. Bearing in mind that the young horses could not be guaranteed to win the betting programme was cautious. It focused on four separate bookmakers. These were Arnold Pudsey from Penrith, Victor Barraclough from Kings Lynn, Teddy George from Consett, and Eddie Edwards from Exeter. Each would be visited before 10.00 en route to the racecourse with the driver calling in to place the bets. Since Holbein and Cunning Joe were thought to face the weakest opposition, these two were entered for the early races of 1.45 and 2.50. They were to be paired in £50 doubles and backed with Arnold Pudsey at the opening show off course. Cunning Joe was then doubled up with The Lamplighter and the bet placed with Victor Barraclough. The Lamplighter was doubled with Kandahar and the bet place with Teddy George. Lastly Kandahar was doubled with Holbein and the bet placed with Eddie Edwards.

In addition four trebles were to be placed and, as the ultimate gamble, an accumulator wagered on all four. For these multiple bets Solly and Bunny split their stakes and chose Tyrone from Tottenham and Mickey Hutton from York. With Holbein and Cunning Joe opening at 16/1 and 14/1 respectively if this double came up, should all the other bets fail the plotters would still be in profit to the tune of £12,350. But if all four won and The Lamplighter were to start at 22/1 as indicated in the morning papers, even if Kandahar shortened into 3/1 then the total pay off would be immense.

Holbein and Cunning Joe duly obliged at the odds predicted. The Lamplighter was backed at 22/1 and Kandahar at 8/1. When these odds reduced markedly and were only 6/1 and 11/4 at the off, Bunny and Solly wondered if they had been rumbled and whether an enquiry would be held. Nevertheless they would have to be paid at the odds struck. In the event all four did win.

The four doubles paid £48,000. The four trebles paid £712,900 and the accumulator amounted to £2,554,300 so giving a grand total of £3,315,200. The four provincial bookies who accepted the doubles paid up without a murmur. But during the afternoon Tyrone from Tottenham and Mickey

Hutton had both spotted all was looking disastrous for them and laid off a substantial share of their loss. As a result the bookmaking fraternity in Yorkshire and London was massively out of pocket with six leading firms all suffering from the heist.

When Smallwoods of York who had accepted the lay off from Hutton chose to investigate, their combined fury was unbounded once they both realised that all four horses were in the ownership of Solly Doull. That had not been immediately obvious for one was in his wife's maiden name and two of the others were in the names of his married daughters. When the Smallwoods sleuth uncovered the fact that all four horses had originally been with Bunny Fearnley they knew they had been had. But there was little they could do, for now that he was no longer a trainer he could not be arraigned. What they did arrange with the authorities was for both Bunny and Solly to be warned off the turf and never again seen at the races. But then after pay-offs to the four drivers and four young apprentice jockeys each was richer by more than £1.5 million and could content himself with watching the racing on television.

The one pundit who seemed happy was Captain Heath, the racing correspondent of the News Chronicle. He had chalked up forty losers in a row and not surprisingly was depressed for he imagined he would be sacked at the outset of the flat season. However on his way to the Newcastle races, as was his practice he stopped off for the night before at his favourite hostelry in Malton. While in the public bar of the Crown and Anchor he had heard the stable boys chatting and venting their views on Holbein and Cunning Joe, both of whom were trained by David Grace. They were immensely positive and joking about their chances later that week. The Captain cottoned on that something was up. So he tipped both horses as worth backing each way. When the two came in he dubbed David Grace as Amazing. And as Amazing Grace that was how he became known to the racing public. These two wins gave the good Captain renewed confidence and over the next couple of weeks he produced a return of 56/1 mainly thanks to Solly's two horses. As for being sacked, not at all! He was kept on for three more years until he chose to retire due to ill health.

By December the Yorkshire police were sure that foul play must have existed somewhere in this betting coup. Within three months all four young jockeys had bought a residence. Three chose a cottage while Ossie Pick purchased a four-bedroomed stone house. The Metropolitan Police too were well aware of the change in circumstances for Solly. Forsaking his Jaguar he bought a Rolls Royce after ordering a custom built one from James Young of Bromley. Word had it that he might move to Portugal and was looking around for a property on the coast. The less honourable people in the gambling game were thought to be gunning for him and rumour was rife that Solly just might be thinking of quitting the world of crime to focus on enjoying his ill-gotten gains in the sunshine. But try as they might, the Met could find nothing which they could pin on him.

Meanwhile Solly was brazen. He had won a fortune at the races and that was that! He even phoned Harry and asked if he could persuade his friend Bart to approach Carel Weight to paint his portrait. Carel declined. He did not wish to associate with someone so undesirable and recommended that Bart put him in touch with Ruskin Spear who tended to specialise in portraiture. Readily he accepted. The resultant picture showed a remarkable insight into Solly's character as indeed did Spear's painting of the much loved weather-worn Cockney comedian Sid James, who at the time was Tony Hancock's co-star in "Hancock's Half Hour". It depicted Solly as a little Jew boy now knocking on seventy but not necessarily well loved, yet who was both devious and powerful as well as blessed with great charm. Solly was delighted. Flattered by the power and charm, any suggestion of deviousness was lost on him.

In Yorkshire the antipathy to Bunny waxed ever more intense. He was treated as a pariah. Even in the best restaurants he was not accorded the gracious reception that a man of his wealth might reasonably expect. No bookmaker would accept any bet from him. No racecourse bade him welcome. Bunny had always been a loner but now he was an outcast ignored by the squirearchy and racehorse owners alike.

Bunny had long been a widower and without the support of family since his son was in Australia and daughter in New Zealand. Neither came to visit him and he in turn after going to Australia once for the Melbourne Cup felt himself cold-shouldered and never went back. He had gone on to visit his daughter and family in New Zealand but as his son-in-law and he were continually at daggers drawn this became a no go area. Although Bunny had not married again he had a female companion called Deirdre who was no more a lady than he was a gentleman. She was neither interested in horses nor in racing and many wondered why the two had ever got together.

However nobody seemed to care either way.

One Sunday evening in December around 7 'o'clock the front door bell rang. The housekeeper answered it to find a man outside with an envelope for Mr Fearnley. She asked him to wait while she fetched Bunny and retired to her parlour at the back. He came to the door in fractious mood to enquire what the stranger had for him at such a peculiar hour. The stranger handed him the envelope then shot him dead. His gun had a silencer. So the shot was not heard. After some ten minutes Deirdre came to the front hall to see what had delayed Bunny's return. Seeing him lying on the floor prostrate poor Deirdre fainted. When the housekeeper thought it was time to let them know supper was on the table she entered the drawing room to find it empty. Thinking that maybe the stranger, Bunny and Deirdre, were all seated in discussions in the study off the main hall she went to see if they were ready to eat and whether the stranger had gone. She nearly passed out too when she saw Bunny lying stiff and Deirdre coming round after collapsing. Pulling herself together she hauled Deirdre up and sat her by the fire in the drawing room with a glass of water. Then she seized the initiative and telephoned the police. Other than the envelope there was absolutely nothing to indicate that anybody had been there. Only the housekeeper's word.

On Bunny's murder being reported in the press the local folk were all asked if they had seen anything untoward that evening. Nobody had for nobody had been out and about. The police scoured the village and the country lanes for the murder weapon. After ten days the gun was found in a storm drain half a mile away. No finger prints could be discerned since almost certainly the assailant will have been wearing gloves. The attention of the police now focused on the envelope. In it on a betting slip of Mickey Hutton's were simply the letters IOU. The police called on Mickey to seek enlightenment but drew a blank. He and all his staff were then subjected to an assessment of their handwriting. But nothing remotely matched the capital letters on the slip. Every member of staff at Smallwoods was checked similarly. Again nothing matched. The entire Hutton team and that at Smallwoods were interrogated to ascertain if they had seen anyone unusual in their premises. But again nobody had. They knew their regulars and as often as not even addressed them by their first names.

The detective inspector in charge drew up a list of the people who Bunny might have crossed. They included past stable boys, jockeys who had ridden for him, and the original four owners of the horses that were the subject of the successful gamble and who had been told these stood no chance whatever of ever even making the frame. All were questioned and submitted to handwriting tests. Once more nothing untoward was detected. The D.I. gave it one last try. He asked Mickey Hutton's family also to undergo a handwriting test. The only member whose handwriting came near to the IOU on the betting slip was that of Hutton's eleven-year old daughter Cynthia.

Mickey was taken to the police station and asked to account for his actions on that fateful Sunday.

'Just the usual,' he replied. 'I played golf that morning in my regular four, had a couple of drinks in the clubhouse before returning home for lunch. In the afternoon I read the newspapers and had a snooze. Then at 6 'o' clock I popped into the Red Lion. Even in winter I often do this on a Sunday evening for it is much frequented by the racing fraternity. It is where I pick up the local tittle-tattle. In return I pass on which horses are being backed ante post for the big events. Nothing wrong in that is there! That evening it was very quiet. So I left early. You can check up if you want. Driving home I got a puncture so stopped to change the wheel. This delayed me but I was still back by 7.15, more or less my normal time.'

'Have you still got the punctured tyre?' asked the inspector.

'No no. The tyre was old and needed replacing in any case. I just flung it on the tyre heap of Herbert Snodgrass later in the week and thought nothing of it.'

The inspector was far from satisfied and approached his senior officer saying he considered that Mickey Hutton should be arrested on suspicion of murder. After all he had a motive, the betting slip looked as if it replicated the handwriting of his daughter, and he had no good alibi for the time that Bunny Fearnley met his death in the village three miles away. His boss was in his last week before retirement. He counselled caution in that he did not feel the case was sufficiently compelling for a jury to convict. But the inspector was adamant and the old man sighed, 'Be it on your own head. I shall not be in office when this comes to court. So it is over to you entirely.'

That is how Mickey Hutton came to be under arrest. The question now was who should be instructed to defend him. Mickey said he knew of a young man in London who was earning a good reputation as a criminal lawyer. This was Harry Fairest, a Yorkshireman. His solicitor made enquiries and in every instance the response was favourable.

Harry listened patiently to Mickey Hutton and recorded the names and contacts for all those he would need to call as a witness to account for Mickey's activities that Sunday. But privately he reckoned that Mickey was being set up and that Fearnley's death was the result of a contract killing by a hired gun. Much as the detective inspector had done, he documented all those in addition to Mickey who could possibly have such a grudge against Fearnley as to wish him out of the way.

His list included the four original owners of the horses that had sprung the gamble, the boss of Smallwoods in York and the bookie Tyrone from Tottenham. He too had incurred a savage loss at the hands of the infamous Solly Doull, the partner in crime in the betting coup masterminded by Bunny. Relying on his intuition, Harry had a word with a junior member of the Kray gang who told him that any day of the week if he went into a particular pub in the East End and said he was looking for a contract killer and would offer around £6,000 to £8,000 depending on the circumstances, as likely as not he would find three volunteers. What is more, he was informed by a policeman who mixed socially with the underworld that a contract killing was the most difficult crime of all to give rise to an arrest and a conviction.

Next May the trial was high profile.

Mickey's golfing pals confirmed he had indeed played with them that Sunday morning in December. Then he had left after a couple of drinks. Snodgrass was his usual unhelpful self saying he did not check on his pile of worn out tyres until he was ready to burn them and that as far as he was concerned he was always glad for people to chuck their old tyres onto the heap. Yes, he knew Mickey. But then who did not? No, he had not seen him throw that particular tyre onto the heap but then why should he when he was far more interested in handling non-ferrous metal. That was where the money was.

When Harry brought in a calligraphy expert the attention of the jury was notably alert.

'Tell me, Mr Davies,' intoned Harry quietly, 'are you able to suggest the age of the author of these words IOU on this betting slip?'

'No' was the response. 'What I could imagine would be the mental age of the writer.'

'And what would that be?'

'I suggest somewhat immature although that in no way signifies his or her physical age.'

'Do you see any similarity between the writing on the betting slip and that of little Cynthia Hutton?' asked Harry indicating the slip and three specimens that Cynthia had written with the same letters IOU.

'Yes, I do. But the two are not the same. Look carefully for you will notice that in every case of the little girl's handwriting the letter O begins at the 11.00 position. On the other hand the O on the betting slip commences at the 15.00 position. So I have to conclude that the incriminating betting slip will clearly have been written by someone other than Cynthia.'

'Thank you Mr Davies. That will be all.' For a moment Harry looked unusually stern.

Then he called every gunsmith in Yorkshire to give evidence on questioning them about the gun that was used. All knew well the type. But not one of them had any record of having supplied this particular number. Harry claimed there was nothing to link the firearm to his client. It was not an uncommon gun and could have come from almost anywhere. So it was the sort of weapon that would easily have been available to a hired killer, a conclusion to which every one of the gun suppliers agreed.

As the outgoing senior officer in the police had predicted the prosecution case was just too flimsy for a jury to be satisfied that Mickey was the killer. Not surprisingly it was dismissed with the result that Harry's reputation was enhanced. But not with Kyros. He continued to deplore that his daughter was consorting with a barrister whose clients were so thoroughly unsavoury. However Kyros was sufficient of a realist to recognise that Veronica was determined to go ahead and marry Harry. He knew if he tried to stop her that she would go ahead in any case and then he would lose her. So he went along with the wedding plans that she and her mother Vera were making.

Until the Mickey Hutton case Harry had not been to Yorkshire for some time. So determinedly he made time to visit his parents. Well aware they barely knew Veronica, he promised shortly to return, spend the weekend with them and to bring her too. This way he hoped they would come to appreciate his choice of a daughter-in-law for them. Come the day his parents were more than welcoming. They even seemed excited. After dinner that first evening, while his father invited Harry into the snug for a brandy and cigar his mother and Veronica got to know each other better on sipping Malmsey before the drawing room fire.

'Harry,' motioned his father, 'I have received an offer for the business from the

Dutch. We have had constant negotiations for ten weeks and they have been both agreeable and not ungenerous. While they are hard-nosed, in my view they have also been fair. Apparently they have their eyes on other acquisitions in Sheffield steel and I suspect do not want to be thought too mean-minded at the start of their buying campaign. This is all most timely for your mother and I will now be in an excellent position to provide you with a handsome wedding present as well as a substantial lump sum for you to invest.'

Harry nodded, smiled and said, 'Thank you. Tell me more.'

His father continued, 'I gather that Veronica's father is a man of property and extremely prosperous. That may well be so. Now if this deal goes through you will be able to look him in the eye and possess a wealth that very possibly will not be dissimilar to that of Veronica's. In fact it may be a darn sight greater since most of his wealth may well be relatively illiquid. Either way I believe you may find him to be less antagonistic than you make him out to be. Let me ask you a question. When you get married will you continue with the criminal law?'

Harry thought for a moment. 'Veronica and I have a big decision to make. We are unlikely to be fully accepted in London society. While this does not bother me a jot it means a lot to her. One thing therefore has crossed my mind. We could go and live in Portugal. Veronica is a good linguist and already speaks reasonable Portuguese. I expect she could become fluent within a year. I am sure she would settle, the climate will suit, and the attraction of life in London gradually fade. However were we to go I will still keep on our flat in Pimlico.'

'What would you do, Harry?' His father's questioning was gentle but thorough.

'One thought is to act as a lawyer for those British who wish to purchase. At the back of my mind I have always liked the idea of being a real estate lawyer. It would make a nice change from the world of crime and I am sure should provide sufficient work to keep me busy enough.'

'Where would you go and live?'

'I think Estoril initially. But you may be aware that considerable development is planned for the Algarve. If this starts to go ahead and golf resorts are built, we will move for we shall be in a prime position to be first in the field. And my escape from defending baddies will absolve me from having to explain myself ceaselessly to Kyros. That I would not regret. One further point, you can never be sure that one day, as and when something does not work out quite right, you are no longer the flavour of the month. And then what?'

'Harry, that is quite drastic. Aren't you copping out? You have the talent not only to be a Queens Counsel but London's very top QC in criminal law. From there you could even become a judge – perhaps one day rise to be a Law Lord sitting in the House of Lords.'

'Dad, you paint a rosy future. Let me think it over.' And there the matter rested.

The deal with the Dutch went through. Fairest razor blades and everything else that they manufactured in sharp steel was offloaded highly advantageously, with Harry and his two sisters provided for, if not exactly munificently, then extremely satisfactorily.

In September 1966 Harry married Veronica. The best man was his old friend Jeremy. The reception was held at Searcey's in Knightsbridge. Those industrious entrepreneurs from Yorkshire who were long-time friends of the Fairest family were outnumbered by affluent Greeks, Hungarians and continental Jews. Merchant bankers mixed happily with property magnates. Ladies competed with each other for showy rings with outsize diamonds and sapphires. Stoles in mink, sable, ermine and silver fox added testimony to the riches that the immigrant community had brought to London on seeking sanctuary from a Europe devastated by Nazi-ism. The air was redolent with heady perfume and the aroma of Cuban cigars.

Every member of that vintage Heathside cricket team in 1947 was invited and each and every one was present to include Vince. After all he had not stood in the way of denying Harry the chance to represent Charlie Richardson when he was accused of receiving stolen goods. For all of us the spectacle was an eye-opener and the opportunity once again to catch up.

I had not seen Mark for some time. He and Myfanwy were still at Lichfield Cathedral School but Mark indicated he would like to move on in a year or two and seek a position as headmaster. Seeing that Marilyn and I had become an item, Jeremy suggested we ought to come up and spend a weekend in Yorkshire with him and Fiona. My gut feeling told me the next wedding would either be between those two, or Theo and Cressida.

The one person who bothered me was Claude. He admitted that progress at the Mallinson diamond mine was slower than anticipated, he now chain-smoked, his fair hair was unprepossessingly lank, and he appeared louche and somewhat distant. He still saw something of Gemma Gough-Wilcox but the family's Wallasey shipping line was struggling. Perhaps life in Liverpool was much changed from when he was Rossall's glamorous captain of cricket and an icon for the young.

Although Harry's father was bitterly disappointed that he was abdicating from the criminal law and made his view very clear, as expected Harry and Veronica did not continue long in London. To the satisfaction of Kyros and Vera, they were to take themselves off to Estoril. The faded elegance of this seaside town near Lisbon maintained much appeal but in due course they followed the serious money into the Algarve. By then Harry had made his mark and was well in with the developers in a region well known for its kindly climate and flowering cherry trees. Once more fortune had smiled for the sun seemed to shine on him.

CHAPTER 11: TEAMWORK

Although I continued to be based in London my visits to Yorkshire became more frequent. Sidney Bassett and Harold Tompkins proved to be highly receptive to sensible suggestions. Clearly they liked Noel and Evie. Dealing with a talented couple a generation younger than them seemed to inspire these two elderly hard-headed Yorkshire businessmen, and because of my connection with Noel and Evie they appeared to accept me too. With their agreeing to the concept of what were to become formal sculpted entrances, I was entrusted with the task of designing all their promotional material. Invariably this was approved with scarcely an alteration. Moreover they were prompt payers. So both the business and personal relationships were fine. Being in their confidence was a real pleasure.

They were also getting on famously with Theo and Cressida. Sidney enjoyed a flutter on the turf and Tip, as he preferred to call him when asking for his opinion on a horse, as often or not contrived to reduce the field to two which in his view stood a chance of winning. With Tip's knowledge and judgement so good, Sidney made extremely handsome pocket money. He was not exactly hooked but he was beginning to become seriously interested.

One day he surprised Noel by saying, 'why don't you and I go into partnership and buy a couple of horses? Your friend Theo has incredible judgement. I am sure he will advise.'

With Noel's business progressing splendidly, he warmed to the idea immediately. So with complete trust in Theo's judgement, that spring two horses were bought in their joint names and lodged with Cressida to train. Harold was supportive but cautious, a canny and wily Yorkshireman sensibly preferring to see how this untried partnership fared before he too considered the vicissitudes of becoming a racehorse owner.

Cressida was cheerful and wonderfully encouraging. She was particularly sweet on the new colt Langbourn Counsellor citing that his sire Cheapside had won six races in all and that his dam Wise Lady, although unraced, had multiple winners in her pedigree. The other purchase, Richmond Dandy, was as handsome as they come but more playful. Cressida thought they might have to wait a little longer with him before he was allowed to race.

Her intuition told her he would need further time to settle down.

Most mornings early on, before taking up his position at Tellings Theo exercised the horses. In particular he work rode Langbourn Counsellor and every week would report to Noel on how the colt was faring.

'I think Cressida is right. We could have a real winner here. This is a strong animal, athletic and intelligent. What is more he seems to revel in striding out. In due course he should develop into a chaser and a stayer but initially we ought to try him over hurdles at two miles.'

Noel agreed. 'Whatever you two decide regarding where he should run and in what type of race to participate, I will go along with it. Just keep Sidney informed weekly with a verbal report too. But tell Sidney to go easy on the betting the first time he races. Make sure he does not get carried away. We don't want to alert the bookies that we have a smart one before he even gets to the tape. Were that to happen the odds would fall to unrealistic levels.'

When Cressida and Theo were happy with the progress of Langbourn Counsellor they suggested his first engagement should be a midweek hurdle race at Wetherby. The two owners both turned up along with Harold Tompkins, anxious not to miss out on the fun. As I happened to be in Yorkshire at the time I too was included in the party. Theo declined the ride which went to Frank Nolan, an up and coming Irishman. He had not ridden for Cressida before but Theo recommended him as having empathy with horses still untried. Frank lived up to Theo's billing and gently nursed him for the first twelve furlongs before letting him enjoy the task in the way he wanted. Cruising up from fifth place to draw level just before the final hurdle, he jumped the last with aplomb and won by four lengths going away.

'That was a very decent performance,' said Noel to Sidney, 'even though the runner up was knackered. However, our horse clearly had a lot in hand.' Theo concurred. As for Sidney, he celebrated the thrill and delight in ownership by lighting a fine Jamaican cigar.

In the next race Dynamic Tom was running. This was the horse which had scored for Sidney on his first day at the races. Cajoling his partner to join him, Sidney and Harold plunged on it. When the horse obliged at 7/2 I sensed that Sidney was becoming very taken with the sport and that Harold might want to become an owner too. He crept over to Theo, congratulated him on his sagacity and asked him to look out for a couple of horses for him too.

Within three months Cressida had doubled the size of her yard with thirty horses in training. For the time being the yard was full. Yet Noel was immensely encouraging. Having every confidence in her and Tip he offered to fund a further six boxes.

'How is that for a wedding present,' he exclaimed on being informed of the wedding date. 'You have waited long enough!'

That summer of '67 the wedding between Theo and Cressida was as happy an event as it was possible to imagine. Noel was best man. No bolt out of the blue there! Jeremy, Owen, Bart and I were ushers. Claude was unable to attend as he was away in Africa but as was to be expected Slim was entrusted with the catering contract with Bart, shrewdly and successfully advising on the wines and champagne. Harry and Veronica needed no prodding to fly over from Portugal. In tandem with the local rector Mark conducted the service. But Vince took no part. So out of that unbeaten cricket team from all those years ago only two were missing the celebration of a union that for so long had been in the offing.

Among the guests were Sidney and Harold. Joyously they had come to be regarded as old friends. A surprise for me until I thought about it more carefully was to see the Earl of Ruabon, silver haired, rubicund, and now a shade portly. Then I recollected how supportive he had been of Gaffer at Heathside and that of course he will have known both Myfanwy and Cressida from babyhood. What is more, he looked upon Jeremy as the surrogate grandson who had procured for him a wonderful investment in Frenshams; and he was enjoying a highly satisfactory relationship with Bart who was managing his Ruabon hotel in London's Kensington. Quite naturally he had been delighted to accept the wedding invitation and to mingle in the company of young people whom he had seen grow up and come to regard as part of his family.

The seating plan at lunch, for it had been a midday wedding, reflected considerable care on the part of Theo and Cressida for the Earl was at the same table as Sidney and Harold. Although older than either he certainly did not look like a fish out of water. While his days of taking physical exercise were in the past, on appreciating the fun the two builders were obtaining from the turf and the amazing impact that Cressida was having with the support of Theo, he listened intently. So when Sidney invited him to be their guest on the Friday of Doncaster's next meeting, the day before the St Leger, he thought that would make for a good day out. Langbourn Counsellor would be running as would Cressida's newest arrival Cool Ronald, whose proud owner and first equestrian purchase was none other than Harold Tompkins. As for Richmond Dandy, he was continuing to be schooled at Malton.

When race day dawned, on studying the newspapers Noel was surprised to see that the ride on Langbourn Counsellor was being taken by Tip for he had kept quiet about this. Frank Nolan was also riding that day and was booked for Cool Ronald in the opening race. So to satisfy his curiosity Noel phoned up Tip and asked him for the low-down.

'It is like this,' explained Theo. 'Frank has been getting on to me asking why I do not race ride more regularly. His view is we both have an equal empathy with horses. As I ride out on Langbourn Counsellor most mornings he encouraged me to take the saddle even though it is a Friday. So let's see how it goes. Certainly Cressida seems happy enough.'

Sidney had included Marilyn and me in the invitation. So we caught the train to Doncaster from London. The plan was to see the St Leger the next day and to stay the weekend with Jeremy at his pied-a-terre in York where we would enjoy the company of Fiona to whom he was now formally engaged. Additionally, Marilyn said she was looking forward to seeing the Earl again. Apparently he had taken quite a fancy to her since whenever he was in town and she was having lunch at the Earl's hotel in Kensington he would come across specially to acknowledge her in the most courteous terms.

There was no denying that both Sidney and Harold knew how to entertain. They hired a private box and ensured the hospitality was lavish. When Cool Ronald won the first race, as champagne corks popped Harold never stopped beaming. Two races later they popped again for Langbourn Counsellor proved equally adept in the hands of Tip as he had done under Frank holding on to win by half a length. I could not help noticing how well both Sidney and Harold were getting on with the Earl. An unlikely combination I thought. But the chemistry was self-evident with the old boy appearing to relish every minute. It struck me as quite extraordinary how racing can bring together diverse characters who then have the greatest fun on level terms. If the Earl could sometimes appear reserved when away from his long-time pals in the military or House of Lords, certainly there was no shadow of this now.

That Friday proved a turning day in the lives of many at this small gathering in the private saloon. A few days later the two builders put a proposition to the Earl. No matter that he was seventy-seven, they invited him onto their Board and asked his permission for the name Ruabon to be applied to one of the finest houses they were about to introduce in an elite range. Its rival for top spot would be the name Langbourn, so thrilled were Sidney and Harold with the chaser. As a sweetener the Earl was offered some debenture shares bearing the generous coupon of 6.25%. Flush with cash, without a qualm he invested £0.75 million.

Over lunch on Sunday with Jeremy and Fiona I learned the date for their wedding. Fiona's ring was a beautiful Sri Lankan cornflower blue sapphire beset with diamonds. The blue matched her eyes. As the couple were so well suited I wondered why they had taken so long to decide on tying the knot. Without any question on my part they freely explained they wanted to be sure that the career of each was heading in the right direction. In Jeremy's case I was in no doubt it always had been and I need not have feared for Fiona either since she was cool, artistic, well balanced and so thoroughly nice. It was little surprise she was kept very busy, her latest assignments being to redecorate both a museum and an art gallery in Leeds.

In retirement her father, the General, had chosen Harrogate as the place to reside. It was a gracious spa town where culture was alive and well. Additionally there was plenty of golf to keep him on the go. Jeremy and Fiona had evaluated the options along with her parents and the wedding reception was to be held at a country hotel a few miles out. Could we be nearing the end of the reunions that "the team" had so enjoyed? Still to marry were Slim, Owen and me, and of course Claude. As for Vince I had rather written him off. In any case I doubted we would see a reunion in Ilford.

I switched the conversation to Claude and enquired innocently of Jeremy how much if at all he saw of him. Jeremy pulled a face.

'Very little I am afraid. I think that Mallinson diamond mine is causing him a shedload of grief. The share price has dropped back and the backers who he attracted are far from happy. He now spends a lot of time in Africa. But I sense the continent is full of chancers and I fear for him in focusing on an area that is so highly volatile. Maybe he should be spending more time in Liverpool looking after clients and putting them into rather less adventurous stocks.'

'Has Claude gained the backing of the Earl for the Mallinson mine?' I asked.

'I think so. And this worries the Earl not a little. I have always understood that when he dies his daughter will be left a life interest in his investments up to a certain amount. This will make her very well off. However she is unlikely to get her hands on the capital even if she wanted to. But actually she is not an extravagant person so that is of no great matter. The point is that there will be income to spare and a large amount to be disbursed one way or the other. And Claude as his great nephew looks to be the first in line. However the Earl may take unkindly to the fact that his investment in Africa is going down the pan and taking Claude with it. I don't honestly know if that scenario is correct. But this is my guess if what I hear from Dad is true. He chats to the Earl virtually every day. And his concern with Claude is apparent.'

'When will you next be seeing Claude?'

'I suppose when he returns from Africa. But he no longer lives at Somersal Herbert. So I shall have to be in touch with him at his office or leave a message for him. He is my oldest friend and with Harry now in Portugal he really ought to be my best man were he to agree.'

Marilyn was delighted to be seeing Fiona and to hear her news. The two had got on well when Fiona was supervising the new décor at the Ruabon Hotel. I was pleased that they enjoyed each other's companionship. Marilyn was easy and she fitted into whatever company she found herself. I realised I was very lucky to have her for a girlfriend and resolved then and there I should take the matter further. On the return train journey to London that Sunday evening we chatted over a bottle of wine and I formed the view she might well be ready to settle down. Having been a bachelor long enough, I certainly was.

Once back in London I phoned Cressida and congratulated her on producing a couple of winners at Doncaster the preceding Saturday. She was bubbling over in happiness, adding she hoped Tip might be able to spend more time with the horses instead of worrying about the range of Good Doctor machines that required attention. Then she said, 'you won't believe it but the Earl so enjoyed his day out he has asked Tip to find him a horse for he wants to be an owner too. Isn't that blooming wonderful!'

Frankly I was astonished. At seventy-seven the old boy appeared to be acquiring a new lease of life seemingly brought about through joining the Board of Bassett Tompkins. This news was quickly followed by Tip phoning me to say he had purchased a three year-old for the Earl called Shameless Eric. With its pedigree similar to Langbourn Counsellor's, Tip could not believe his luck. Cressida's efforts at training looked as though they really might be smartly rewarded on the back of her string gaining strength and depth.

Some weeks later Tip phoned me again. He was thinking of giving up working with Noel to become a full time jockey and assistant to Cressida. I asked if he had spoken to Noel. Indeed he had at which time Noel was ambivalent. Having broached the subject, the conversation had gone something like this.

'Tip, are you mistaking the substance for the shadow? You are planning to forgo a lucrative career for one that, as you know, is hazardous and hazardous on many counts. Not just concerning your health and well-being, but also your dependence upon the support of owners plus of course the good fortune of having super horses in your yard. There are so many variables. At the moment you can have both your cake and eat it at least as far as the riding is concerned. That might not be so in future.' Noel was doing his best to bite his lip, hide his frustration and dispense wisdom.

'Noel, you are quite right. It is not as though with Tellings and the Good Doctor I feel trapped in a *ménage à trois*. After all the business is your creation, pride and joy. In my case the two real loves in my life are Cressida and the thrill of the chase when in the saddle. And the two are inter-twined. If I do not now involve myself with horses full-time I shall forever regret it. As to your appointing a new Technical Director, this will surely be a minor problem.'

'That is as may be,' retorted Noel. 'Look, we are a great team. We always have been and I don't want to lose you. Dammit, if you really are determined to chance your arm and life as a jockey I shall certainly support you as best I can. By the way, for some time I have been toying with the idea of having a customers' day at the races and financing a race that we would call The Good Doctor'.

'An alternative is to purchase a horse and call it The Good Doctor', was Tip's rejoinder.

'Yes, indeed. But if it turned out to be a failure the image of the Good Doctor machinery would suffer accordingly.'

'True, Noel. But the press coverage you obtain from one annual jolly at the races, if any, is as nothing compared to a successful chaser. Think it over. This could have the propensity to win over a period of, say, five to seven years and in the process capture the imagination of the racing public among whom will be a host of your customers and their customers too.'

Noel said that he would think it over.

Clearly in phoning me Tip was not actually seeking a second opinion – since I detected that in reality he had made up his mind. Surmising he had another agenda as well, I thought I would forestall him.

'Look, if you do go ahead and switch career I shall be more than happy to write this up and see what coverage we can achieve in the national and sporting press. After all it is not every day that a successful businessman and talented amateur takes up the reins full time.'

A fortnight later Tip phoned again to say the die was cast. He was leaving Tellings and would be announcing his new full time post with his wife Cressida. What I did not know at the time was that Noel was offering him a lifeline in case things did not work out.

Noel was not only loyal to his friends but he was a shrewd judge of character. He trusted Theo to the nth degree, recognised his ability as a top-rate engineer and communicator and perhaps more importantly as someone with whom he could work in a totally relaxed manner. Frequently the ever proactive Noel had used him as a sounding board and bounced ideas off him. Then he had listened carefully before making his decision. Out of the blue he now offered him the title of non-executive Deputy Chairman with a modest salary to boot. On promising him that Board meetings would be arranged around Theo's timetable, Theo accepted. For all kinds of reason Noel was determined not to lose him. By keeping him involved in the fortunes of the Good Doctor range of equipment, he felt that as and when the thrill of the turf palled Theo would not have lost touch. What is more he could think of no one else whom he could trust so absolutely in fulfilling the role of his confidant and number two. Quite simply Theo was his best mate and probably always had been.

Some weeks on Noel phoned me to say he would be in London and wondered if I would be free for dinner. 'Jeremy will be in town too and will be able to join us.' He wanted to take us both to the Connaught. As that was an invitation that needed no repetition, I assented readily and altered my diary to avoid a clash. Noel was seeking finance from a merchant bank and his accountant had travelled with him. Hence the reason for his trip south. In the event, the meeting had gone so well that the accountant had returned on a late afternoon train for York.

Over dinner Noel was upbeat. 'Evie is transforming Owen's garden centre and the two of them have plans for a second one. She is also well in with Bassett Tompkins for I am happy to say both Sidney and Harold are content to deal with her fully knowing she is my wife. Happily this appears a blessing rather than a hindrance. Jeremy and Nigel, I have a confession to make. I too am getting the racing bug. Tip is now looking for a colt at the sales that will do justice to the Good Doctor name. I am getting quite excited.'

Clearly Noel was well on his way to making a fortune. He elaborated further, 'you must know I am thankful I have extricated myself from Father's Rolls Royce franchise. Dad is retired and he and Mother now spend most of their time in the south of Spain. Tennis, golf and bridge have taken over their lives. As for brother Russell who is running it on his own, he is finding the business tough going and frankly I fear for it.'

Other than Vince he maintained touch with all "the team". Harry appeared to be happy enough in Portugal. But like me Noel was worried by Claude. 'I suspect he may not last long with his broking firm. And if he leaves he is going to find life tough. His travails in Africa have done him little good and I think in the process he has shown signs of desperation. He approached me to invest in two extremely questionable exploration outfits as well as saying that the Mallinson shares would never be so cheap again. I was polite but firm, explaining I required all my spare cash for the Good Doctor business as it is growing apace. I could tell that Claude was unhappy. I think he may have been trying to offload a portion of his shares onto me for he had difficulty in concealing his desperation. But I am not going to hold it against him. I believe he could be in deep trouble and may have been sounding me out as a last resort. Anyhow that's how I read it.'

I detected that Noel was being realistic and forgiving. At the same time he had all his wits around him and was going to be nobody's fool.

Jeremy had listened carefully. 'I am afraid, Noel, you are only too right. Claude has sounded me out as well. The Mallinson mine is not the only share he has been pushing, although arguably it is the most glamorous and so the most appealing since it has features in common with the mighty Williamson mine. He has travelled far and wide in Central Africa and come across some highly speculative outfits, some of which may of course ultimately succeed. The largest one is the Fungurume copper mine. I got Father to check on this with the stockbroker the Earl uses. It has management problems and the broker advised to steer well clear. However it is always possible Claude knows better having actually spent time there.

'Other ventures over which Claude has enthused are Kolwezi Gold, Makoni Minerals, and the Gwaai River Ranch where a breed of cow is said to thrive due to the altitude and alluring climate. Other than white settled Africa the continent is short of good quality meat, so the ranch's future is thought to be exciting enough to warrant a chain of butcher shops in capital cities such as Abidjan in the Ivory Coast where Gwaai steak should sell like wild fire.

'We did not exactly fall out but I reminded him of my own experiences in Kenya. I don't wish to be a Jonah but I sense that Africa will long be a basket case. Fortunes may be made although in my view will more easily be lost. What is certain is that it is dangerous and I doubt this will diminish. Some may choose to chance this and wish to invest but I for one want no part.' As ever, Jeremy's viewpoint was sound – almost boringly so.

That night Noel and Jeremy stayed at the Ruabon. Over breakfast they were joined by Bart who updated them. As foreseen all was far from well with Claude. The two had met for dinner a fortnight earlier. More happily he reported Slim had been asked to do another TV show. The idea was that this would be filmed in London and a pair of celebrities would participate, relish the meal, and comment on what Slim had cooked. Bart was quick to offer the Ruabon's kitchens and private dining room. He could see this as a win-win situation.

'Clever concept,' I said when Bart told me. 'Let me sound out my contacts to see if we cannot get a well-known actor and his wife.' The obvious choice I thought would be John Clements and Kay Hammond. Kay was a glamorous actress renowned for her part as the ghostly Elvira in Noel Coward's famous play Blithe Spirit. Playing opposite her was Margaret Rutherford as the eccentric clairvoyant Madame Arcati. This ran for nearly 2,000 performances to establish a record at the time for a straight play. My pal in the theatrical world was lucky first time. John and Kay were tickled pink to be approached and asked for a further two dinners *à deux* as their fee. When Harry heard of this he quipped, 'well if they had not accepted you could always have had those gourmets Charlie and Ronnie Richardson'.

In January '68 Jeremy and Fiona duly got married. Succumbing to much persuasion, Claude was persuaded by Jeremy to be his best man. After all the two had grown up together in the same village of Somersal Herbert and Jeremy, ever charitable, wished to recognise this fact regardless that life was not treating Claude as kindly as his other old friends. But prudently Jeremy asked Noel to be the Master of Ceremonies, a position he chose to share with Theo. The two carried this off with the assistance of a slide show – a duo who proved utterly masterly. It was just as well for Claude did not seem to be quite the man that once he was. Uncharacteristically his eyes now betrayed a vacancy. However his hair had been cut at a smart salon and with his upright carriage he looked the part in his morning suit. His speech was delivered in well-modulated tones. Tact predominated. He was only reasonably humorous since there was no history of misbehaviour that he was prepared to divulge of Jeremy. Was he really too good to be true? Perhaps wisely there was no mention of Jeremy's exploits in Kenya. Yet Claude lacked spark. I could not put a finger on why. I rather suspected he might have involved himself in drugs when in Africa. I honestly do not know but certainly I was not alone in being a shade disappointed and just a mite concerned for him. Thankfully he did not step out of line.

Marilyn was with me and I decided the time had come for me to propose to her that evening as we danced. I had flunked the opportunity when travelling with her on that train south after Theo's wedding but was now determined to make amends before she gave up on me. Romance would be in the air and I sought to share it with her. Owen must have been of the same mind for he was with a sweet girl called Penny. She worked at the garden centre and I suspected that rather like me came from very little money if any. I heard within the week that like Marilyn she too had said Yes. Brilliant, I thought. They will make a great combination.

Noel, Theo and Jeremy, were now well on their way. I felt fortunate to have all three as friends. While I saw all too little of Owen I sensed he was a round peg in a round hole. Certainly I kept up with Bart though I did wonder when he would pop the question and forsake bachelorhood. I had always thought he might be the first of us to reach the altar since doubtless every girl with whom he became intimate will surely have been won over. But you just never can tell. As it transpired I did not have long to wait.

A couple of weeks later Bart phoned me. 'Come and have lunch at the Ruabon. I have a lot to tell you.' Well, that was an opportunity one could not resist. What was Bart up to now?

Over a Campari and soda he confided he had fallen for the loveliest of all German girls.

'Her name is Giselle. She is blonde with short curly hair and speaks impeccable English without a trace of an accent. We met at a Deinhard's wine tasting in one of the arches below Waterloo station.'

When Bart mentioned he had once spent a week in Germany courtesy of Deinhard and the Hasslacher family, she responded positively in saying the next time she went home she hoped he would accompany her. Then she would show him round further so he could gain first-hand experience of even more leading estates.

'This girl is going to be my soul mate. I would like you to meet her especially now that you are no threat thanks to your fiancée Marilyn!'

'Thanks a lot. I suppose that is a compliment but I have never thought of myself as a competitor to you, Bart,' And that was true.

Over lunch Bart explained his plans. 'We are going to revive the BMW consultancy and my partnership with Jeremy and Slim. Plans are now well forward for Owen to open a second garden centre. This will be adjacent to the racecourse at Wetherby. As it is just off the A1 it will be easy to access. Jeremy is dealing with the land aspect, Slim is to manage the catering, and I shall work with Slim to procure the kitchen equipment, china, glass and cutlery. Fiona will be overseeing the interior décor to include lighting, furnishings, chairs and tables and, as you can well imagine, Evie already has the concept of landscaping well under control. In all Owen will be well supported. He is a workaholic and we will make sure he is off to a cracking start. And fear not. When the moment is ripe you will be entrusted with the public relations drive. Nigel, the esprit de corps of that vintage year lives on.' I nodded in pleasure, recognising that my fears on leaving Heathside prematurely had happily been confounded.

Giselle turned out to be a honey. She was bubbly, intelligent, well informed and fun. She knew how to relate to people and immediately struck up a rapport with both Marilyn and me. It was agreed that we would go away for a long weekend and visit a wine growing area. After some discussion Alsace was chosen. The plan was to fly into Basel and hire a car. This way we could visit the Kaiserstühl first, the small area with a dozen or so villages in the extinct volcanic area on the German banks of the Rhine where the characteristics of the wine from each village appeared so utterly different to that of their neighbours. By travelling at the end of April we were sure to experience "spargelessen". Here fresh asparagus piled high in the form of a pyramid and doused with liquid butter, would be tied together with brown string at either end and served with slivers of smoked and unsmoked ham. By the side of the plate a pair of scissors lay to cut the string. The dish would be accompanied by the local wine just disgorged from the previous vintage. And if the weather permitted we could be sitting al fresco under red chestnut trees on wooden benches and eating at wooden tables.

Indeed that was the case. After that initial lunch in Emmendingen we had a fascinating three days on the western bank of the Rhine visiting "vignerons" in Riquewihr, Ribeauville and Hunawihr, and many other villages besides. Despite having been overrun by Germany twice since 1870, Alsace had been restored magically. Ramparts, towers, gateways, municipal buildings, shops and houses had been rebuilt just as they had been before they were ravaged. On many of the taller buildings metal hoops were constructed to allow storks to nest. From there they looked down on mankind with a detached contentment. The atmosphere was truly medieval.

Over our final lunch in the beamed and gabled town of Colmar, Giselle pointed out that the sales of Alsatian wine in Britain had never taken off in the way they deserved. She laughed when she said, 'it is what the wine trade in the City drink when they entertain each other. If we come to this part of the world again and I hope we will, I suggest we visit the Moselle where the wines can be flowery, delicate and ever so feminine.'

'Rather like you,' I thought to myself.

'Good idea,' I agreed, 'for I could return here happily any day of the week, especially in the spring. This is so much warmer than in Yorkshire or even London.'

Marilyn and I saw more of Bart now that he was linked up with the lovely Giselle. Indeed the more I saw of her I thought what a really sweet girl she was. Wasting no time he proposed to her and was accepted. It was some years later I gleaned that Giselle's long considered plan had been to work in London with the primary aim of finding an Englishman as a husband. Apparently German girls dream they could be kinder, or maybe more malleable, than their own race. Anyhow it had paid off. Another wedding on the way, I thought, but this time most probably in Germany. I wondered whether we would beat them to the altar.

A few days later Bart was not just surprised but horrified to see the Robber Baron and Charlie Richardson arrive for lunch at the Ruabon. He did his best to disguise his displeasure. These two were not the kind of clientele he either sought or required. Equally, he did not wish Bob Barron to see Carel Weight's original painting of greyhounds in action at his Catford stadium believing this might provoke the most frightful scene on the part of Barron who, he imagined, would assume he possessed a unique original. Fortunately this was hanging in the private room so not readily visible.

'Bart,' enquired the Robber after lunch, 'have you got a room available for private lunches?'

'I have,' Bart explained, 'but this is solely reserved for the Earl's personal friends, the local museums and college worthies. Try as I might, I have been able do nothing about getting the Earl to change his mind on this. I am sorry but you will appreciate I simply cannot help.'

That settled the issue since the last thing he wanted was for the Ruabon to become the haunt of the underworld when hatching conspiracies. In fact he did not want anyone of that ilk anywhere near the place. It had been an awkward hour and a half for Bart in placating two such unsavoury characters, an event he hoped would never be repeated. As they departed he let out a sigh of relief. It was after this experience that he insisted all luncheon dates had to be booked in advance. Nobody in future would be served who just arrived unannounced. His regular clients did this already. They thoroughly approved of the new rule too for even more than before it conferred on the Ruabon the atmosphere of an exclusive club.

CHAPTER 12: NEW HORIZONS

Owen's plans for a second garden centre had proceeded smoothly. Building on his experience with that first venture at York which was exceeding expectations, at Wetherby he provided a playground boasting a helter-skelter and a cunningly contrived track where young children could have fun in pedal cars. Additionally there were two further areas for roller skating and skateboarding. Alongside these were trampolines, a bouncy castle and a small lake big enough to support half a dozen pedalo canoes. A further divertissement was an inflatable cylinder not dissimilar to a hamster's wheel and capable of housing four little people. Every time one of them moved it rolled around in the water causing loss of balance and much hilarity. Paint ball and laser shooting were also on offer to appeal to older children, as was a Zipliner. This was a high wire assault course where one swung from one challenge to another before descending via a second and even more tortuous helter-skelter. Naturally, the mainly student staff wore uniforms and were versed in first aid. The shop was stocked with books on cooking and gardening, together with garden tools, lawn mowers, hedge clippers, greetings cards and toys for tots. The restaurant too aimed at a broad clientele. An extra which had not featured at York was a well-appointed function room which it was hoped might attract birthday parties and the like. Another market for which they were going to cater was the coach party where people could come and choose their pot plants or whatever, enjoy a tasty meal and have a day out to remember. I detected that Owen had had the gumption to enlist the advice of Jeremy in determining what facilities should be provided. Even I had added my two ha'porth at his request. Gratifyingly all had been taken aboard.

The opening coincided with Wetherby's biggest racing day of the national hunt season. To provide a carnival atmosphere Owen engaged the steel band that had played at the twenty-first of Claude and Jeremy. Yorkshire Television showed off the facilities in two minutes of prime time and Jeremy's father-in-law, General Sir Ramsay Southerness, performed the formal act of cutting the tape to declare the garden centre open. Champagne corks popped and there was a raffle for hampers, plants, vouchers at the restaurant, entry tickets to the next race meeting, and much else besides. On behalf of Chatsworth I was happy with the way things went. Owen was thrilled and the consultancy of BMW well pleased.

I was glad for Owen particularly as he had had the courage to branch out on his own rather than work with the Whyte family at Semleys. I feared that had he done so, most probably Freddy would have destroyed him regardless that Owen was thorough and hardworking. I liked Penny and imagined she would be good for him if only he would be bold enough to tell her he wanted to share his life with her and ask her to become his wife. She was uncomplicated, friendly, and had both feet firmly planted on the ground. I hoped he would do so and needled Jeremy to steer him gently in that direction. Jeremy laughed and said that both he and Noel had been on to him for months to take the big step forward. Perhaps with the Wetherby centre up and running he would at last focus on Penny and seize the moment. We both crossed fingers in wishing him a new horizon.

In this respect I stole a march on him for Marilyn and I now decided on a wedding day in that summer of '68. Well, actually she chose it. Her parents lived at Silchester, a village on the Berkshire and Hampshire border that had once been a Roman settlement in excess of a hundred acres known as Calleva Atrebatum. Renowned for good weather, it was never subject to flooding for the Romans chose their sites with considerable acumen. Her father was a boffin at the Atomic Weapons Research Establishment at nearby Aldermaston and her mother Hilary a potter. She worked at the Aldermaston Pottery and specialised in lustre ware. Any item bearing her signature became much sought after. So I guess that Marilyn will have inherited her artistic leanings from her. Their house in Soke Road was extremely pleasant but the rear garden, although attractive, was left largely wild and wooded so was unsuitable for a marquee. The church service was held in the tiny church dating back to the late twelfth century possessing a bell turret with a ring of five. Four of the bells had been cast in 1744 with the fifth more than a century later. As guests filled every pew to the full extra chairs had to be brought in to accommodate everyone. The reception was at the nearby Romans Hotel, a charming venue with manicured gardens and eye-catching topiary.

Every member of that 1947 cricket team was present including Vince who I had not wanted to omit. He had changed a lot. He wore a finely tailored morning suit that I suspected he will have owned so well did it fit. One could not avoid the fact that he appeared to be prospering judged by his neatly groomed hair and showy cravat. His days as a brass-necked military policeman were long behind him. While he was not especially friendly he was nevertheless keen to let us know he was doing well, not that we found out exactly how. Then I suspect none of us was sufficiently interested other than possibly Owen who had been so good to him in Nairobi and with whom he chatted at length. Guarded courtesy prevailed overall.

Thanks to Harry and Veronica our honeymoon was being spent in Portugal, a country neither of us knew. Rather than donate a wedding present they paid for Marilyn and me to spend three nights in a hotel in Lisbon and then enjoy a few days with them in Estoril and the Algarve. Lodged in a time warp Lisbon was fascinating. Plying the twisty narrow streets that were frequently precipitous and shabby were ancient toy trams. These offered seating for only twenty passengers. However a further thirty-eight could be accommodated if huddled together and standing in discomfort.

On our second morning we visited the museum of ancient carriages near the monastery at Belem where disappointingly not all had been restored. Threadbare and forlorn their grandeur was diminished. Matters now took a turn for the better. Virtually opposite the city's most famous watering hole – where with a sonorous clatter a waiter dropped a tray of drinks while we waited ten minutes for a simple drink – was one of three gracious churches whose benefactors must have vied with each other for prestige at the time when enormous wealth was being acquired from Portugal's colonies. Outside this extraordinarily elegant building hung a discreet poster which announced that that very evening there would be a sung Mass in Fado style. Fado is missing from the Oxford Dictionary so how to describe it? Arguably, as the original soulful folk music of old Lisbon conveyed so utterly magically by the spellbinding Amalia Rodrigues. In the early 1960s her dramatic bearing and haunting voice stole rave reviews at the Edinburgh Festival. On the sleeve of one of her recordings is an enigmatic explanation:

> *'The Fado means the nights one wastes…and the shadows…*
> *Where voices sob to the rhythm of guitars.*
> *The Fado is love and jealousy, ashes and fire, grief and sin.*
> *The Fado is all that exists, all that is sad.'*

Our luck was in for we obtained the last two seats out of a total of 240. A further 200 worshippers thronged the aisles or were moved to a small auditorium at the side. The contralto opening proceedings possessed a timbre sufficiently rich and riveting as to captivate international audiences. Along with her female companion their interpretation of the Fado's bewitching melodies emphasised the sufferings and sacrifices of Christ. A hand plucked guitar and cello provided backing as did an electric guitar. Mass was said followed by the Peace where all were welcome; and when the clerics came to depart the congregation clapped. In a little over an hour we had been enthralled. Whoever would have contemplated that a Fado Mass would be such a revelation!

On leaving Lisbon and reaching Estoril we met up with Harry and Veronica. Over dinner Harry was forthcoming. 'You won't believe it,' he explained, 'but also living in Estoril is that one-time rival of the Kray brothers, London gangster Solly Doull. He was the fellow who pulled off that astounding gambling coup with Bunny Fearnley. Bunny was later murdered and Mickey Hutton, the leading bookie in York, charged with the crime. You may remember I defended him and he got off. Correctly as it happened.'

'How can you be sure?' I asked.

'Well, Solly spilled the beans to me one evening when we happened to be in the bar of the Palacio Estoril Hotel Golf and Spa. Solly is living out his days in splendid affluence. He plays golf – not very well but enthusiastically – has forsworn crime and acts the Jewish gentleman, albeit still with a cockney accent. For some reason he wished to unburden himself on me and told how the man behind the plot to see off Bunny was Tyrone from Tottenham.' Harry mimicked the conversation which had gone something like this.

'Tyrone was the bookie who had to fork out a million and a half to me,' confided Solly. 'But Harry, he could not touch me,' he continued in his gravelly tone. 'Everyone would have known he was behind it had he done so. And he would not have lasted long as my boys would have seen to that. Tyrone was not stupid. He could appreciate this a mile off. But then Tyrone knew that I alone could not have pulled off the coup. He understood as night follows day that Bunny was the brains behind this while I was merely the lucky guy who he needed and was happy to be in on it. Bunny had taken Tyrone for a ride once before. Now here he was again, instrumental in Tyrone's huge losses even though the bookie was as wide awake as they come and had laid off a substantial amount. Believe you me, Tyrone was absolutely livid and swore to rid the racing world of Bunny who he regarded as a perennial threat.'

Harry continued the saga that Solly had related. 'It was easy enough to engage a hired killer. That was achieved at the Blind Beggar pub in the East End. But for it all to work Tyrone needed an accomplice. And that simply had to be the bookie in York who like him had been badly affected, none other than Mickey Hutton.

'The plan was that the assassin would motor to Yorkshire that Sunday and park his car near the A 64 trunk road at the Cross Keys. This is a public house with a large following for Sunday lunch. So neither would he have been conspicuous nor would his vehicle attract any attention. Mickey met him that evening before going to the Red Lion for his usual Sunday snifter and dropped him off in a wooded area a quarter of a mile from Bunny's Victorian house. The timing was carefully agreed. The killer would sidle up the drive shielded by mature rhododendrons, present himself at the front door at precisely 7 'o'clock, proffer the envelope and shoot Bunny dead at point blank range. Discreetly he was then hurriedly to creep away.

'With the deed done, as arranged at five past seven Mickey duly picked him up. On the way to the Cross Keys he pointed out a storm drain and urged him to chuck in the weapon. Mickey was home at his usual time of a quarter past seven and shortly after eleven 'o' clock that evening the killer was back in London.'

'Two points,' Harry had said to Solly. 'What about the IOU on Mickey's betting slip and what about the so called puncture?'

'That was all taken care of,' Solly had replied. 'Mickey's daughter had indeed written IOU on a betting slip but that was not the slip that was inside the envelope. Mickey had handed the killer another slip for him to write IOU. This was planned because Tyrone could not be sure that whoever was selected as assassin would be able to read or write. He was not far wrong either for this fellow chose to copy little Cynthia's childish handwriting. As for the puncture, there never was one. But next morning Mickey drove to a garage in Selby where he was not known. He had two new tyres fitted and left behind two worn ones. He never did fling a tyre on Snodgrass's old pile.'

Harry now explained to Marilyn and me that all along he had suspected Bunny was disposed of through a hired killing. What he could not be sure of was whether Mickey was involved and if so how. Certainly he always doubted that Mickey was the killer. In fact of course he was not. But he was guilty as an accessory before the fact.

Next day Harry and Veronica took us to the fashionable neighbouring resort of Cascais. At their suggestion we were then to travel to the Algarve where Harry wanted to show us the site and the architect's drawings for the house that he and Veronica were having built for them at Penina. As soon as it was ready they planned to move in. Fortune favoured them for they had been lucky enough to obtain a stunning situation. Originally this had been snapped up by a German. But he had died suddenly and as his widow was not interested in living there on her own it came back onto the market. With Harry in the know since he was friendly with the developers, he grabbed the opportunity. As for the house, even Veronica's father Kyros could not have failed to be impressed. Of particular appeal to Harry was the fact it overlooked the golf course that Henry Cotton had designed and which had opened two years earlier in 1966. Harry explained that because he was well in with the developers he hoped to be first choice as legal adviser for any Briton wishing to purchase. It was pretty clear he had fallen on his feet as there were several score plots still available awaiting buyers.

That September of '68 Bart married Giselle. Bart's wedding was held in the Black Forest with the reception at the Adler Hotel in Hinterzarten overlooking Lake Titisee. Now called the Parkhotel Adler, in the 1960s and 70s it was said that if you stood at its bar for a year you would see all your old friends pass through, such was its international reputation for quality and ambience. What I had not realised till then was that the attractive Giselle came from a family both well-connected and well-heeled. As far as they were concerned, money was no object in providing their beloved daughter with a lavish wedding. Giselle's father had an engineering business in Stuttgart which was a major supplier to the Germany's highly successful motor industry. But their country home had long been in the Black Forest which was where they preferred to hold the wedding.

Everyone from "the team" was invited and apart from Claude and Vince we all accepted. Slim especially was keen to see how well-to-do Germans celebrated the occasion at the dinner dance. He was not disappointed and recorded the details in a pocket book. After a light bouillon with noodles served with a delicate Moselle, came fresh trout garnished with spinach and enlivened with a glass of Alsatian Riesling. The main course was suckling pig accompanied by an intense golden three-year old Ruhlander wine from the Kaiserstühl village of Achkarren, something totally novel to Slim who waxed lyrical about it.

'This will go well with venison,' he suggested.

In traditional fashion we finished with Black Forest gateau washed down with Trockenbeerenauslese, the sweetest dessert wine that Germany produces.

Afterwards with Jeremy, Noel and Harry, Fiona, Evie and Veronica, Marilyn and I spent two days exploring the area. It was new to three of the girls. Indeed only Marilyn and I had a nodding acquaintance resulting from our trip with Bart and Giselle earlier to the Kaiserstühl and Alsace. As we all got on so well we said we ought to try and repeat another short break next year. Alas, with other priorities intervening, this particular dream went unfulfilled.

'Better to dream I suppose than go through life without purpose or ambition,' I reflected in due course. After all that might well have been my lot had I forever stayed a journalist with the Kent Essential.

CHAPTER 13: CONCERN OVER CLAUDE

Back in London I found myself increasingly busy and it was several weeks before I saw Bart and Giselle again. Then one day in October Bart called to ask if Marilyn and I would dine with Giselle and him at the Ruabon. Over dinner Bart announced he had received a visit from Claude.

'All is very far from well with him. He has left the Liverpool broking firm of Perkins, Cooper and Leighton – known to the wags of Liverpool as the perky copulator – and is not joining his father's firm either. Just as serious, he has broken up with Gemma Gough-Wilcox. Her father has taken unkindly to Claude recommending him to invest in Mallinson. Word is the mine is going to fail and a lot of the puff behind the story has been speculation and exaggeration. The same goes for Kolwezi Gold. I suspect Claude has been taken in and very possibly is guilty of conning his friends and acquaintances. Whatever the truth, these stories reflect no credit on him at all with the wags now dubbing him Claude the Fraud. It is all very sad.'

'What is he now doing?' I asked.

'He is working for Argosy Life selling life insurance on commission. He operates in Belgravia and Knightsbridge where he imagines he might mix with a load of idle money and is touring certain pubs where many of the potential customers are – how does one say – spoiled Hooray Henrys, in other words loafers of no great repute.'

'This is very unsatisfactory. But what to do to stop him ruining his life?'

'Nigel, I think he is unlikely to listen to you or me. I suspect the only person who may have any effect on him will be Jeremy. They grew up in the same village and although they went on to different schools were in the same regiment in Kenya. They know each other well and at one time were bosom friends. After all, Claude was his best man. Jeremy comes to town from time to time as he keeps a watching brief on the work that Surridges is doing. And when he is in London he always stays here at the Ruabon. I will try and bring him up to date but in the meantime perhaps we ought to visit these dives where Claude hangs out and see for ourselves what in heaven's name he is up to.'

'Which are they?' I persisted.

'As far as I know there are three: the King Charles off Kynaston Place which is his lunchtime haunt, the Falcon in Earls Court and the Troubador in Belgrave Square.'

'That sounds like a jolly lunchtime although not altogether a prepossessing evening. But I guess you are right. Look, I will visit the King Charles on my own. Then another day we can go together to the Troubador and if he is not there on to the Falcon. We can show support even if we do not fall for any of his patter to buy a life policy.'

I duly visited the King Charles. This was a tiny pub run by a man who used to work for Avon Tyres in East Africa and who answered to the name of Leo. His domain had been Tanganyika and to say the least he was quite a character. Signed photographs adorned the walls depicting well known film stars on safari. Among them were William Holden, Ava Gardner and Spencer Tracey. He kept the beer superbly and, although he offered only a limited range of finger food, specialised in simple spicy dishes that reflected his colonial past. These included samosas to die for and small curried shepherds pies that were easy to eat and did not require a knife and fork. Most days there were also pieces of chicken, pork or turkey cooked "piri piri" style on a cocktail stick with assorted exotic dips into which to dunk them. To get a seat or a bar stool one had to arrive before 1230 so popular was it. I arrived a quarter of an hour earlier and found Claude already there. He saw me immediately and could not have been friendlier.

'Buy me a drink, Nigel, and I shall have some very good news for you.'

My heart sank but without a second thought I honoured his request for a Balblair malt, a light beguiling Scotch matured in Bourbon barrels and possessing discreet tones of apricot, butterscotch and citrus. Asking where he was living, Claude replied he was sharing a flat with a Scot called Roddy Burnside who also worked for Argosy Life. Often the two paired up in the evenings and split the commission when a prospect bought. As to his address Claude was vague. He just said Maida Vale. I let the matter drop as his reluctance to divulge further was obvious. Rather as expected Claude tried to sell me a life policy. But I was having none of it and told a little white lie that now I was employing four staff some months they took home more in their pay packet than I did.

I bought Claude a second dram and paid for his lunch too. He was expansive before turning his attention to a well-dressed man who he will have recognised. Excusing himself he ambled across and engaged him in conversation. Realising that Claude was now turning on the charm in an endeavour to make a sale, I bade him goodbye and promised to look in on him one evening when he would be at the Troubador. On reporting back to Bart, he agreed that we should call in at the Troubador to assess the situation and to see whether this Roddy Burnside was a good influence or, as we suspected, a downright bad one.

Two days later we arrived around 7.00 pm. Claude was present and introduced us to his friend Roddy. Personable, persuasive and younger looking than his years since he barely needed to shave, he struck me as dangerous – all "bullshit and handkerchief" while he waved his spotted silk hankie around to emphasise a point. In his lilting west of Scotland accent he told us over a pint how he had been a member of Troon and Prestwick Golf Clubs and off his handicap of three had played with such luminaries as Morty Dykes, Dick Smith and Reid Jack. All three had been Scottish internationals and Walker Cup players. Answering why he had left the comfortable life that a family business provided in such an idyllic place, he explained the company had failed and for this he placed the blame squarely on his two cousins. It was a sad story.

'The family firm used to make canvas hose pipes and at one time was the major supplier to the nation's fire services. This had done us well over the years. Branching out in to deck chair covers, shop awnings, camping equipment and even Bedouin tents, all helped to provide a lucrative living. The problem arose when my cousins resolutely refused to employ synthetics. I had championed these for they were lighter, easy to clean, longer lasting and cheaper. Once canvas was seen as "old hat", the business went bust for it was found there was insufficient capital for diversification and the necessary machinery. I was furious that they had not listened to me and we fell out in a big way. I am utterly blameless – the victim of wretched circumstances. But I have put all that behind me now. London is the place to be and life insurance has to be an integral part of all our lives. Don't you agree!'

Both Bart and I were then subjected to the most high pressure sales spiel with Claude chipping in to assist. On departure we both agreed that the life those two were now embarked upon was profoundly depressing. How or whether Jeremy could help gave me cause for concern and doubt. We would have to see. I wondered if that romance with Gemma could ever be revived and floated the idea with Bart who was far from optimistic.

When Jeremy was next in London the three of us had a quick lunch at the Ruabon. The moment we mentioned the affinity between Claude and Roddy Burnside, Jeremy groaned.

'That was the fellow behind the scam at Kelso racecourse. In conjunction with Dickie Birkmyre it replicated the scam at Cartmel. If you remember, another feckless and spoiled Scot was involved who sought to switch his horse Gay Future with a similar animal but one far more talented. Why Roddy could have been so stupid I don't know. But he was. The scam failed this time too and as you can imagine the outcome was predictable. He was warned off the Turf for life and banned from the Golf Clubs of Prestwick and Troon. Claude could not be keeping worse company if he tried and this is a tragedy. From what I hear he has become a scrounger and is drinking like a fish mainly at the expense of other people. I think the only way out will be to arrange for him to go to Alcoholics Anonymous and seek professional help. But of course he will have to be willing to undergo this. I'll see what I can do to help.'

In stark contrast, within the year Owen married his girlfriend Penny. He was now on a roll. He had gone ahead with his desire to develop garden centres and cultivated his old friends who could assist. All in all he was not putting a foot wrong. At York and Wetherby the two centres now sold garden furniture, books on both gardening and stately gardens, a broad range of casual clothing, and homemade preserves along with the original offering of old and much loved English apples. As for his two restaurants, together with the play centres these were drawing in the crowds almost regardless of the desire to purchase shrubs and plants. I was delighted for him. He had shown much inventiveness and was reaping the reward.

Claude did not attend the wedding but he was the sole exception from our vintage team. One memorable innovation at the service was a solo from Theo who sang Stand by Me. He focused on Owen and Penny but I noticed that briefly he also looked across at Cressida and then at his friend and support, Noel. In that instant I was reminded of the occasion when Noel threw a punch at Luigi at Pen Island. A wonderful thing is chemistry, I thought. And now it was working out to the advantage of both. Years later in 1987 Stand by Me became a Number One hit in Britain, sixteen years after the former lead singer of The Drifters, Ben E King, had made it the cornerstone of his career as a solo artiste in the USA.

The surprise attendee was Vince, not only because he actually took the trouble to come, but because he was there with his wife. She was an unusually tall Sri Lankan lady of magisterial bearing and undeniable elegance and, although somewhat restrained, I sensed that behind her polite manners was a character of steel who could well drive Vince forward. Whether this would be in the right direction or not, my guess was only time would tell. Perhaps I should not have been that surprised at seeing Vince for he had worked with Owen in Nairobi's Buller Camp in helping him as a film projectionist when he had been suspended from his duties as a military policeman. Tactfully Owen was never once critical and I suppose Vince will have wished to show his gratitude.

As for Slim, he produced a girlfriend in Jessica who none of us had previously met. But we all knew her from the big screen. She was clearly good news, being a striking girl who worked in television. Slim had run across her originally when he featured in that programme on BBC TV extolling Canadian recipes in support of the Good Doctor. But now that she had become a presenter with Yorkshire TV she was a familiar face throughout the county. I did not have to ponder long why the two had got together for one could see at a glance they were on the same wave length. I was delighted for them.

Once again Harry and Veronica were happy to have an excuse to return home for a few days and maintain their connection with family and old friends. With Veronica pregnant and blossoming, Harry whispered she was expecting twins.

'I might be on the lookout for a godparent or two,' he laughed when he told me about this.

'Well, count me in if you are desperate,' I answered. 'A trip to Portugal will always be an attraction,' I added, 'especially if it involves a round or two of golf.'

'I shall give it long and serious thought,' was his reply. 'But Marilyn might be first choice for the duty role. Would that matter?'

'Not at all as long as I am permitted to accompany her.'

And we left it like that.

CHAPTER 14: DRAMATIC CHANGES

That March on the advice of Theo Noel had bought a young horse at the yearling sales that he called The Good Doctor. As it would not be running for some years and his business was prospering, he decided on sponsoring a race at Wetherby to be called The Good Doctor and to take a private suite in which to entertain friends and clients. Sidney Bassett and Harold Tompkins were still the best of friends with Noel, for he was the type who once he had forged a relationship would never willingly allow it to lapse. The two builders both wanted their horses to participate that day too so Cressida trained all three with this meeting in mind.

Although a winner first time out, Harold Tompkins' horse Cool Ronald was something of an enigma. But Langbourn Counsellor was on everybody's lips as a sure-fire good thing so short in price. To add spice to the afternoon, Richmond Dandy, the other horse that Sidney and Noel had purchased, had run only once. And that was in a minor event at Carlisle. There it had come a distant third but was in no way disgraced. Almost like schoolboys looking forward to a treat out, the three businessmen were pumped up in a state of happy anticipation.

Theo was to have the ride on the Counsellor and Richmond Dandy, while Frank Nolan took the saddle on Cool Ronald along with three other rides as well. Frank was a popular jockey and was often asked by a number of trainers to perform when Cressida did not have a runner.

Richmond Dandy was in the second race which was the one sponsored by The Good Doctor. Although he was little fancied at 15/2, the TV pundits remarked on how well he looked and considered he was one to keep an eye on. Tip, as he was known to punters, rode it patiently as was his wont and the horse responded in an encouraging manner. The favourite was two lengths ahead going to the last but was clearly hard pressed by the Dandy. The favourite stumbled. The Dandy performed an immaculate jump, then to undisguised near hysteria won by a head. Noel looked composed as ever but Sidney was almost overcome with excitement.

Cool Ronald ran in the next race and was going well when he was brought down at the fourth by an errant horse which fell in front. It was crushing luck. But Cressida was not dismayed and comforted Harold by saying this was all part of the jumping game. The important thing was that both horse and jockey were unhurt and she doubted that the fall would seriously dent Cool Ronald's confidence once he was given time to get over it.

The big race of the day was the 3.40. This was the Yorkshire Ewer, hugely prestigious and with prize money of £36,000. The favourite was Red Uppity at 5/2, unbeaten for two seasons and arguably the best bred horse in the race since he was by two multiple winners in Red Fort and Up the Khyber. But Langbourn Counsellor was in receipt of four pounds and with Tip benefiting from the amateur allowance of seven pounds, the horse was thought of as well in. Many punters must have reckoned so too. The odds came down from 9/2 to 11/4 although in places it could be backed at 3/1. Noel, Sidney, and those in the know had backed it ante post two weeks earlier at 6/1 and 5/1.

The race unfolded much as planned. Red Uppity and Langbourn Counsellor were respectively in fourth and fifth position throughout the first circuit biding their time nicely. Whereas in his previous race the Counsellor had held on well to win by half a length, this time he was a head down coming to the last fence. Red Uppity scooted away from it but Tip was not to be denied and was after him cajoling his mount to perform wonders. He drew level. Excitement in Noel's private salon was electric. His fan club was hoping that Tip's weight allowance would make all the difference when it came to the line. Langbourn Counsellor inched ahead but Red Uppity retaliated to be a nose in front. Then Tip galvanised one final effort from the Counsellor as the two horses passed the line locked together. With the camera angle not precisely opposite the finishing post, on CCTV it looked as though the favourite had possibly got up and certainly the bookies must have thought so for immediately they posted 8/11 on Red Uppity and 6/5 against Langbourn Counsellor.

Now Noel knew two chaps who specialised in assessing photo finishes whose interpretation could take some time. In fact they made their living doing this on the northern circuit in both the jumps and the flat. He understood the tic tac code they used to signal their gamble to the bookies. Noel was equally quick and pounced on Langbourn Counsellor at 6/5 placing £500. The outcome required a magnifying glass and the counting of pixels. After nearly a minute the judge gave his verdict. First, number 9, Langbourn Counsellor. Second, number 3, Red Uppity. Sidney went wild. Harold was exuberant. Even the Earl allowed himself a beatific smile. Jeremy seemed amazed by it all. He was not an aficiniado of the racing game but confessed this had been a wonderful baptism. Noel just looked knowing. And apart from a face grinning like a Cheshire cat said hardly a word, except to the barman. The celebrations were long lasting. When the Earl's horse Shameless Eric obliged in the last race at 7/1, all agreed they had never experienced a race day like it. And Ruabon announced he had never enjoyed an afternoon so much in all his long life.

Next morning the sporting press was unanimous in praise of this "new" lady trainer Cressida Manners and her young husband, the amateur jockey from nowhere, Tip. He had fought a battle with Jason Pitt, the champion jumps jockey and got the better of him. Jason had the graciousness to congratulate Tip as they journeyed to the winners enclosure and even looked in on the revellers in Noel's box after the last race to add his congratulations to them too. He was not just being thoroughly courteous. He thought it was in his best interests to make his mark with these new owners and indeed with Cressida, who he determined to get to know better.

At the end of April I got a phone call from Harry. Veronica had duly been delivered of her twins, one a boy, the other a girl. I was asked to be godfather to little Anthony and Marilyn was asked to be godmother to Celia. Naturally we were happy to accept. With Jeremy also invited to be a godfather, we flew to Faro and spent a happy three days during which we managed a round of golf at Penina in a threeball with Harry.

Harry and Veronica had settled in by then and he had played with Henry Cotton twice. What really pleased him was that Henry's Argentinian wife Toots had taken a liking to Veronica. After our game Henry came over and could not have been more pleasant. He turned to Harry saying that Gerry Cutsam who was his regular Friday afternoon partner had fallen down and broken a hip, and he wondered if Harry would take his place. You can imagine how honoured Harry felt. Now off a handicap of four he reckoned he could hold his own and not let Henry down. The opposition were also single figure handicappers off seven and eight. One was from Zurich, the other from Stockholm. Both were wealthy and aged around sixty. They were also extremely competitive. As neither of them was fully retired each still kept his finger on the pulse of their business in visiting the office mid-week whenever they considered it necessary. In no way flamboyant the two were shrewd. They offered Henry good investment advice and with Harry privy to this naturally he found these afternoons not only stimulating but highly profitable too.

Back in London life went on at a hectic pace. I was asked to produce a public relations article for an exhibition in the Tate Gallery at which Carel Weight and some of his friends from the Royal College of Arts had new works on show. Bart was there at the opening party with Jeremy as his guest since he was staying a couple of nights at the Ruabon. Discreetly Jeremy took me on one side.

'Nigel, I saw Claude at lunchtime and am profoundly sad. He is still in league with that wretched Roddy Burnside who remains seedy and all "bullshit and handkerchief". Claude retains a smattering of his elegance but is a pale shadow of how he used to be. He has put on weight, takes no exercise, and is drinking even more heavily. Just possibly he is beyond helping. If I am wrong, the opportunity to do so might be relatively brief. What is apparent is that Claude is not proving a good gambler, something I surmised long ago even before Claude became a stockbroker. He is now wagering on the horses under the tutelage of Roddy yet without the latter's intuitive flair. How he is making out selling insurance for Argosy Life is unclear. Rather more transparent is that Claude shows little interest in how any of his old friends from happier days are doing. Incidentally, Gemma has got married and Claude was not invited to the wedding. So it looks as if Liverpool society has ditched him.'

I shook my head saying I would try to maintain touch with him and keep Jeremy informed.

In the late summer of 1969 I received a phone call from Jeremy. The Earl of Ruabon had been taken ill. He had had a heart attack and was confined to his house at Somersal Herbert. Jeremy's Dad was on hand to help and to supervise the nursing staff. The Earl's daughter Millicent had been informed as of course were Cressida and Theo who had the custody of Shameless Eric. The Earl had asked to see Mark and Myfanwy and they were due to visit him the next day. Jeremy himself had been round where he found the Earl at seventy-nine weak and a tad confused. He did not think it appropriate for Bart or me to attend but he wanted us to be aware of the problem.

The next day Jeremy ushered in Mark and Myfanwy. Weak or not, the Earl seemed composed and remarkably coherent. With him was his lawyer. In front of these four he itemised just how he wanted to change his will. This had been in favour of both his young relation Claude and Jeremy after ensuring that Millicent had a generous income for life but no further capital. In his view she was already nicely provided for. She had no dependants nor would she at her age of fifty three. However to bolster her fortune as she grew older he wanted her to have a life interest in his holding of the builders Bassett Tompkins who he considered were riding the crest of a wave. This was paying 6.25% on his investment of £0.75 million. That would make for a hefty supplement so that if she wished to spend the winter cruising or indeed required medical treatment, she had ample funds to do so yet still attend to charitable bequests out of income. More importantly from her point of view, there should not be any question of her ever having to leave her bijou flat in London's Mayfair because of funds being depleted.

The changes were material. He now wished to leave £1.5 million each to Myfanwy and Cressida. He had been a huge admirer of Gwyn their father and realised that this talented and godly man never had the accumulation of wealth as a goal. He knew therefore that on his death there was very little to pass on other than memories. His objective was two-fold: for Mark and Myfanwy to be able to purchase a prep school and for Cressida and Theo to expand their training establishment.

In addition he wanted to leave an appropriate but significantly lesser amount to Claude to pay off his debts. He did not know what these were but hoped that a trust sum of £75,000 would suffice and still allow a handsome surplus to help him rehabilitate himself. He stressed he did not wish to leave him any more since he suspected this could result in throwing good money away after bad. He asked Jeremy to take on the responsibility of becoming a trustee and confirmed what had long been apparent, namely how he had long looked upon him as his surrogate grandson. After all, his only son Christopher had been killed in the War.

To Jeremy he would be leaving the Ruabon Hotel which was now debt free. Moreover, as he was to be the residuary legatee, once death duties and outstanding expenses had been cleared with his pictures sold or not as appropriate, he should find there was a reasonable sum in the kitty. In any case Jeremy, rather than Claude, would be inheriting the substantial estates in the vicinity of Somersal Herbert which for so long his father had been managing with prudence and acuity and where there were two tenanted farms. There was one proviso to this. He had not forgotten that Bart had given him the painting of those racing greyhounds that hung in the private salon at the Ruabon in Kensington. To recognise this he left Bart two of the late nineteenth century impressionist paintings from his orangery in Somersal Herbert. I don't quite know why but the Earl remembered me too. I can only suppose it was because I had been on the scene for so long among the young men he had come to know and admire that he will have accepted that I had been fully admitted to their coterie. He left me £5,000 and a silver George II cream jug hallmarked with the leopard's head of London and dated 1757. Finally he proposed leaving his horse Shameless Eric to Tip plus £4,000 a year to keep him in training and deal with veterinary fees – but only for so long as was deemed sensible.

The Earl must have had a sixth sense for he survived just another ten weeks, dying in September. Happily and rather marvellously he had the satisfaction of knowing that he had managed to sort out his affairs in the way he now wanted. He was only too thankful that he had not left it too late. Jeremy could not believe his good fortune. He knew his benefactor was wealthy but nobody had really had any inkling as to exactly how rich for he was modest in his tastes. Whether Claude's nose would now be put out of joint is anyone's guess. It is difficult to know if he had had great expectations only for these to be confounded. My own view was that Claude had never paid that amount of attention to the Earl and so presumably never really thought about it. Then a certain lackaday had always been Claude's trait!

When probate had been granted surprisingly speedily Mark got in touch with Jeremy.

'You have your ear to what is going on in the property world. For my part I hear strange happenings in the world of education. The prep school Cholsey Heights has been struck with scandal. You know the usual thing – two masters abusing boys. Old Roger Howitt, the Head, is beside himself. The school has been his creation in large part. In my view he is too old to rebuild confidence in it. In any case I hear he wants to retire and is even thinking of selling the whole thing, lock stock and barrel, in the belief it can become an old people's home. If he does, that will leave a lot of parents in the lurch and looking frantically to see how best their offspring should be catered for.'

Jeremy agreed. 'Mark, actually I happen to know Cholsey Heights and Roger could be right for it would well transform into an old people's home. As for the existing pupils that is indeed a problem. But you may know that only last week Stokehill has been severely damaged by fire. If that school were to close too, then there is the opportunity for a new school to arise rather like a phoenix from the ashes. Well not quite literally. But you get the gist.'

'Yes Jeremy. I had indeed heard that Stokehill had a problem but was unclear just how serious its fire has been.'

'Very serious, Mark. I doubt it will reopen any time soon if at all. In the short term the boys will have to go somewhere and maybe Cholsey Heights is one answer even if a temporary expedient. Should Roger proceed to close Cholsey down as one might now reasonably expect, then that will leave a lot of parents seeking a solution. Some will opt for Middleham but I am not sure how well considered it is.'

'My understanding in a phrase is "not very". So perhaps this could be the time to create a new school, Jeremy. Do you know of any estate that could be coming onto the market and might be suitable?'

'Leave it to me. I do have an idea that could suit rather well for the Oliphants property of Ragley Hall is a possibility. Josiah II's widow Julia is finding it all too much and her son Ruan is thinking of moving to the Cotswolds. He has an interest in a thriving engineering business in Malmesbury. Were he to become actively involved in this then he will probably move south. He is an engineer of some inventiveness. In any case he is a clever guy. He really ought to bite the bullet and do this instead of keeping Mum company in what so easily could pass for a mausoleum. After all it does resemble one thanks to its wonderful basilica.'

'Tell me the story behind this,' interposed Mark.

'The Oliphants grew cotton in Egypt in the late nineteenth century. Old Joseph was a friend of Lord Cromer who was Britain's Chief Representative in Egypt at the time and who encouraged British investment in the country, particularly in their cotton. Other than the relatively scarce sea-island cotton, Egyptian cotton was widely esteemed as the world's premier long staple variety and thanks to British and French investment it was not long before it was readily available in quantity. Joseph, as a landowner in the Peak District, was enthused by Cromer. He could appreciate that not only would the sun and an empirical life style be more attractive than the cool and misty days of the Derbyshire hills, he reckoned that with Lancashire's cotton industry waxing strong on the back of exporting to the dominions and colonies, a fortune was within his grasp. A persuasive man, he found little trouble in obtaining backers. So he brought with him ample funds from a number of influential friends. In 1876 he was therefore able to purchase good land in the choicest of areas. Due to hard work and careful husbandry, Joseph and his son, twenty-two year old son Josiah I, soon possessed what came to be seen as the finest and most progressive cotton plantation in the country. Just after the 1st World War the Oliphants sold out to an Egyptian family of good repute backed by a French consortium. They did indeed make the fortune that Joseph so confidently had predicted. With it they bought Ragley Hall a few miles from Bakewell. This is late Georgian, rather stately and with lovely proportions. The grounds are capacious and well hidden from the surrounding roads. It is not an easy property to value but I will talk to Ruan and his mother and see what they have in mind.'

In a matter of weeks Jeremy worked his magic. Julia Oliphant had a small cottage on the estate that she had long hankered after. It was let to an elderly couple but sadly the wife had begun to suffer from dementia. The husband could not cope. Jeremy arranged for her to go into care in time for Christmas and for her husband to be accommodated in sheltered housing at nearby Baslow, where a newly built close featured the first development of this type in the area. Jeremy now ensured the cottage was renovated and decorated to Julia's satisfaction. Then that spring he sorted out her move in conjunction with Ruan. She was thrilled.

Now Ruan felt he could relocate to the Cotswolds, happy that both his mother and he no longer had the ceaseless worry over the upkeep of the hall. Neither Ruan nor Julia was rapacious in seeking an enormous sum for it. Both professed to be delighted that their beloved hall would become a prep school, hence in their view a seat of learning. They were pleased too that the grounds would be used for sports facilities. For generations they had been ornamental – gorgeous in their way but truly not of much use to anyone.

Mark and Myfanwy honoured the family name in building an extension to be known as the Oliphant Wing. Cholsey Heights duly closed at the end of the summer term in 1970. Together with some boys from Stokehill, at the start of the school year in the Michaelmas term there was a sufficient nucleus of pupils to provide a foundation on which to build. Naturally Mark was able to cherry pick the best staff from both schools in addition to taking on two excellent teachers from Lichfield Cathedral School who he had liked and respected. The dream of Mark and Myfanwy came to fruition well within budget to leave a handsome sum as a contingency fund. To commemorate the Earl, the name of Ragley Hall was changed to Ruabon Hall now that it was no longer a private house but a school. Were the Earl to be looking down from above he must have been mightily gratified.

Further fortune flowed Mark's way for in July 1971 Middleham shut down. Some of the boys went to the local state school but about one-third sought a place with Mark. Quite fortuitously he now had 160 pupils. Jeremy, as chairman of the governors, sensibly counselled that they open a junior school so as to provide the seed corn for the future. They obtained a bank loan and built two classrooms to take forty youngsters. With a total of 200 boys on their books the school was not only viable but profitable too. Equally satisfactorily, the contingency fund remained intact.

For her part, in the autumn of '69 Cressida had been overwhelmed by the Earl's generous legacy. Thankfully she was a realist and recognised that the fortunes of a racehorse trainer are liable to fluctuate all too often in a volatile fashion. Theo was both conservative and forward looking. Having discussed expansion with their three most important owners, they decided to phase in bit by bit any plans they might formulate. Noel was the most upbeat. But even he considered that eight horses might be about as much as he would wish to have in training. Theo reckoned that one day an all-weather surface was a possibility in which case he would introduce it on one of his gallops. But that time had yet to come. He also contemplated building an equine swimming pool. But before he did so he determined to ascertain just how successful these had been where they were newly established in Australia.

With Jeremy travelling to London every month on business for Beale Thompson while he still kept a supervisory eye on Surridges, in the spring of '70 he sought out Claude. Leo at the King Charles said he had not seen him for a week or so but thought he was still around. And 'No' he did not know where he lived. Jeremy left his card with Leo and asked him to get in touch should he ever put in an appearance again since he did not fancy spending time searching for him in either the Falcon or the Troubador. As luck would have it Leo called him the next day at 1215. Claude had just walked in.

'Buy him a drink on my account and keep him amused, will you. I shall be along in half an hour to forty minutes.'

When Jeremy entered the small bar Claude was still there. Leo must have been discreet for by the look of surprise on Claude's face he was not expecting him although he was quick enough to accept the drink proffered.

'Make mine a Balblair please, Jeremy. A fine lunchtime malt if ever there was one.'

Jeremy bought him lunch too and they sat together quietly in a corner while he enquired after his life in general. Claude was noticeably edgy but put on as brave a face as he could.

'I am now working solo for Roddy Burnside has left Argosy Life. He is not well. I think he might have inoperable cancer. We have lost touch since the fellow ratted on a deal we had struck. A big one too for we often shared commission on a 50-50 basis on working together when a prospect thought we were partners. Dammit, I was due the best part of £4,000. In any case he was getting on my nerves and leaving our flat in disgusting condition. Shameless he was. I think the bastard would have double-crossed his own grandmother!'

'I am sorry to hear that,' said Jeremy. 'It is always a pity when a partnership goes wrong and trust is broken. Tell me Claude, are you owing any money to anyone?'

'Things are not good and this last month matters have escalated. I am now in debt to the tune of £6,000. I can't really see my way forward, what with the extortionate rates that the moneylenders charge.'

'Look, you may well have heard that the Earl has died. The good news is that you have been remembered via a small trust fund and I have been appointed a trustee. There is enough cash to discharge your debts and still leave some over. But first you will have to earn it. Claude, you need to get the hell out of London where you seem to be killing yourself. What is more, I propose you enter a clinic in Bakewell where you can dry out. There are sufficient funds to warrant a stay of at least three months. That should be ample time to sort you out and allow you to regain your good health and confidence.'

Claude listened with an ashen face. He twiddled his glass and looked pensive while slowly stubbing out a half smoked French Gitane. After a little while he found his voice.

'Jeremy, I have been a failure. Living among those roughnecks in the African mining world was not for me. I felt like a fish out of water and became bemused. Everywhere each boss man would talk his book in trying to instil confidence in his venture. I was gullible and fell for their hyperbole and hospitality. I even came to believe the tales I was told. My judgement was poor. Some of the characters I met were chancers with highly dubious backgrounds. It was obvious even to me they were controversial. Among them were Iranians, Greeks and some very plausible utterly amoral Australians – the worst of all – each one out for the quick buck. I also totally ignored the corruption affecting the local politics and to curry favour with the senior partner rashly promoted grandiose schemes. All along I knew in my bones these were highly speculative. Sometimes, buoyed up by the prospects, I actually bought their shares. Then when they turned sour I sought to offload them regardless of their intrinsic value. I have been a disgrace.'

Jeremy resisted any temptation to comment. His role was not executioner. With Claude's wellbeing at heart he continued as he had intended.

'Look Claude, the Earl detected all was not well and thanks to him you are now being offered a lifeline. If you accept, on leaving Bakewell I shall find you a job with a reputed firm of estate agents, probably in Sheffield. Your understanding of mortgages, insurance and finance will hold you in good stead and you will be back more or less in that part of the world where you feel at home. What is more there will be a small nest egg by way of a monthly income sufficient to assist you in paying for accommodation and to make ends meet while you are learning the ropes, which I have no doubt you will do and do so quickly. I urge you to start afresh. I will be there to help.'

For a few moments Claude said nothing and drained his glass. While he was cogitating, Jeremy wondered whether Claude would grasp the lifeline he was proffering or fail to find the inner strength and just give up. He desperately hoped he would seize the opportunity as he could foresee that if Claude refused he might crash down the slippery slope so fast there would be no chance of recovery. For what seemed an age Claude sat looking at his empty glass. Then he glanced up to see Jeremy waiting patiently.

Never mind learning the ropes, Claude now recognised he was on the ropes. 'Jeremy, you are right.'

With a sigh he gave Jeremy his contact details and agreed that afternoon to let Argosy Life know his time with them was over and that they needed to settle up. With the decision taken he seemed relieved. Jeremy abandoned his plans for the rest of the day and accompanied him to Argosy's London office since he was unwilling to let Claude go alone in case he flunked it. Jeremy had prepared the ground well. He knew the Bakewell clinic had a space for

Claude and that afternoon he confirmed it. The next day he helped Claude pack and that afternoon the two travelled up to Derbyshire by train. They spent the night at the Midland Hotel in Derby and by noon Jeremy had seen Claude welcomed into the clinic.

The question now was whether Jeremy's solicitude would be repaid by the required behaviour from Claude. Jeremy crossed his fingers that this would be the case and silently prayed so.

CHAPTER 15: THE GAME OF LIFE

It was the long awaited wedding in the autumn of 1970 between Slim and Jessica that gave rise to the next reunion. Slim was now a well-known chef on television. He had developed into an amusing character, showing off recipes that were easy to follow and so proving popular. His link with Jessica, who continued with Yorkshire TV as a presenter, will have been advantageous. At his request I had ghost written a cookery book for him. This was more ambitious than his first book detailing Canadian recipes which had come about as a promotion for Noel's Good Doctor range of equipment. The photographer I hired took the most gorgeous pictures and the book was beautifully produced on high quality paper with an attractive sheen. This sold well in the established bookshop chains and was particularly favoured at Owen's two garden centres in York and Wetherby. Slim was still active in looking after the restaurants at these. As both garden centres remained well patronised Owen invested in a third one. Opting once again for a site near a racecourse the choice was obvious, namely Doncaster. As before, the décor was undertaken by Fiona and the restaurant franchise entrusted to Slim. Work on the centre had run late but it opened in time for the St Leger in September. That was the year when Nijinsky triumphed and in doing so pulled off the rare event of the Triple Crown, having won the 2000 Guineas and the Derby in May and June.

Doncaster may not have been an especially glamorous location at which to host a wedding reception but an internal marquee in Owen's landscaped garden centre achieved wonders and it was to prove most popular. Slim and Jessica had chosen well. At the opening reception one guest to surprise me was Bernard Whyte, Owen's contemporary at Semleys when they had been trainees. On the other hand Owen was relaxed and without hesitation went across to greet him and took me with him. Bernard could not have been friendlier towards us both.

'Owen, I am delighted for you. Well done. For my part I can report all seven stores are doing well. But Freddie and I feel we could smarten up the restaurants at Leeds, York, Harrogate and also at Giffords in Sheffield. So I am here to learn a trick or two.'

However something was preying on Bernard's mind and he made a clean breast of it. 'No, no, Owen. We are not going to poach Slim from you. He will act as a consultant to us which he says he can do without affecting his existing ties.'

'I am sure that will be possible' said Owen graciously. 'By the way, if you want to change the décor at all or any of the restaurants, then why not ask Fiona. She is over there and is the wife of Jeremy Broughton. In Yorkshire he is known as Mr Property.'

We left it like that and as we repaired to chat among the other guests Owen said simply, 'I am glad it was Bernard who made the overtures rather than Freddie. If ever I had to, I could work with him were there to be a project in our mutual interests. He is straight.'

I then ran into Claude. I had not seen him since he had left London and been rehabilitated in the clinic at Bakewell. He looked a new man. Thank goodness those three months had produced the desired effect for he had stopped smoking and was no longer drinking alcohol. His colour was better and his hands had stopped shaking. His eyes were bright and, although reticent, he had regained some of his old confidence albeit tinged with a becoming modesty. He had commenced work in an estate agent's office in Sheffield which specialised in good quality family houses possessing a reasonable amount of land. He claimed he quite enjoyed it, while Jeremy said he had taken to the task well and was happy not to be under any pressure of the sort he had endured as a stockbroker and at Argosy Life.

The extraordinary thing about members of the 1947 team, all of whom had taken the trouble to attend, was that so many of the wives were expecting, namely Myfanywy, Cressida, Fiona, Veronica – aiming for just one to add to the twins – Penny, Evie, my wife Marilyn, and Giselle for the second time. Vince was present and his wife Leila was expecting as well. She must have been good for him as he had mellowed. I think he was continuing to make a very good living out of the law in his practice at Ilford. Claude was the only remaining bachelor. Provided he did not stray from the straight and narrow I wondered how long he would stay single. After all in his laid back way he still possessed a charming if diffident attraction.

On behalf of the Yorkshire Evening News I was commissioned to write about "The Team". The editor was most enthusiastic and gave it a double page spread complete with photographs.

Three years on life for all had changed. Like the rest of us Slim and Jessica had wasted little time in starting a family. That meant ten of the team were fathers.

We all had two children apiece other than Noel, Harry and Owen who had three. The odd man out was Claude. But finally he too had married. It had been a quiet wedding with Jeremy reciprocating the part Claude had played for him as best man. His wife Mavis was a nurse and with Claude earning a modest salary she had no wish to give up her job unless and until she had to. That December Marilyn and I were invited to Penina to stay with Harry and Veronica. They wanted us to be present at the nativity play in which our godchildren Anthony and Celia were playing the roles of Joseph and Mary. The night we arrived Harry told us at dinner that he had not shaken off Solly.

'When Veronica and I left Estoril for Penina we thought that perhaps we had. But not a bit of it. Not only has Solly followed but Rosie, his daughter by his second wife, is living here too with her husband Roly. He did extremely well as the owner of Upminster Car Deliveries, a tricky business if ever there was one. His orange car transporters and their drivers in orange livery were a regular sight around Ford of Dagenham and at the ports which handled cars imported from the Continent such as Harwich, Felixstowe and Ramsgate. When Roly received a handsome offer for the company he snapped it up promptly knowing the fragile and ever fluctuating fortunes of the motor trade. Now, living half a mile away from us are Solly with wife number three, Roly and Rosie and their family. There is nothing I can do about it other than to acknowledge Solly and Roly on the golf course and steer as wide a berth as possible from the whole lot.'

As luck would have it, the host to Joseph and Mary in playing the part of the innkeeper was Solly's grandson, four-year old Billy. Allegedly a large proportion of the morning had been spent in rehearsals. So by the time that the play commenced at three o'clock the participants were somewhat jaded. When Joseph and Mary, remembering their lines to perfection, knocked on the door of the inn and asked if there was any room, the response was not as anticipated. With a sharp retort the innkeeper shouted, 'How many times must I sodding well tell you there is no fucking room at the inn!' There was a sharp intake of breath followed by deathly silence. The curtain then descended while Billy was carted off before he could do any further damage. Coming to the rescue was a little Portuguese girl. Taking the part of his wife she deputised for the rest of the scene and "ad libbed" most skilfully.

As they motored home Harry said, 'you see what we have to put up with here. There are some very rough diamonds around. It may seem all sweetness and light on the surface but it can be very far from that. Goodness knows what language Roly and Rosie use at home.'

I wondered if Harry and Veronica would stay for ever and a day at Penina. I detected they might not and in fact this was prescient. Within eighteen months they had sold their fine house and bought a smaller but totally delightful one at Quinta do Lago where a new course had sprung up. They planned to use this as their Portuguese base from where Harry could continue to act as legal adviser to the developers and aspiring clients. In addition they bought a house on the St George's Hill estate in Weybridge to be near to good schooling. With Harry joining the golf club there, he bid farewell to Wentworth.

Running through the rest of the team in the batting order of that summer of '47, there was invariably good news. Mark's venture with Ruabon Hall had clearly been blessed. Now into its fifth year, it was already recognised as the leading prep school south of Sheffield for miles around. It continued to go from strength to strength in scholarship, sports and music. Myfanwy had provided him with two sons, Giles and Paul. With that they were content.

Theo and Cressida had a son and daughter, Michael and Angela. Somehow Cressida was still able to continue as a successful trainer, although generously she gave most of the credit to Nicholas Broadbent who had joined her since he was finding it difficult to make ends meet as a trainer on his own. He recognised that perhaps his stables were not in the mainstream of the racing world. And in this he was probably right. A thoroughly good chap, he just did not have sufficient capital to see through the tricky times. But as a number two he had many qualities. What is more both Theo and Cressida liked him. He had been good to Theo at the outset of his riding career and the two were more than happy to repay that kindness now that Cressida had been left so well off. Theo remained an amateur jockey and with his weight allowance was favoured with rides in the north by a select number of discerning trainers.

Jeremy and Fiona appeared to lead a charmed life. They had a son David and a daughter Annabel. As Number Two in Beale Thompson, at forty Jeremy was now the partner in charge of both Surridges and Rawlings Clifford. The two continued to trade under their original names. He still owned the Ruabon Hotel in Kensington and looked on this as a long term investment. Noel had long valued both his experience in property and wisdom and had asked him to go on the board of Tellings where Theo remained as Deputy Chairman. The trio worked uncommonly well together. Boardroom discussions were frequently hilarious while they dealt with the ever present commercial problems with agility and ingenuity. Noel knew how to get the best out of his team. Once problems were resolved and policy agreed he then made sure his fellow directors enjoyed themselves. One of the great marques of champagne was always to hand nicely cooled. And as often as not it would be Billecourt Salmon.

Claude seemed to have got back on the straight and narrow. All agreed that Mavis was remarkably good for him. While he did not appear in any way ambitious he looked settled and claimed that Mavis was hoping to start a family now that her parents had died. Her inheritance was modest but timely, so her need to work was no longer all consuming.

Owen was thriving. He continued to throw himself into whatever task confronted him. He had also been busy as a father since Penny had produced two sons, Thomas and Oliver, then followed up with a daughter Mary. What was apparent was that Owen had found his niche. Moreover, he must have inherited his father's flair for business. Yet never for a moment did he regret not working with the Whyte brothers and in extricating himself from the complexity of running department stores. He was just thankful to be doing his own thing in his own way without having to answer to anyone else.

Noel we all knew was prospering. He and Evie made a fine couple. They had two sons in Daniel and Stewart and a daughter called Florence. Then on Noel's fortieth birthday in 1975 Evie presented him with a final daughter in Amelia. Like Jeremy, virtually everything Noel touched turned to gold. Both possessed an enviable magnetism and judgement enabling them with apparent ease to attain success and win friends at the same time. The quality they each possessed was grit. Delightfully hidden behind a veil of charm, nevertheless it was still there.

Bart had made a good choice in marrying Giselle. Not only was she sweet but highly capable too. Their two children Stephen and Helga were a delight. The family lived in Chiswick, an area at once peaceable and prosperous. Bart had an easy commute to the Ruabon. In fact all seemed good. But Bart had been in charge of the hotel for a long time now and was beginning to have itchy feet. He felt he needed to extend himself instead of just coasting along. Giselle understood this and was supportive with one proviso, namely that they continue living in or around the London area.

Life in Yorkshire was not really for her. She thought the people could be dour. On one occasion Bart and she had visited a pub in the dales. Above the bar a sign read, "A pie, a pint, and a friendly word". The pie and the pint were ordered then served by a surly landlord. 'What about the friendly word?' said Giselle. 'Don't eat t' pie,' was the reply. Giselle had been unimpressed and failed to catch the humour if humour there was.

At home in Chiswick they debated whether they should set up business as a wine merchant or open a restaurant with the idea of developing this into a small chain. But neither concept hit the button exactly. Even if they specialised in the import of quality German wines, there would be more than enough competition as well as any amount of hassle. What caused them to have a double think was that the big brewers were selling cheap German wine like it was going out of style. In the process this was affecting demand for quality German wines. Almost by definition these could never be cheap since the better estates tended to be in small parcels on steep schist so were inappropriate for mechanical harvesting. In recognising the quandary Bart and Giselle reluctantly decided to bat the idea into touch.

When Jeremy was next in London, at Bart's initiative the two discussed how he should move on. 'Jeremy, the family is anxious to step back from the greyhound track at Rotherham. I never wanted any part in it so am in total agreement. Dad wishes to retire. If the business is sold I shall receive 33% of the proceeds.' Giselle chipped in. 'My family is willing to back a new enterprise as long as London is the location and the figures add up. Bart is keen to develop his expertise and do more in life and I think he should.'

Jeremy listened carefully. Then addressing Bart he advised, 'I do not see any need for you to leave the Ruabon altogether. Felipe is a conscientious under manager and as long as you are contactable and look in two or three times a week that may well suffice.

'You could of course be most successful in either the restaurant trade or the wine trade which I know has tempted you. But I agree they are hideously competitive and the former can be fickle. Giselle, even with your knowledge and background I would back your judgement in avoiding any tie up with German wine producers. That day could long be behind us. I believe there may be a better opportunity in a totally different field, one which Bart knows and which once in action ought not to require your full time.'

Jeremy had gained the attention of both Bart and Giselle.

'There is going to be an ongoing demand for simple basic hotel accommodation. The forecasts for travel growth show this to be increasing at an exponential rate. If you can find a suitable location and modify an existing building appropriately you could be on to a winner. However, it is more likely a new build will be the answer. Either way you will have to consider the basic essentials that a short term visitor will be wanting by way of furnishing the en suite bedrooms and dietary requirements at breakfast. Steer clear of any other meal. Top priorities will be sound proofing, heating, a comfortable bed, television, a fridge, electric kettle for tea and coffee, a trouser press and maybe an iron with ironing board.

'Remember you and Nigel did a capital job on finding the Ruabon. Scout around again with this entirely different brief. I will get Surridges on to the task as well if you wish.'

Bart thanked him while Giselle added her approval.

On his return to Yorkshire Jeremy mentioned the subject to Sidney Bassett and Harold Tompkins. The two showed considerable interest. They had yet to build in the south but did not reject the concept out of hand. In anticipation Jeremy explained to Bart that if the project looked a runner he would be glad to be involved in some small way too. But he wanted Bart and Giselle to be in the initiative. With their pedigree and a hands-on approach right at the outset, he thought backers would be found. In any event they should reckon on a long time frame.

Slim was continuing to do well. He had picked up the catering franchise at Wetherby and Ripon racecourses and assembled a willing team of helpers who had proved themselves at Owen's garden centre restaurants. He had assisted Semleys and worked well with both Freddie and Bernard Whyte. Neither had interfered with him since catering was not their metier and both had been grateful. Jessica was an admirable mother to young Douglas and Emma, contriving to double up as a Mum with being a working girl at Yorkshire TV. In addition Slim had sold seven of the old family milk bars but cunningly retained the two he had always wanted to develop as fine restaurants. He remained cheerful and hard-working and was counted a great success – an astute businessman and popular into the bargain.

As for Vince all had gone quiet. He had not responded to phone calls and quickly became the last person on my mind. I was not sure what was going on for the most recent conversation I had with his office was that he was in Colombo. So I left it at that.

Much more fun to witness was the expansion of Noel's business. In the summer of '76 he was visiting Canada as the guest of Bob Buchanan and Peter Toogood to see the latest range of Good Doctor machines. They were just delighted at the progress that Noel had made in the UK and could not do enough for him. Although Noel scarcely played any golf on professing a lack of time as well as interest, both Bob and Peter did and when they insisted on taking him out for lunch at their Country Club they showed him the very latest in golf carts.

'Noel, these are our newest toys. We have seen the increase in popularity of these and hired the best of the young engineers we could find. We are now developing a golf cart which will offer features that to date are rarely available even individually. We are putting brakes on all four wheels. Currently they generally have brakes only on the rear ones. Ours will be safer. We are also offering detachable windshields and side-screens so they will be weatherproof in inclement conditions such as we experience here in Canada and you do in Britain. We will also incorporate ball cleaners as well as four bottle holders.

'We think you could do very well with these in due course. In Britain what you term buggies are seldom evident. Your golfers all profess they like to walk. But as people live longer they may begin to think otherwise. The current aversion to them for fear they might do damage to the course will slowly disappear. In fact one or two Clubs are already thinking of creating golf cart tracks. If you market these carts you will be more or less the first in the field so in a dominant position. We will be offering them in electric or petrol driven form. At present these are marketed under the Diplomat and Ambassador brands. Discuss it with your Board. As a novel feature we can offer you either under the banner of the Good Doctor. If you are happy with that they can then be in our house colours of blue and yellow instead of the more usual white or drab green. This is an exclusive offer to you naturally. No one else will be able to use the brand name or be supplied with these colours should you opt not to proceed. So the brand recognition of your existing range of machinery will not be compromised.'

Noel smiled and nodded before suggesting the present market was likely to be tiny but might one day take off, maybe in another twenty years. He could see the good sense in being in early on and would raise it with his Board. He appreciated that in a sunshine state there would be other markets. But he doubted that this would be so in Britain outside holiday camps and, possibly, country houses with rolling grounds open to the public.

Back in Yorkshire Noel put the proposition to his Board. By now Harry was a director on account of his legal knowledge, so making the fourth member of the vintage team of '47. Theo recommended that were they to proceed they focus on electric traction rather than petrol.

'Fewer moving parts so less to go wrong. Quieter too. The secret will be to convince Golf Clubs to have a buggy store.' Recognising this could possibly be a downside he added that, once they were persuaded, the supply of electricity will be a "sine qua non".

Harry backed him up in preferring electric to petrol, emphasising that an important factor would be to ensure there is sufficient power to cope with dunes and hills since a lot of courses in Britain are not as flat as those in the USA or along the 51st parallel.

With no serious counter arguments Tellings decided to add golf buggies to their range and go for a top quality at a top price. Theo said that to try and do this on the cheap might be self- defeating, citing that as this was relatively new technology teething problems ought to be less frequent the better the build. He was also concerned that if the machines were sub-standard in any respect at all, the market for them would fail to take off in the way their Canadian friends were reasonably expecting.

That September when the first consignment arrived Theo examined them carefully. Reporting to Noel he was both optimistic and constructive, reckoning they would not be too difficult to manufacture under licence in which case the profit margin should be greater.

'You know it is not just Golf Clubs that might be interested. What about hospitals, railway stations for attending to the needs of the disabled, as well as your idea of holiday camps and historic houses? The Good Doctor will be an excellent name any which way. And if we make them we will be better able to modify them according to need. I don't see a problem.'

Noel was sanguine. He could appreciate the opportunities. But as he was far from being an avid golfer he sought compromise in suggesting that perhaps they could persuade Harry to take charge of this venture.

'He is virtually out of litigation now. He does not have enough to occupy himself. He loves golf and this will give him every excuse to travel the country, make friends and play courses that otherwise he might never have the opportunity to do. What is more we will not have to pay him an enormous amount. Generous expenses ought to entice him, don't you think. If he excels then we can whack up the directors' fees for us all. After he has dealt with the golf market, maybe he can be persuaded to look at other opportunities too but my guess is he will turn these down. Still by then we will have a better idea whether we have a potential winner on our hands or not and, if so, we will go ahead and hire an enterprising salesman.'

Harry was not difficult to persuade. He agreed to concentrate solely on golf at the outset. 'It is rather like a paid holiday,' he said to Veronica. Not surprisingly he was admirable at it. In any case he was under no pressure. Noel saw no point in putting him under any either. After all in his view the project would either sink or swim. Frankly he was not that bothered. His bread and butter was selling and servicing machinery of a far greater capital value and that was where he would continue to focus.

As ever, Noel showed loyalty to the friends he could trust. I was given the task of producing the brochures for their range of golf carts and the various modifications that were available. The following spring Harry wanted me to accompany him to those Clubs which thought of themselves as progressive and where we were offered a game. This was too much of a temptation to turn down but I was highly selective and chose just two. I would have loved to play more but honestly I had too much work on hand and thankful this was the case.

It was after obtaining formal permission for the brochures I had designed, that on the train home I thought about our team members from '47. On the whole they were playing the game of life well.

In his own sphere Mark, who I had known the least, had got off to a flying start. Moreover, in marrying Myfanwy he had chosen wisely. What no one had anticipated was that she would be left such a fortune by the Earl. But for this Mark might never have been able to make the break and own and run a prep school himself. Yet in no way was he the image of a typical prep school headmaster for he did not resemble an Oxbridge outward bound extrovert dedicated to foster team spirit and the pursuit of sporting activities. He left that to a well chosen staff. Rather, he was more of an intellectual who focused on the desire of a pupil to study and to learn tolerance. In this way he evoked respect from both his staff and prospective parents. What was important to him was to establish a strongly felt Christian sense of morality. If in some ways he was thought of as austere, he certainly was not narrow-minded. For he encouraged the supervision of billiards on a half-size table and on Sunday evenings delighted in playing table tennis with the senior boys and teaching them technique. In the process he was watchful of talent and character. With music his first love, he found local musicians who were prepared to visit and instruct. As for his second love of tennis, this was readily available on summer evenings. All in all he offered a rounded education.

The remarkable thing now was that history was repeating itself for most of our old cricket team were sending or about to send their own sons to him. So in place of Heathside and Gwyn Evans read Ruabon Hall and Mark Atherton. The long standing connection between us cricketers from that vintage year looked set to continue with the next generation nearly thirty years later. That happy teamwork dating back to 1947 appeared to roll on. Or would this be a mirage?

CHAPTER 16: CONSOLIDATION

Naturally, from our old team it was Mark's two boys who were the first to be at Ruabon Hall. These were Giles and Paul who in the autumn of '77 were twelve and eight. Next in line were Noel's boys Daniel and Stewart aged ten and eight. Also eight years old was Theo's boy Michael, Jeremy's son David, my godson Anthony, my son Francis, and Bart's boy Stephen. A year younger was Owen's elder son Thomas, with Harry's second boy Charlie and Slim's son Douglas both six. Finally the babe of the batch at five was Oliver, the second son of Owen and Penny. So out of that 1947 cricket team, nine players were represented by thirteen lads. But there was no offspring from either Claude or Vince, not that Claude had any.

When we nine old boys were at the school play that Christmas we all agreed that we would meet up at next summer's Speech Day. The day in question would be June 18, the date when Wellington beat Napoleon at Waterloo whatever the visuals at the battle site in Belgium depict. As Bart and I were the only ones living in the London area, with Jeremy and Fiona now ensconced in a fine old Yorkshire rectory they offered to put us up. Consequently both Giselle and Marilyn were more than happy to make the trip north.

That morning at breakfast Jeremy was the first to be studying the morning papers. Suddenly he put down the Daily Telegraph and said, 'my goodness, listen to this under the headline of "London solicitor found dead in pool".

Let me quote, "Vincent Winterton, a prominent solicitor in Ilford has been found drowned in the pool at the Galle Face Hotel in Colombo. The pool attendant Fernando described Mr Winterton as an excellent swimmer and considered he must have suffered a seizure. With difficulty he and his colleague Lorenz managed to raise him up and apply mouth to mouth resuscitation. However as he never regained consciousness it is presumed he was already dead."

'Well, I bet there is a story behind this,' he added before continuing to read. "It is thought Mr Winterton had strong ties with the Tamil community. He had visited Sri Lanka three times during the previous twelve months. A post mortem examination has been ordered and his Sri Lankan wife living in England has been informed."'

Bart was quick to speak. 'There will indeed be a story. My guess is that

Vince will have been helping disaffected Tamils to relocate to London and find employment while at the same time assisting the funding of the group known as the Tamil Tigers. This lot are seeking independence for the largely Tamil territory in Sri Lanka's north. There will be more to this than meets the eye. And it may never be fully resolved.'

'How can you be so sure?' asked Jeremy.

'I can't,' he replied. 'But when we were in Kenya and Vince was damn near court-martialled for accepting a bribe, I heard in the Kenya Regiment that an officer in the military police was partial to "a bit of brown" as it was indelicately put. It never came out in the open or if it did was hushed up. Yet in marrying Leila it looks as if this rumour could have some foundation. At any rate his Ilford practice is renowned for its Sri Lankan and Indian customers. You just wonder what exactly has been going on.'

The popular press was not as discreet as the Telegraph and three of the more irrepressible tabloids were bursting with comment. Clearly their reporters had been active in Ilford seeking to uncover whatever story they could possibly latch onto. The text of all three was highly speculative. Nevertheless, one had to conjecture how much truth there was in the innuendo that Vince was the principal conduit for funds to pay for armaments deployed by the Tigers as Bart had hinted at breakfast.

Over a picnic lunch that day by the cricket pitch where Mark and Myfanwy were hosts, once the talk of Vince had been exhausted I noticed Mark in quiet conversation with Jeremy. Apparently he was explaining their matron was leaving so he would be on the lookout for a replacement.

Jeremy listened attentively. 'Do you know, this might be an opportunity for both Mavis and Claude. If she were appointed matron should she have a child would that be a problem?'

Mark said he did not think so as Myfanwy could step into the breach. 'She has done this before and performed well as a stop gap.'

'I raise the matter, Mark, since I am not entirely sure that Claude is achieving full satisfaction in selling houses. Could you make use of him as a master?'

'Possibly. Remind me of his background.'

'Remember, he was captain of cricket at Rossall having been in the team for three years. And he was an ace swimmer. Would you be able to use him as an English and Geography teacher as well as being in charge of cricket and swimming? As for geography, his experience in Africa could be put to good use. That ought to be fascinating as well as educational. One other thing, I think he was also pretty good at hockey if that was ever to be on the agenda.'

'Regarding your question, Yes. Up to a point he could fulfil a role here admirably. However on the downside he lacks an academic qualification and in due course most parents will be looking for that. Do you reckon he would be prepared to study for a Diploma in Education? That would do. It might be asking too much of him to sit for for a degree.'

'One can but ask. Perhaps the first thing is to approach Mavis before trying to interest Claude. If she were to join you and he came up to scratch and followed suit I honestly think this could be the making of him. Mavis, I am sure, would be massively supportive.'

'Fine. I shall follow this up with the initial enquiry restricted solely to the post of matron. If she likes the idea we can then explore how Claude might fit in.'

'Thanks Mark. I'll leave it to you now for the time being.'

With that the two adjourned to the other picnickers where the wives were busy chatting about careers and children, all of them genuinely glad to be in each other's company.

'I suppose there will be a memorial service for Vince,' said Jeremy later that afternoon. 'If so I shall go south and tie it in with my normal business meetings. I don't think we all need to be in attendance but it will be good to exhibit some solidarity and show loyalty to Leila. Theo I guess that this could be difficult for you. What about you Noel?'

'No real problem for me, Jeremy. I can always find an excuse to go south.'

Owen said he would like to be present too for on Vince's recommendation he had two Tamils working for him. Both had come from the renowned botanical gardens at Peradeniya outside Kandy and were excellent workers. I remembered that Owen had been solicitous towards Vince when he had been suspended and had gone out of his way to help rebuild his confidence. Perhaps this was Vince's way of repaying him. As for Bart and me that would be no problem. Nevertheless, Bart sensibly posed the question whether any service would take place should Vince be thought to have been implicated in criminal activities.

Next day Mark got in touch with Mavis. She expressed herself honoured to be approached and agreed to come and see Ruabon Hall with Claude. No mention at this stage was made of any possibility of engaging him too since if she was accepted as resident matron it would not be impractical for him to commute to Sheffield.

In the event Mark was impressed both with Mavis and her background. In the course of the interview he discovered that she was an artist and would be more than happy to teach art.

'That would work really well,' said Mark. 'What else might you be able to teach?'

'Don't laugh, but I will happily try my hand at teaching handicraft, first aid and cooking. One day the young might be glad of two out of the three. It could be worth a try.'

Mark did indeed laugh. 'Well, why not? You have a point. And we would be unique for a boys prep school if cooking is on the curriculum too.'

Offering her the job, she accepted then and there. Mark then broached the issue of whether Claude would like to join the staff and if so in what capacity. Jeremy had judged the situation well. Claude was not unhappy as an estate agent but admitted he could not envisage a lifetime in selling houses. So when he saw how Mavis would be welcomed he responded positively. On agreeing terms, Mark showed them the accommodation that would be theirs. This was a small but well-proportioned house some a hundred and fifty yards from the main building. It suited perfectly. Before they left, Mark recommended a crash course at Durham for aspiring teachers with which he had been acquainted when he was at theological college. Again Claude was receptive. Later that evening Mark phoned Jeremy to give him the news.

'I feel we may be on the way to getting Claude thoroughly back on track. Let's cross fingers if you will permit a rather unspiritual expression.'

When Marilyn and I were next at Ruabon Hall that autumn visiting Francis we saw a huge difference in Claude. The contrast between him now and how he had been in London and even at the estate agent's was manifest. I took him on one side and congratulated him but not before I had had a quiet word with Mavis. She was blooming, pleased to be matron and clearly happy with Claude and life in general. Asking me to be quiet as it was so early in her confinement, she confided that she was expecting.

I had not forgotten about Leila. She had been polite on the phone but unwilling to discuss anything or to meet up until, as she said, the truth has come out. I gained the impression that she thought I was being inquisitive and intruding on her personal grief and private tragedy. I imagined this was a natural reaction from having to deal with reporters far more intrusive than I would ever be.

In fact, in due course Vince's body was shipped back by plane and a private funeral service took place unceremoniously in Ilford. None of us was invited or knew about it until it was over. It was not as if there was a blanket on the news of how Vince met his death. But the media seemed not to be that interested. It was merely presumed that Vince will have been up to no good. One theory going the rounds was that, one way or another, a Government representative will have supplied with him a harmful drug of which he was unaware and that this will have precipitated his demise when swimming. The Colombo Clarion hinted at this but on the whole the Colombo papers were pretty tight-lipped. It was seen as just one of those things. More important items took their attention and were deemed noteworthy. And with one exception this appeared to be the case in Fleet Street. Only the News Chronicle sought to impute blame on the opponents of Tamil separatism. It was not long before this sad affair was forgotten and shelved. I wrote to Leila expressing my deep regret and offering to be of assistance if she needed any help. She responded politely if briefly but made no further contact. So I concluded that was the end of the matter.

A month or so later Bart phoned me and asked me to lunch at the Ruabon.

'Do come. Jeremy will be here as will Rupert Lyall. You may recall he is the chartered surveyor working for Frenshams and also that he was a former colleague of Jeremy's in the Aberdare forest in Kenya – the fellow who was wounded.'

I certainly did and was delighted at the invitation and the thought of linking up with Rupert again. When I arrived Bart ushered me into a private room saying we would be undisturbed there. Drinks were poured while we chatted and played "catch up".

Over lunch the purpose of the get-together became clear. Addressing Jeremy and Bart, Rupert took the initiative. 'Our Chairman, Sir Jocelyn Frensham, is now seventy-eight and has decided to retire. The Managing Director Ben Goddard has indicated this would be a good time for him to take his leave too. After all he has been in the job for twenty years and is now looking forward to a healthy and happy retirement. On behalf of the Board I would like you to know we are seeking a new Managing Director and a new Chairman. Both your names have been well considered. So I am now exploring the proposition that you Bart join full time as MD and that Jeremy takes over as Chairman. Board meetings are held some half a dozen times a year – perhaps a little more if necessary.

'Nigel, thank you for coming too for under a new regime Frenshams will be seeking a major publicity splurge to cover the progress made and the plans for the future. Gentlemen, those BMW recommendations all those years ago have been both successful and remembered. Now we seek a property man at the helm to oversee further expansion and a full time executive who understands the hotel and entertainment world. Experience in the brewing industry is not important since we are happy with our head brewer who will be staying on as director in charge of production. I also shall be continuing with the firm as Deputy Chairman and be glad to work with the two of you,' he said looking at Jeremy and Bart. Handing them the proposed terms he added, 'in my view we have the makings of a wide awake and thoroughly agreeable team. What do you think?'

In thanking Rupert, Bart and Jeremy said they would need to ponder this offer. Rupert knew well Jeremy was busy but what he had not appreciated was that Bart was about to open his first low cost hotel to cater for visitors to London. While this would not offer catering other than breakfast, Bart had in mind it could contain a pub to be let out under franchise.

'Would Frenshams be interested in taking this on?' he enquired.

'For that matter would Frenshams be interested in taking over the Ruabon Hotel?' asked Jeremy somewhat surprisingly. I looked at him in mild astonishment and left them mulling over the options after thanking for lunch and asking to be kept in touch. What struck me on departure was how well Rupert and the two of them would hit it off, with each able to bring a strength to the partnership that the other did not necessarily quite possess. I rather felt that were Jeremy and Bart to join Frenshams, the atmosphere in the boardroom might replicate that at Tellings in being thoroughly friendly and supportive even if Noel's brand of hilarity were to be missing. Moreover I sensed that as a team Jeremy and Bart would drive Frenshams further along the road already perceived as being the right route for them, namely to become less dependent on beer and more involved in property particularly with plans to provide low cost tourist accommodation.

Once Rupert had departed, Jeremy and Bart stayed on to discuss the offer. Bart was the first to say this could well work out right. He could see Frenshams might be willing partners in his dream of bringing to fruition a successful low cost hotel operation. Jeremy agreed saying, 'while beer sales in the country are pretty flat and there is a swing to wine, the effects of any drink drive regulations could make the case for diversification ever more compelling.'

'Jeremy, I hear you but why would you be thinking of selling the Ruabon?' asked Bart.

'If I am to be Chairman of Frenshams I shall want a slice of the action. Currently I am in a partnership at Beale Thompson. This is great for salary but not exactly for capital appreciation. Owning a share in a public company where one has influence is altogether a different ballpark. If Frenshams were to buy the Ruabon I shall then have substantial funds to invest in them. At the moment the value of the hotel is illiquid. Arguably you could say it is high risk for it could be subject to a terrorist attack or all kind of acts of God or mammon. What is more, by the time one has spent the necessary on regular refurbishment and reparations the return looks scant on the balanced sheet even if it is ultimately high in capital appreciation. But then of course only when sold! By investing in Frenshams and working with you to realign their portfolio, I shall be acquiring a share in a far broader enterprise. It makes sense to me. In any case, the connection with the Ruabon will be ongoing should they buy since it will be something we can continue to enjoy.'

A week later Bart phoned to say he and Jeremy had commenced a discussion of terms and conditions with the Frenshams Board and asked if I might be willing to undertake a stimulating public relations campaign. He added the question, 'would you have time to present the framework of this in a fortnight?' That was no problem to me and I said so.

Progress was now swift. By the spring of '79 Sir Jocelyn and Goddard had departed and Bart was in position as was Jeremy. The new team were settling in well. Jeremy and Bart had paid a visit to Hadleys of Aldeburgh to see how a family concern was successfully running a brewery, a hotel or two, and a wine business. They discussed the prospect of offering each other's products as guest ales. Readily they agreed terms. Bart could also see the sense in strengthening their wine business if this could be run by a wine expert. He knew a woman in the trade who might fulfil that position admirably. Within three months Bart had secured the services of Janine Innes, the very lady he had in mind. As to his low cost hotel operation which he continued to own, this had opened near Covent Garden and was doing well. Jeremy had long forecast that one day the area would be ripe for improvement. Now with backing from Frenshams the need for outside financing had been reduced enormously. If this proved a winner then they would look around for other sites that Frenshams could develop. Jeremy had the Kings Cross area in mind, a part of London that deserved – and one day would surely see – a spectacular upgrading.

The City liked the way Frenshams was developing under the new management and within months the shares climbed 20%. I had invested a few thousand pounds the moment I knew Jeremy and Bart would be joining. I was more than happy for I had got in on the ground floor under the new team in which I had the greatest confidence. So I decided to let the investment ride, forget about the daily gyrations and just allow my holding to motor on. When it became public knowledge that Frenshams had bought the Ruabon the City liked this even more. The shares rose again. It was sensed they might spread themselves and be after further boutique hotels. The concept was thought avant-garde and not unattractive, for it was not lost on the brighter of the investment analysts that a property man was now at the helm instead of a "patrician of the old school and the beerage" as Sir Jocelyn had been.

In the event in March 1980 Frenshams bought one other boutique hotel at the back of Park Lane, the Lilliput. This proved a masterstroke on quickly establishing itself as the favoured haunt of Hollywood's stars when lured to London. Both Jeremy and Bart reckoned they were incredibly lucky with this find and held back on further purchases for a while. Rather than pursue a third upmarket proposition they now focused on another low cost operation. That summer after much devilling they secured a plot less than a quarter of a mile from Kings Cross. This suited admirably. In the autumn shareholders were asked to subscribe to a one-for-six rights issue at a not very heavily discounted price. The response was nearly 100%. Clearly Jeremy and his advisers in the City had judged the terms to a nicety.

Checking on the register, it was found that Germans connected with the family of Bart's wife Giselle were in on the action too. A little research revealed this was Stuttgart's Gutesheim Brewery, best known for its Schonberg lager. Bart took the initiative, got in touch, and arranged to visit. Soon Frenshams were offering this light and tasty lager so unlike anything brewed in Britain. Next May both Bart and Rupert were happy to entertain two of the brewery's directors on the golf courses at St George's Hill and Royal St George's Sandwich. By now Harry had put Bart up for membership at the former since Bart had become keen on receiving lessons from Leslie King. He was achieving fame in operating his Knightsbridge golf school at 47 Lowndes Square from what was formerly a pair of squash courts.

'Bart,' Harry had said, 'you simply must go and see Leslie. He has worked wonders with me and helped me reduce my handicap from four to two. Gary Player studied under him before winning his third Open in 1974. The best amateur of our time, Michael Bonallack, has had lessons from him too. His only regret, he says, was that he did not visit Leslie when he was younger. Mind you he won pretty well everything in his time. So perhaps a late arrival at Leslie's was not such a serious blow!'

So twice a month on a Friday which was his regular day of the week for Bart to look in at the Ruabon and see all was still well and that Felipe had matters under control, once the lunch crowd had been well looked after, Bart enjoyed the opportunity to nip along and learn from the master on pre-booking the four thirty slot. 'Poets Day,' he would say with a smile.

The Board was now delighted at the progress Jeremy and Bart were making. They had broadened the Frenshams range significantly thanks to the addition of certain Hadleys products along with those from Stuttgart plus, of course, the new wines that Janine was rapidly introducing.

That autumn of '79, when Marilyn and I visited Francis at Ruabon Hall we were introduced to young Christopher, or Kit for short. This was the infant son of Claude and Mavis. All three could never have looked happier. Claude showed us a new feature in the grounds. This was an amazing aviary with assorted bird cages alongside. These housed a variety of African birds. Exotic and extraordinary, they ranged from bee-eaters and barbets to a hornbill, a black chested snake eagle, a goshawk, striped kingfishers and a white bellied go-away bird. One species of particular charm was the Banglafecht weaver with its yellow and black cheeks. There were two types of fiscal, a lilac breasted roller, and a Hildebrandt's starling resplendent with its orange belly, a body of dark green and a brilliant blue head and tail. Also on show were a purple grenadier and a spotted thick-knee – this latter actually with slender legs to support an agile forager boasting a plumage of brown and white spots. Naturally no display could be complete without the inevitable but adorable lovebirds, ring-necked parakeets, and a talking African grey parrot of questionable temperament. By good luck this one, Felix, was quite amicable and loved to show off on imitating Claude's well-honed drawl. Resisting temptation, Claude had been meticulous in ensuring the parrot knew no swear words. Nor was he taught any. His catch phrases were benign: "Who's for cricket?" and "Well bowled".

I enquired how all this had come about to be told that the idea was entirely Claude's. He had built the cages and designed the aviary which Noel had commissioned. Noel had also paid for each and every exotic African bird and the brass labels that gave their names in both Latin and English. Mark and Myfanwy were of course over the moon with the concept and took on the task of paying for the birds feed without a murmur, although I rather think that every six months Noel put his hand in his pocket and made a sizeable contribution. Mr Claude, as he was uniquely known to the boys, made it his responsibility to explain where the birds hailed from and what their habits were. It formed one of his many enthralling geography lessons in enlightening his pupils on the diversity of Africa.

Not surprisingly, Claude's collection proved a magnet for parents looking round the school while contemplating its suitability for their offspring. More often than not they were won over. When this was so, they were presented with a handbook he had commissioned from me. This depicted colour photos of each and every bird with a brief description. Mark understood that from time to time this little volume was passed around and shown to other aspiring parents. He joked it was one of his prime marketing tools. And perhaps it was.

Good days were in abundance. Mark's school was achieving the desired results. By and large, when boys were ready to move on at the age of thirteen they were able to attain the school of their parents first choice. Head boy was twelve-year old Daniel Telling, elder son of Noel and Evie. Next summer joining him in the 1980 cricket team were Harry's lad Anthony, Michael Manners son of Theo and Cressida, Daniel's younger brother Stewart, Mark's younger son Paul, Bart's boy Stephen, Jeremy's boy David, our son Francis and the youngster of the side at ten, Thomas Gifford. That made nine sons from the famed Heathside team of '47. Waiting in the wings were Charlie Fairest, Douglas Marston and Oliver Gifford.

It struck me that among the fathers who were making out very nicely thank you, the two stars were Noel and Jeremy. But Theo in his way had done marvellously, as had Slim, Owen and Bart. And of course Harry had succeeded hugely before the good life wooed him and he succumbed to the gentle option of an easy affluence devoid of pressure. In many ways who could blame him other than his late father who had been gravely disappointed.

Three years after that introduction in '77 of the golf carts from Toogood Buchanan, Noel accepted Harry's advice that there could be a ready and growing market for them. So he approached the Canadians saying he wished to set up a plant and produce them under licence. The Canadians were not unhappy. They felt they could now further concentrate on the USA, Mexico and Latin America. Moreover, they expected to sell every cart they could make.

So it was that golf carts added a new dimension for Tellings since this would be their first venture into manufacturing. Theo now indicated that his time as an amateur jockey was drawing to a close. Noel had been waiting for this day. Apart from keeping an eye out for new bloodstock, it was agreed Theo would now give his undivided attention to the Telling business at least four days a week. At the outset Noel had given Theo a generous 10% of the shares. He now stepped this up to 15%. Only these two had a sizeable shareholding outside Noel's family. All the other directors were on 1%, a salary and bonus.

'Theo, golf carts are your baby now. Carry on with the blue and yellow livery, the same as the Sri Lankan cricket team. They look distinctive and continue the image of the Good Doctor. But, Harry, will you examine the potential for single seaters. They don't seem to exist here. If there is a demand we could be first in the field.' Noel was one for delegation.

Tellings now had three strings to their bow: earth moving equipment, agricultural equipment and golf carts. What neither Noel nor his colleagues had foreseen was that this move into golf would attract the attention of a reputable Japanese manufacturer of hedge and grass cutting machinery. Knocking on Tellings door came Kichi from Osaka.

'Would they be interested in the agency for their power mowers and hedge cutters? You do realise Kichi translates as fortunate.'

In no time Noel, Theo and Harry had been to Japan as Kichi's guests, seen their enterprise, been impressed, and before their return signed up as their UK agent. That gave Tellings a fourth string to their bow. Jeremy congratulated them.

'Next you know you will be wanting to go public, Noel.'

'Jeremy, that is some way off. And believe you me I am not too sure I wish to be bound to shareholders. Let's see how we get on the way we are with the support of our friendly bank,' was the rejoinder.

'Noel, allow me some lateral thinking. Why not persuade Owen to display at his garden centres the single-seater golf carts and the range of Kichi domestic mowers and hedge cutters. Check first the age profile of his customers. I imagine a fairly high proportion will be verging on the elderly and that your new products will appeal to that market in some measure.'

Noel smiled and said he would pass this on to Theo and Harry to examine. 'Jeremy, you may have a very good point there. Thank you. Your ideas are always welcome, you know that.'

As for Jeremy, the next January he was promoted to senior partner at Beale Thompson. His charm, his judgement, his erudition and sheer ability to get on with people and encourage them to give of their best had long been evident. He knew the business through and through, having run Surridges and Rawlings Clifford, the two firms which had been absorbed into the partnership so successfully. He was now chairman of Frenshams and thoroughly useful to Noel at Tellings, as he had been to Owen when developing his garden centres. He was chairman of the governors at Ruabon Hall where his sage advice was appreciated by Mark. No matter what he turned his hand to he was liked and respected. Moreover, he was valued.

The more I thought about it most of the team of '47 were making their mark through sheer hard work. Luck had scarcely been involved. Equally importantly teamwork had played its part. Admittedly Harry was now coasting for he and Veronica had enormous private means and he did not need to work. Introducing golf carts for Noel was a breeze. He was not under pressure to succeed but succeed he did. He found it just so damned easy. When offered the opportunity to introduce the Kichi grass cutters he declined saying this was best left to a hard nut sales team. As for the rest of us, thanks to Jeremy Claude had at last found his niche; and I could be reasonably proud of my progress on ceasing to be a paid hack as my PR company now numbered sixteen employees. I was hugely grateful to so much support from our vintage team and blessed the day I secured that prestigious address in the City at Frederick's Place off Old Jewry. Other than the late Vince I wondered what if anything could go wrong. Maybe fortune would continue to smile upon us and all would proceed swimmingly.

CHAPTER 17: UPS AND DOWNS

Theo was not idle after giving up steeplechasing. While putting in the agreed four days a week for Noel he was still helping Cressida and Nicky Broadbent. These two were now looking after forty eight horses and with that number were satisfied. It proved economic. Moreover, in the eyes of the racing fraternity they were considered the most successful of the many northern trainers.

Theo had an excellent eye for a horse and specialised in selecting young unraced ones at the sales. On average he purchased six to eight a year either for Cressida and himself or, more likely, for aspiring owners. The most prominent of these was Noel, who having limited himself initially was now happy to own as many as ten. Bart had commissioned Theo to find a couple. Even Jeremy had taken the plunge and followed suit with two. Owen had joined them and agreed that Theo buy him one. Not to be left out, Harry also now had two. So did Slim. I was tempted but refrained in the knowledge I was the only one of these who did not come from money. No fairy godmother had favoured me in any will. So what cash I did have could scarcely be called loose change.

'Stop feeling sorry for yourself,' said Theo. 'Look, you have helped every one of our old team except I suppose Vince who chose to dissociate himself from us. You have been a success. What is more you deserve to enjoy it. Go on. Come in 50:50 with me. I shall find us an up and coming horse at a fair price. Not only can you afford it, I shall make it my business to ensure that you can. It will be my aim to see that it wins at least three times. Your contribution to the training fees will be as nothing – mere pocket money if at all. Don't forget that summer in the slips when we each made thirteen catches. It was 50:50 then so why not 50:50 now!'

I wavered for if truth be told I had to rely on my earnings. Regardless I capitulated. Theo's offer was not just considerate since he did not want me to be left out but highly generous too. His judgement was impeccable. Practical Alice won four times and was to prove valuable at stud on producing multiple winners in Rory Boy and Fearless Fergus. So to some extent we were in the money. As ever in character, Theo was entirely straight. His eyes told you so too.

Conversely, quite out of character it was around this time Noel and Theo had a disagreement. I doubt they ever had many if indeed any. The reason had nothing to do with business. Instead it was over their horse called The Good Doctor which specialised at 2 miles 5 furlongs but could and did win at 3 miles. However Noel was ambitious for it to win the Hadrian trophy at Carlisle. Run over 3 miles 2 furlongs this was the big prize of the year. Noel had never before interfered with Theo's plans for the horse but on this occasion he was adamant it should participate, saying, 'it may be eleven years old but is still virtually in its prime and as fit as a fiddle. Let's have a go.'

'Noel,' argued Theo, 'I have my doubts. Yes, he is certainly as fit as any eleven year old in the north. But this is a tough race and if there is a headwind staring the jockey in the face over the last two fences this just might be a furlong or two too far. I would not advocate it.'

'I hear you. But to win this would be the icing on the cake. Theo, please go ahead.'

Theo looked at Noel. 'Very well,' he volunteered grimly, 'but be it on your own head.'

'Thank you for being so understanding. You know I back your judgement implicitly but on this occasion on my own account I want to accept the challenge.'

The afternoon went ahead as planned with Noel and Evie taking a party of clients and entertaining them in a private box right royally as was their wont. Very graciously Marilyn and I were included. Naturally enough the Hadrian Trophy at 3.10 was the star event of the day. Off to a steady start The Good Doctor was never out of the first four. Three fences out he moved into second position and was proceeding smoothly enough up the incline. He now jumped this with aplomb and edged ahead by a neck. At the second last he was a length in front but took off a mite too soon. Stretching valiantly, his rear legs caught the top and he took a crashing fall. Then he somersaulted and lay prostrate on the turf while the other contestants thundered by. For a minute or so he stayed there seemingly motionless. A hush overtook our box. With Noel for once lost for words, Evie cried out, 'Oh! My God, I think he may have broken his neck.' She looked distraught, anxious not for herself but for Noel.

In no time both ambulance men and vets were quickly to hand since the jockey too was slow to stir. With the authorities preparing to cordon off this fence for the next race, The Good Doctor arose, shook himself and allowed the handlers to lead him off. Theo, also speedily onto the scene, reported that instead of a broken neck or a heart attack the horse was merely winded. It had been a traumatic moment. Noel, still ashen, gasped a sigh of relief. His guests overcame their solemnity and congratulated him on the fortuitous outcome given all the circumstances. Tragic though it was, tragedy in its final form had been averted.

Later, Noel apologised to Theo. He was abject and ill at ease for humble pie was not on his menu. 'I have never insisted over a horse before. I am sorry and will never do so again. You will always know these animals better than me.'

Theo was meek. 'Noel, one cannot always get it right. There are so many variables in this game. But if he runs again we will stick to a distance under 3 miles, don't you think.'

Noel nodded. And that was the end of the matter.

By now Sidney Bassett and Harold Tompkins had retired. They never did build in London. Their firm was now run by their two sons Simon and Gary but not as ably as their fathers. When the two approached Noel to ask if he would buy them out he was flattered and said he would put this to his Board. But it did not take them long to decide this would be a diversification too far. They lacked the expertise and recognised that building is a cyclical trade which would not act as a counterbalance to their existing interests. They preferred to rely on the two well established bases of construction and agriculture and now that they had a couple of new ventures with golf carts and Kichi on the growing empires of golf and municipalities.

Jeremy was surprised that the invitation had ever been put and questioned whether Simon and Gary knew something they did not. Was the market for construction machinery going to be less buoyant, he wondered? Noel debated this with Theo. Cautiously they decided to go easy on the import of the heavy stuff until the future was clearer since the last thing they wanted was an excess of inventory over a weakening demand. In any case they found the Good Doctor equipment was so well made that most machines were worth reconditioning. Even clients who rented were now offered this option.

As time went by Harry said to Noel he had done as much as he reasonably could to market the golf carts. He now wished to spend more time in Portugal seeing that their economy had recovered from the revolution which had deterred overseas house buyers. As this appeared well set for the future he resigned from the Board with good feeling all round.

Shortly after his fiftieth birthday Jeremy was knighted in the 1985 New Year's honours list. The formal reason was his charitable work about which he seldom spoke and concerning which I knew very little. But I think that with all due modesty this was a front, for the general view was that he was acquitting himself extraordinarily well at whatever he undertook. The progress at Frenshams was a case in point. It was his overall success that will have earned this honour. If golf had been a casualty of good honest toil, he now determined to put that right and drive at weekends to Ganton outside Scarborough always provided Yorkshire was not playing at home in a needle county cricket match.

Like Bart, Jeremy had visited Leslie King in Knightsbridge to sharpen up his game. By this time Leslie was getting on and only teaching golf one or two days a week, even then just for half a day to selected clients. But he was more than happy to welcome Jeremy once he learned of the connection with Harry and Bart. Rather than stand, he resorted to a comfortable folding chair from where he dispensed advice when not actually demonstrating the technique he was endeavouring to foster. Leslie appeared infallible. He focused on the plane that a golf club should travel. Jeremy's handicap had slipped from three to ten due to so little play. But in the space of a few months he was back to five and was content with this – especially on Ganton's time honoured links that has been home both to the Ryder Cup and Walker Cup and goodness knows how many English championships. It was great to see him once again pursue the sport at which he was so adept as a teenager and young man. I was sure that had he concentrated on golf at Cambridge after winning his Blue as a freshman he would have been honoured with the captaincy in his final year. Still, he won a second Blue – at cricket. I marvelled at just how gifted he was. But then I had always been in awe of him.

Five years passed peaceably enough. Alas, from the standpoint of our old team a number of dark clouds now appeared on the horizon. Slim had been working far too hard and had suffered a heart attack. He was not the sort to slow down, and when his doctor insisted that he must Slim did so most unwillingly. He faced a choice of whether to forgo one or both of his two restaurants in Sheffield, withdraw from his connection with Owen's garden centres, cease racecourse catering, or go easy on his TV work. It was a dilemma to puzzle him. In the event it was the garden centres that were dropped since one way or another they were a seven day a week commitment. Racecourse catering at the seven northern courses where he had won the franchise was not so time consuming. It was also more prestigious and kept his name in front of a well-heeled public. Owen accepted this with equanimity. Graciously he claimed he had been fortunate to have had Slim's services for so long.

As ever, Owen too was a glutton for work. I wondered if the time had come for him to slow down. Running the six centres he now possessed was taking its toll. He had to delegate more. When I was next in Yorkshire I prevailed upon Jeremy to join me and have a word with him. Very gently he did so.

'Owen. Your old friends and I consider it is time you slowed down. There is little point in being the richest man in the churchyard when only in your fifties.'

Owen did not disagree. 'Good point, Jeremy. But my ambition is to hand on a thriving business to my two boys, Thomas and Oliver. Right now they are both still at school and a long way off being able to participate. But that time will come soon enough and Penny and I are gently encouraging them to think of this as their birthright.'

'Owen, you need good qualified help in the meantime, believe you me. Look around and see who could fit in who really knows his stuff and is fully qualified, not just a good chap and a willing pair of hands.'

In his heart of hearts Owen knew Jeremy was correct and without further ado the matter was dealt with.

Having discussed it with Jeremy, I let Harry know that both Jeremy and I thought Owen needed a break. I suggested he invite Owen and Penny to Portugal for a holiday despite the fact neither played golf. A kindly soul, although one who was possibly drinking rather more than was good for him and putting on weight, Harry accepted the challenge. He and Veronica took the two to some ancient palaces whose gardens had the most sumptuous exotic plants and shrubs. Apart from one extraordinary incident the visit was deemed a great success.

It was on their last day this arguably unparalleled incident occurred. Harry and Veronica were invited to the wedding of a young nephew of that old-time gangster Solly Doull. Harry was considered a catch, so famous had he become when acting as counsel for ne'er-do-wells in London's underworld. Accordingly his presence, regardless that he was long retired, was thought to confer respectability on those for whom such a term was quite likely highly inappropriate. Initially Harry and Veronica demurred saying they had guests staying. But they were prevailed upon to bring them too. And Harry, being the diplomat that he was, thought it best to accept for to decline might cause ructions. So it was that Owen and Penny found themselves as esteemed outsiders among a motley crowd, many of whom will have harboured experience of London's less savoury side.

With the wedding party in full spate, the best man – a roguish character called Hymie – was both vulgar and amusing. Finally it was the turn of the groom, Bradley, to address the throng now happily lubricated on champagne. After suitable pleasantries, to many hurrahs he announced with generous jollity he had a present for his bride Ruth. Offering her an envelope he said to further applause, 'this is a first class ticket on the Ocean Gladiator for a fortnight's cruise to Madeira, the Canaries and the Azores.'

As the cheers and clapping subsided he added, 'Now I have another present too. This is for the best man Hymie. He and Ruth have been having it off twice daily for the last week so I think he should accompany her.' And with that he promptly handed him the second envelope and sat down.

Uproar erupted. The parents of all three, Ruth, Hymie and Bradley, were taken aback. Horror and sheer incredulity were shatteringly obvious. Not one of them had seen this coming. As for the younger set, there was a stupefied silence broken eventually by gasps and an intoxicated shout, 'And the very best of luck to you both.'

Eyes now fell on Bradley as he was besieged by three or four special mates then ushered out of the marquee to have his sorrows duly drowned while the party broke up in pandemonium. Mouthing 'what to do now?' Owen glanced at Harry, who responded with a wave of his hands suggesting it was time to move on. Quietly they bade discreet farewells and made for the exit. Harry knew only too well his sunny days in Portugal, already blighted once, had been afflicted again.

Owen was later to report that Harry appeared a trifle bored with Portugal. He intimated too many crooks were spoiling the scene. Veronica though had been supremely content, playing bridge three times a week and happy to be a lively and charming hostess. She had tried golf but decided correctly the game was not for her, other than pottering about with lady friends on an early evening when the serious pundits had had their fun and were safely back in the bar. So in no way was she a spoilsport. While I sensed that blip affecting Harry might be a one-off, I was wrong. He knew the time had come to move on and quietly resolved to do so.

As it was I continued to see quite a lot of Bart and Giselle. Following the sale of the family's dog track at Rotherham, they had bought a delightful Tudor house on the edge of the North Downs not far from Sevenoaks. Nearing retirement Bart had joined Knole Park golf club where he was able to relax in sociable golf with likeminded folk. After golf he often enjoyed a game of snooker with the veteran Sam King, the only member of the British Ryder Cup team in 1947 to win a point in America when the British team were trounced. Sam was treated almost as a deity so popular and highly respected he was. The club professional for many years, he had long been elected an honorary member. As a boy he had lived in neighbouring Godden Green, the son of a charcoal burner. His natural athleticism had enabled him to confront the difficult choice of whether to become a professional cricketer or golfer. After much prevarication golf had won out. Almost his whole career had been spent locally in this attractive part of Kent, a decision which Bart understood perfectly since it was far preferable to Rotherham where he had grown up.

Bart had made a signal impression on the wellbeing of Frenshams. Very simply he was a round peg in a round hole. Three times the company was sought by the big players in the brewing industry. Even Gutesheim of Stuttgart made an offer. But with Jeremy's support and that of the founding families Bart resisted all such invitations for they had a steady business and, with the tie ups such as he had instigated with Hadleys, Frenshams saw no need to become enmeshed in a mammoth combine. In any case they were facing a fine future with the prospect of more investment in low cost hotels where these could be strategically situated. Somewhat as a bonus Janine was developing a flourishing wine business which was finding favour with other small provincial brewers to whom they were happy to wholesale. Friendliness and goodwill abounded. Each year a further back to back deal was cemented. Now Frenshams and another brewery were agreeable to swap beers on a regular basis so treating the ales of their newly found partner as guest beers. Happily and without hiccups, business was moving forward very satisfactorily. I could not be other than impressed. Somehow Bart had solved the game of life and through focus and imagination appeared to be succeeding in every way just like Noel and Jeremy.

I reflected that if Gaffer could see us now how happy he would be and to muse on the legacy of teamwork that remarkably had stayed with us throughout life. For apart from Vince and Claude a lot of things had gone very right for the rest of us. Alas this satisfactory state of affairs was not to last long.

Dark clouds returned bringing bad news from the most unexpected direction. Mark's wife Myfanwy was poisoned and died. Very simply, she had been gardening. Apparently she had been working in the grounds of Ruabon Hall and pruning, firstly, roses and then a thorn bush. Unbeknown to her or anybody else, this bush was a rarity that had come from North Africa, most probably from Egypt. It must have been imported by Josiah Oliphant when he returned to England on selling his cotton plantation. A thorn had become impaled on her thumb. She had been unable to extricate it despite the application of hot water and salt. Thinking no more of it she retired to bed. In the night she suffered searing pain and next morning the thumb was red and swollen. Mark was away and she decided not to fuss. But on day three when he came home and saw the problem, straightaway he drove her to hospital. Confusion reigned among the staff and the correct remedy failed to be forthcoming. Within twenty-four hours Myfanwy was on a drip. However she never recovered. The poison had invaded her system to such an extent there was nothing further they could do and a further two days later she died.

Naturally Mark was bereft. Even before the funeral Jeremy saw that the thorn bush was dug out and removed. Clearly it was far too dangerous to have around no matter how rare and becoming it might have been considered. Mark continued to take Myfanwy's death badly. She had been a support to him not just as a wife but in the rigorous role of a headmaster's wife. Jeremy sized up the situation smartly and came up with a plan. He approached Claude and Mavis. With Claude's blessing he asked Mavis to take on the duties of showing prospective parents round the school and performing the tasks that previously Myfanwy had undertaken. Mavis was a capable lady and in no time proved herself up to the job.

Not long afterwards it was apparent that Slim was again unwell. Jessica had a word with Jeremy. Like everyone else she valued his opinion and recognised that decisions were necessary. Jeremy outlined the options after learning that she and Slim were toying with the idea of retiring to the south of Spain. In a conversation with the two of them he volunteered,

'Slim the time has come for you to go easy. Yes, go and enjoy Spain. But go there without too many worries. Divest yourself of some of your enterprises. Why not start with the catering business that serves those seven racecourses and which you won from the previous incumbents, Eshelby & Percival. But first, the clever strategy could be to employ a super chef who will carry on and maintain the standards you have so long set. Then the chances are that any new owner will capitalise on the goodwill and continue to employ the members of staff you recommend and who have served you so well.' As ever, Jeremy was thoughtful of others.

'Next, you could sell one of your two restaurants in Sheffield. In keeping back just one, if you ever felt well enough to return and run it then you could.'

Both Slim and Jessica took Jeremy's advice to heart. A super chef was hired who proved an instant success. As his reputation was sky high and he was part of the package, the racecourse business was readily sold to a buyer who was more than happy to give first refusal to those staff wishing to continue. With Slim opting to retain the Magnolia Tree restaurant, further cash was raised when another purchaser snapped up the brasserie Gisbournes.

Slim and Jessica could now retire to a village not far from Alicante where they found the climate and the relaxed pace of life suited them admirably. Here Slim perked up, so much so that when Yorkshire TV sought him out and sent a crew to film how he was doing with ethnic Spanish dishes, Slim performed with the flair to which his viewers had long become accustomed. Having enjoyed the stimulation of once more being in the limelight, he was tempted to open a small restaurant. But Jessica counselled against it and came forward with a less demanding suggestion. After all she and Slim were friendly with Miguel. He was the owner of a characterful café in a hilltop situation overlooking a bay to Alicante's north yet set well apart from Benidorm. So following a quiet word from her with Miguel, he agreed to invite Slim to be his guest chef once a week in the high season. Cunningly he charged twice his normal price but as he advertised well he had no trouble in obtaining a full house every night Slim was performing. All three were delighted. More to the point, Miguel proved to be an apt pupil and in learning from Slim quickly enhanced his repertoire and burnished his reputation.

When this good news percolated through to me, Marilyn and I decided on a short break near Alicante to catch up with Slim and Jessica. Owen and Penny were more than pleased to join us. All four of us were impressed with how they were doing and indeed with the area, our preference being for a mile or two back from the coastline. Owen was so enthused he was sorely tempted to buy a place but Penny suggested they bide their time until all three children had completed their education. Son Tom was at university while Oliver was in his final year at Repton. The Methodist school near Matlock that Owen had attended had failed to survive and Owen had taken Jeremy's advice as to where his two sons should go. Daughter Mary was still at school too. Thrifty and practical was Penny and a great help to Owen.

I passed on the encouraging news to Jeremy. Then a few months later when he came south for the December board meeting of Frenshams he invited me out to lunch at our long-time favourite haunt, the Ruabon. He had an ulterior motive.

'Nigel, you ought to know that Mavis has done a sterling job in assisting Mark. I propose to recognise this by sending Claude and her on a ten day skiing trip at Zell-am-See in Austria. Would Marilyn and you like to join them at my expense? I owe you a real thank you for all the work you have done for me over the years. If you accept you will be the ideal companions for them and just the kind of support they need.'

Since it was too good an invitation to pass up we cheerfully accepted, happy to assume the role expected of us as well which we considered absolutely no hardship.

The little town of Zell was a revelation. It boasted numerous four and five star hotels. Ours was one of the former. It was family run by the Heitzmans after whom the hotel was named. We had one day of heavy snow but otherwise the weather was excellent. All seemed highly satisfactory. Alas on the penultimate day Claude lost control and crashed into a tree. He was concussed, smashed a shoulder and broke a leg. When the doctors had done all they could, some days later he and Mavis were air lifted to Munich airport and flown home. If truth be told he was lucky not to have been permanently disabled or even to have lost his life.

Claude was in a poor way for several weeks and on light duties back at the Hall. But he did not waste his time. He started writing. When I enquired of Jeremy as to what he was engaged in, his reply astonished me.

'Nigel, he is writing children's stories. What is more, as you know Mavis is a talented artist and she has undertaken the illustrations. Three of the tales have already been accepted for publication by an enthusiastic publisher.

The titles are unusual to say the least, namely "The Piggy that Crossed the Road", "The Cloud that Fell out of the Sky", and "Clarissa the Hen that Liked People". Claude is as surprised as anyone else that he has this creative ability, which for so long has lain dormant. He claims to be mystified.'

After all these years it appeared that Claude had truly found his metier. In due course he recovered fully. Mavis had been wonderfully supportive. Jeremy was more than delighted. Some years on he was overheard to say he had never expected that Claude would one day become a veritable Mr Chips. But he won respect and esteem and was the only member of staff ever to be known by his Christian name, namely Mr Claude. What a change from a chancy stockbroker, an unscrupulous insurance salesman, and a reluctant estate agent!

Come the millennium, I became sixty-five as did the other members of that Heathside team if they had not already attained it. It was a time for reflection. Should I start to take it easy, carry on regardless, or sell the business? Marilyn and I discussed the matter at length. She vetoed number two option while I could not see how I could stay and take it easy. It just would not work out in my book. For two years I did actually try. But in public relations you accept an assignment and give it your all. There is no halfway house. And when people ask you to do a job they mean you and not necessarily someone else. So in 2002 I sold the company to the most talented of my team. At thirty-eight and having just inherited family money, he was in a position to make a satisfactory offer for Chatsworth with the help of his bank. I wondered if I would be at a loss, relieved of the incessant hard work and responsibility. But not a bit of it! Within a couple of weeks I was at ease with retirement and as each succeeding week went by dwelt less and less on the firm I had so painstakingly built up.

The same year Bart decided to leave Frenshams, find time for golf and travel. Giselle was in agreement. She reckoned Bart had earned his retirement as did Jeremy. A young Frensham and a young Dixon, a nephew of Rupert, were waiting in the wings and showing themselves to be hardworking and adaptable. The wine, beer and pub business was doing fine. But it was the low cost hotel outlets that were providing a head of steam with sites at Heathrow, Gatwick and Stansted as well as three in London and a further three in the pipeline. With members of the Board unanimous that they wanted Jeremy to carry on as Chairman, they recognised his judgement and were impressed that he had stoutly repudiated the advances of Sir Philip Creed in wooing him to take the helm at British Home Securities, a mortgage finance company which then promptly and spectacularly went bust. The Press dubbed Sir Philip — a rare bird in that he was a Bristolian Tory — as Sir Full of Greed, citing he had plundered the once robust pensions fund in favour of a lavish life style embracing a private jet and an island in Fiji. Shades of the publishing tycoon and yacht owner Robert Maxwell!

Mark had now been a widower for some years and was contemplating retirement. Somehow running a school without Myfanwy was never going to be quite the same. Indeed it was not despite the stalwart help he received from Mavis. He discussed this with Jeremy. One problem was that the school was now a trust. Although he had invested wisely in a pension and was entitled to a house within the grounds, he claimed he was not too keen on that. If he was going to retire he wanted a clean break. The subject of his succession was broached. Mark's elder son Giles was a nuclear scientist so was out of contention. But his younger son Paul was working as a schoolmaster in Western Australia. Mark doubted he would want to return and take over. However at thirty-one Paul might just be ready for it. Jeremy said he and Noel were planning to visit Australia since they were minded to invest in McCarthys, a family firm in Melbourne. This made single person golf carts and vehicles for the disabled as well as bespoke tractors for use in vineyards. Early in November they would then be spending a day at the races as guests of the McCarthys for the Melbourne Cup. Afterwards on their way home they offered to sound out Paul and report back to Mark. Theo was invited to go along too. But he ducked it having once been to the Melbourne Cup at a time when he was focused on investigating the merits of an equine swimming pool. In any case he thought it would be overkill and that somebody had to mind the shop. Contrary to what many assumed, Theo never had been a playboy. Once he was committed he never wavered.

When Noel and Jeremy had concluded business with these affable Australians and so were set to participate in the expanding market of catering for the elderly and disabled, the two flew to Perth. Then they headed south for Busselton where Paul was teaching and he and his wife were more than willing to make them welcome overnight.

Over dinner Jeremy took up the cudgels. 'Paul, your father's best days are now behind him. I am sure you appreciate this. He has created wonders at

Ruabon Hall and the one thing he would like to see for sure is that it is going to continue and prosper.'

Paul understood this readily enough and nodded assent.

Jeremy continued, 'Paul, would you and Rosalind consider leaving this exceptional part of the world and taking it on? You have absolutely the right credentials as well as being your father's son!'

Noel added, 'the Hall is a fine business, well established and highly regarded both in the world of education and by aspiring parents for miles around. It is without equal in this respect and enjoys a well-to-do catchment area. Your Dad has done a great job.'

To their delight Paul's immediate reaction was not averse.

'I have loved it here. Western Australia is very special. In my view this is the choicest area in the entire continent. But you know we are somewhat detached from the world of academia. Our school, Dundas Grange, is all very well but it emphasises physical fitness and sports to an almost overwhelming extent. There are times when I feel an intellectual challenge is lacking.'

His charming wife Rosalind who came from Fremantle agreed. To the surprise of both Jeremy and Noel she appeared positive on a move, particularly as the wife of a headmaster. Gently, Jeremy ran through the kind of life she might expect in England for privately he wondered if she would miss the fine climate, the swimming, and the tennis that was available in abundance in the area bordering the vineyards of Margaret River. He need not have worried. She was very much in love with her husband and fully prepared to up sticks and take on the responsibility that would come her way. As for Paul, he possessed an impressive pedigree with a fine degree from Oxford, had been an athlete of note, and now was an enthusiastic walker and photographer when not coaching swimming and hockey. What struck both Jeremy and Noel was his love of theatre too, for they could see that he might arouse artistic talents and interests in the young rather earlier than would be the norm.

The following September, having given the due notice required, Paul and Rosalind joined Mark for a term. He had decided to retire at the end of the year. The hand-over worked well. Then Mark took his leave with a certain sadness and regret but with gratitude as well. He was just so pleased the school would remain within the family and thrilled that Paul and Rosalind seemed enchanted with the ambience and were up for the challenge. Rosalind's no nonsense and "what you see is what you get" attitude went down well with the northerners as did Paul's disarming friendliness. With Jeremy obtaining an alms house for him within the curtilage of York Minster, Mark opted to move there rather than residing on the school campus in the house that was available. Weary from years of endeavour, he could now concentrate on his love of music and undertake research into the music and instruments of the Tudor age without pressure or interruption. His ambition was to write a book that would appeal to scholars of the period. Retirement he hoped would prove peaceful yet stimulating.

If Jeremy was now considered affluent, even wealthy, in contrast Noel was seriously rich. His golden touch had even been evident with his horse The Good Doctor, for apart from that one incident at Carlisle he had dominated the world of steeplechasing in the north of England and Scotland these last five years. As for the Good Doctor range of equipment, this had expanded from the competitive world of agricultural and earthmoving machinery to be preeminent in golf carts, disabled mobility, and grass and hedge cutting. Noel had entrusted the latter aspects of the business to his younger son Stewart while the elder one Daniel was looking after their customers in farming and construction. Carefully he was being groomed to take over when Noel thought it was time to step back from the dual role of chairman and managing director and hand over to him the day to day job as MD. As far as he was concerned that day could not come quickly enough. Loyal as ever to Cressida and Theo, he wanted to spend more time on racing.

Meanwhile Cressida was in the process of handing over the reins of training to her son Michael. Theo was still active and more than delighted that Michael was proving such an adept learner. Blessed with the right attitude he was marvellous with the owners who were impressed with his vitality and knowledge. Theo continued to focus on buying horses for his clients and was known for his intuition and ability to select an animal without having to pay through the nose. The number of stables in their yard had long since grown from forty-eight to more than seventy. Nevertheless their principal owner remained Noel.

That Christmas of 2004 Harry and Veronica invited Bart and Giselle and Marilyn and me to join them at Saman Villas south of Bentota in Sri Lanka. 'Fly out under your own steam,' he had said, 'but once in Bentota you are to be our guests.' That was extraordinarily generous for while I was more than happy to visit Sri Lanka I would have opted for less luxurious accommodation and Harry knew this. On the other hand Bart and Giselle could have well afforded it but Harry was emphatic this was his offer was intended to be a treat for the four of us. The plan was that after Christmas we would all spend time in Galle, then Tangalle and the game park further east at Yala. Next we would proceed to the tea country surrounding Nuwara Eliya. The final stop before a day in Colombo was to be Kandy and the fine Donald Steel golf course on the banks of the Victoria Dam.

Saman Villas is built on a rocky promontory with views to the north, south and west. It is discreet, forgoing any portentous sign from the highway and is not overlooked. It aims and succeeds in being a peaceful retreat. Three days before Christmas the four of us joined Harry and Veronica who had preceded us and knew the place well. The weather was peerless as was the hotel and the service. We were in seventh heaven, hugely relaxed, and being thoroughly and rather disgracefully lazy. Christmas Day was celebrated in style with the staff seeming to love it just as much as we did.

Early next morning on Boxing Day it was remarkably calm. The sun was up as usual, the sky an untroubled blue. Marilyn and I ventured onto our sun loungers before breakfast and read. There was no sign of Bart and Giselle while Veronica was quietly in the bedroom attending to her make-up. However, as was his wont, Harry was full of energy despite arguably overindulging the evening before. But for some time now Harry had been putting on weight and living well while still aware of the desirability of keeping fit to some extent. Up with the lark, he had gone for a moderately brisk walk along the beach to the south before it became too hot to consider. He must have traversed well over a mile towards Induruwa and was some way beyond the Royal Beach hotel when he noticed the waters withdraw to an unbelievably low point. Birds were flying in some profusion, swooping and soaring in an effort to attract latecomers to their flock. Little shellfish that previously he had not noticed dotted the sands. Village children were running around artlessly anxious to see who could reach the distant sea first. Even if it was strangely different it still appeared normal and quiet. Utterly unconcerned, Harry strode on.

Then to his horror a giant wave welled up and invaded the sands carrying all before it. Like everyone else Harry was swept up by it and knocked over. Briefly he must have lost all sense of time before the waters retreated taking him with it far along the shore out towards the sea. By the time he gathered himself together another monster of a wave, even more threatening, was cascading up the sands. There was no chance of escape. The shoreline was hundreds of yards away. Again he was powerless. He understood the inevitable. Moments later he was pummelled, submerged, and helpless in its wake. He lost consciousness and never recovered. Too far out to have sought the sanctuary of the Royal Beach, even this would have been false security. That saw its swimming pool wrecked, the beach furniture shattered along with the magnificent picture window fronting the ground and first floor, and the computer equipment irretrievably ruined along with the sophisticated kitchen. Four years on the hotel had still not reopened. Smaller hotels suffered much the same fate. Insurance companies invariably denied responsibility claiming an Act of God. All along the coast the devastation was utterly appalling. The scene was one of random spoliation as these two unprecedented waves had encroached upon land then on occasion curiously bypassed a few hundred yards either side.

More than thirty thousand lost their lives in Sri Lanka to the tsunami, Harry among them. The whole episode was traumatic. A train taking holidaymakers from Colombo to Galle was swamped by the second wave when not far short of its destination. In excess of 1,700 passengers perished to render this the worst rail incident the world has known. Naturally our plans were shot. We rallied round Veronica who was mesmerised. She just could not believe it. How could such a perfect morning usher in such tragedy? For her it did not make sense. Against all expectations the sun had finally ceased to shine on her beloved husband.

Bart and I were asked to verify Harry's body. Officials declared that Veronica be spared the gruesome task. Understandably for swollen beyond comprehension he was a mass of bloated and discoloured pulp. Due to the heat the stench was both sweet and nauseating. Other victims were in a similar state. It was considered best if after identification all were buried promptly and locally. We explained this to Veronica. Too pained to argue otherwise she submitted meekly. Once it was apparent that there was to be no recurrence of destruction, Bart and I offered to help clear up. But as tourists the offer was declined, so letting aid workers alone to try and resolve the impossible. This refusal was difficult to fathom. On the flight home I confided to Marilyn I now felt both a sense of total inadequacy and humiliation in the face of such catastrophe.

Some months later a memorial service was held for Harry at Weybridge where for many years he and Veronica had lived. Mark came down from York to give the address, which he did beautifully. The little church was packed. Harry had probably never made an enemy. He was cheery and generous. I pondered his life during the service. A glittering career had been abandoned in favour of a desire to pacify Veronica and her parents and to sustain effortless respectability. That was arguably a laudable ambition but scarcely one to breed fulfilment. Not that Harry was self-satisfied or racked by misgivings of self-reproach. Far from it. Rather, one could but sense their combined inherited wealth must have contributed to a lurking indolence and this prevailed over any compelling need to achieve. I conjectured that had matters been otherwise, who knows how far he could have gone in the world of criminal law! Had he been lucky when defending Ronnie Kray, for everyone needs a slice of luck sometime? Or was he simply innately clever? Either way, my not so charitable view was that he failed to pursue the path on which he had first embarked with such elan, and that his father will have died deeply saddened that he never sought to be a QC and then aspire to become a judge. The former he would definitely have achieved. Who can say about the latter?

Marilyn and I never returned to Sri Lanka. We never saw Yala. Indeed, had we been there instead of at Saman Villas we might well have been among those to perish. Seven members of staff died as the hotel was overrun and literally ransacked by the tumultuous sea. We never got to the small highland town of Nuwara Eliya, much loved to this day by those seeking to escape from the heat of the coast, or to Kandy – home of the Temple of the Tooth – or to the golf course at Victoria. For us time moved on to be accompanied by regret. What we were to learn later was that not one animal died as a result of the tsunami. Apparently they were privy to underground tremors. Four days in advance they, rather than humans, were forewarned of this tragedy. While snakes reacted by slithering inland, elephants were filled with foreboding. Grudgingly they too sought sanctuary in trudging towards high ground on their tippy toes. Nature looked after its own. In contrast the manmade early warning system failed abysmally. Whether this was through defective design or human error and complacency, or a combination of the two, was never fully divulged. Japanese technology has since replaced it.

CHAPTER 18: CAUGHT OUT

That summer of 2005 the unhappy news continued with Slim suffering another heart attack. His years in the south of Spain had been soothing and pleasant. Jessica and he were grateful they had made the move and counted their time there a success. Alas he was to undergo a further attack within the fortnight. This was too much for him and he died.

Every one of his remaining friends from that 1947 cricket team attended his funeral a week later. Even Claude made the trip which covertly Jeremy had paid for. Owen was accompanied by Penny. Alas he was losing his sight and walked with the aid of a white stick. The rest of us seemed hale enough with Noel and Theo positively bursting with energy and rude health.

Once again Mark gave the address. He recalled how Slim mimicked the patter of a jovial London Jew, be he bookmaker or tailor. Yet he doubted Slim even knew the location of his local synagogue. His audacious teenage flirtation with the drugs scene was never replicated. Instead his goal was a determination to develop and harvest his talents in which he succeeded magnificently. Too often he denied himself relaxation in the quest to satisfy his clients. His energy had been infectious. He had worked himself to the bone and in his own way had achieved fame. To laughter he added he was only so glad that finally Slim had succumbed to the delights of horse racing and had the winner of the Yorkshire Hurdle in Lucky Ludo, bought for him needless to say by Theo.

The bad news continued. Claude was now starting to fail. Reluctantly, Paul as headmaster of Ruabon Hall confided to Jeremy that he thought he might be losing the plot. Claude was still upright and still incomparable at narrating children's stories. But his personal efforts at composition were dwindling. In class quite suddenly he would appear vague. He seemed to be wondering why he was there and what he was able to impart to young minds were they to be concentrating on the task in hand. He considered himself too old to officiate at swimming classes in a supervisory capacity. Yet he managed to coach the under nines at cricket and to bring on any talent that might be open to fostering.

Mavis was rightly concerned and had a long discussion with Paul and Rosalind. As a nurse she detected Claude might be on the verge of Alzheimer's disease. Paul was very patient. He and Rosalind would watch out and make every effort to ensure Claude was not placed under any pressure. The school doctor was consulted. Tactfully he offered a medical examination for every member of staff and suggested that Paul intimate to them this was merely a routine if infrequent practice. In this way Claude would not be singled out as wanting in any way. In the event, as feared, he was found to be wanting.

Mavis had sensed correctly that Claude was on the cusp of being far from well. What no one foresaw was how quickly this would gather pace. Claude was retired at the end of the summer term. By Christmas he had died. Once more the funeral service was conducted by Mark. His address was discreet. Any lapses were passed over. He dwelt on Claude's attributes, his athleticism, his talent at swimming and cricket, and the fun he had instilled in the young through his tales of derring-do in Africa as well as with children's stories. Mavis was stalwart. She had proved to be a tower of strength on fulfilling her role as a nurse admirably. Not surprisingly Paul was only too pleased when she agreed to stay on.

The following summer Owen and Penny went on a cruise aboard the newly launched SS Harmony. This was an Italian boat with an Italian skipper. Owen had been retired for some time now and his two boys Thomas and Oliver had taken over the garden centres which by then numbered eleven. The business that Owen had built up was proving a staggering success. Three times the boys were confronted with takeover offers. Three times they batted these into touch for they had no intention of selling. They had been trained by their father most carefully and each had degrees in horticulture and possessed more than a passing knowledge of botany. One bidder had sought to attract them by promising them the opportunity to amalgamate his garden centres with theirs and to let the two run the joint empire. They discussed this with Jeremy for they were tempted. But he counselled them to ponder their future if they were to be mere managers rather than majority shareholders. Using his contacts he sounded them out on the probity of the bidder. The responses were far from enthusiastic. To Owen's relief Thomas and Oliver declined.

Owen's eyesight now failed. So Penny had to be his eyes. For someone who had all his life worked hard and fundamentally been healthy it was galling. With Owen restless at home, Penny sought to maintain his interest in life and as far as she could to invigorate him. A cruise on the Harmony in the Adriatic, Bosphorous and Mediterranean seemed an ideal solution since it would combine history and culture with fresh air and relaxation. She asked Noel whether he and Evie would like to come too.

'Give me twenty-four hours to come back to you on this,' was the reply. While Noel was tempted he wondered if this would really be his scene. He mentioned the idea to Jeremy, adding that he did not consider himself intellectual enough to enjoy the lectures as much perhaps as Owen would. 'But why don't you go instead?' he suggested. 'I am sure Fiona would find the concept ravishing.'

'You are probably right,' Jeremy laughed. 'But she is engaged on a fascinating project for the Duke of Devonshire and, no joking, I am just too busy over the dates on which Owen has booked. So I am afraid we are non-runners. But I'll tell you a couple who might not only enjoy such a trip but benefit from it in no small way would be Mark and Mavis. Let me put it to them. Although they are both on their own I think the chemistry could well be right. I am more than happy to fund this.'

'Look, if they agree,' said Noel, 'I will go 50:50 with you on this. It will be a jolly nice way for us both to thank them for the selfless work they have given our families over the years.'

Mark and Mavis were delighted to accept. Mark was enthusiastic as the lectures would boost his modest sense of scholarship concerning that part of the world, while Mavis was thrilled at the prospect of such a holiday and recognised that if the need ever arose she might be able to offer Owen assistance. As for Penny she was gratified that she had sought the additional company in the first place. Owen thoroughly enjoyed the lectures prior to each onshore visit. These helped him to visualise spectacles that he would never actually see. Although weary he was more than happy with the programme and the company. One afternoon he retired to his cabin adjoining that of Mavis who had also opted for a rest. Penny stayed on deck reading and chatting to Mark. The ship had recently left a small port and was passing an island where the intention was to allow passengers to line the deck and wave at any inhabitants who chose to wave at them. For the islanders the day was special as it marked the Saints Day of their patron saint and the ship's captain thought this would be an appropriate way to honour the occasion and show respect. Suddenly there was an awful rasping sound as metal struck rock. The ship's port side was gouged. In moments the Harmony began to list.

Apparently the captain was not on the bridge. His deputy was in charge. The ship's bell was sounded and passengers asked to stay where they were while lifeboats would be made ready. All were advised to remain calm, there being absolutely no need for panic. The action planned was merely a precautionary measure for it was envisaged they would be able to berth offshore a mile or two on just off a small harbour to which rowboats would take them if need be.

Penny and Mark were unimpressed. They failed to comprehend how the ship could be evacuated fully in such a manner. Penny defied the request to stay where she was and rushed towards the staircase leading to their cabin on the port side. To her horror a member of crew stood in her way.

'Madam, you must return on deck. You cannot come here.'

Penny screamed at him, 'my husband is down there in his cabin. He is blind and will need assistance.'

Still he would not let her proceed. 'I will do the necessary. Leave it to me. Get back on deck.'

And with that he shouted at a fellow crew member to escort Penny upstairs. Tearful, kicking and shrieking she was manhandled roughly and dragged back. Penny was desolate, knowing that never again would she see Owen for she calculated their cabin was perilously near where the rip in the metal occurred. With the ship now lurching and in the throes of sinking, the crewman – panicking and distracted – failed to fulfil his promise. The ship went down. As for the captain, he succeeded in escaping. So did his deputy. The British press were quick to castigate the way the captain and crew had behaved citing it as scandalous, while the shipping line's owners saw their shares fall overnight on the Milan bourse by more than 10%.

With Penny totally overwrought and in floods of tears, it was on taking to a lifeboat that she gasped in relief. Unbelievably, in the one preceding hers she saw both Owen and Mavis. Now she wept in uncontrolled joy. Only on arriving at the island was she was to learn how Owen had been saved. Mavis had been quietly resting on her bunk reading. Immediately on hearing the collision she came to. Vigorously she banged on the cabin wall knowing that Owen was the other side also resting. Begging him to unlock his door which mercifully he managed to do, she then hustled him away as quickly as she could in the opposite direction from where Penny had tried to reach him. Somehow the two stumbled onto the forward deck where both then collapsed in utter shock and from where they were rescued.

This appalling scenario with the Harmony was the forerunner of the Costa Concordia six years later. Afterwards it was revealed that in similar fashion to the Concordia at her launching ceremony, when the bottle of champagne was first swung onto the bows it remained intact. Only at the second attempt did the contents froth and flow. With this taken as a sign of ill luck all concerned kept very quiet. As a result the matter was known only to the few who had witnessed it. No way was this for public knowledge. The outcome for the Harmony was tragic. Along with four members of the crew, eleven passengers died. But for Mavis, her quick thinking and resolution, Owen would have been number sixteen.

Owen had never been other than a good guy. He understood his limitations and determinedly developed his strengths. Never flamboyant, he was industrious in the extreme. So the success he achieved was hard won and in no way fortuitous. In contrast, the loss of sight that so marred his later years was ill-deserved. It was then that the inner steel long detected within Penny was to mushroom, for she was constant in the kindness and attention she showed to Owen as his need ever increased. I rejoiced for her and their three children that Owen might now be due a few extra years.

One was now only too conscious that those of us remaining from that 1947 cricket team were growing older even though five out of the seven of us were in good shape. The one who was visibly ageing was Mark. He had never really got over the loss of Myfanwy. While he was pleased that his son Paul was running Ruabon Hall with conspicuous success, his self-appointed exile in York had proved a mixed blessing. I was not alone in considering it was too far away for him to be in regular contact and had wondered just how wise this was. Paul and Rosalind must have thought so too for with Jeremy's continued support as chairman of the governors they had persuaded him to return to the Hall and take up residence in the cottage that was originally earmarked for this very purpose. By now not one of the boys at the school had been there when Mark was headmaster. So the ties that he had for so long enjoyed were merely to be remembered. Back home, so to speak, Mark appeared to gain a second wind. He continued with his research in to Tudor music and finally finished the book on which he had so long been working. His scholarship received critical acclaim both from musicians and the musical press. His satisfaction at completing the task he had set himself was total. Yet as ever he remained ineffably modest.

2008 saw the unexpected. Recession stormed the land. Under a Labour government the country had lived beyond its means. Not that the United Kingdom was the only one to suffer. Spain and Italy in particular were seriously affected. France continued its long decline while Germany's strength helped keep the Euro from floundering. Yet the fellows who had made a success of life like Noel, Jeremy, Theo and Bart soldiered on more or less undisturbed.

Although Bart had retired his lifestyle was little changed. When moving to the North Downs and giving up membership at St George's Hill he had joined Knole Park. This was ideal for his regular golf. Moreover, he was now a member at Rye as well where so many years earlier he had been introduced by Rupert and formed an attachment for the people, the place and the inimitable atmosphere. Life was good. Then catastrophe struck. One fine summer evening as daylight gently dimmed, he was returning from the Club at Knole Park where he had been playing in their snooker tournament. As he was driving sedately in his 1933 cream and black Singer 9 Le Mans drophead coupé and plying the narrow lanes contentedly that led back to his Kentish weather-boarded home in the North Downs, suddenly a deer sprang across the lane followed by two more. Presumably they will have escaped from the deer park abutting that most awesome of Tudor mansions, Knole House, and in which the golf course is situated. Bart swerved to avoid the first one but was struck by one of the other two on the shoulder. He lost control of the vehicle which shot into the embankment hosting the beech trees towering overhead. The car overturned. Bart was crushed. His beloved coupé was a write-off.

As for Bart, his left leg was so damaged that even after two operations it was an inch shorter than the right one. His shoulder was slow to mend and caused him ongoing pain. It was thought he might never again play golf. The whole fiasco was wretched luck and thoroughly ill deserved. Giselle was a wonderful support but effectively his life looked as though it would be changed irrevocably. Arguably Bart now drank more than he should have. Then he went on the wagon. But that soon palled. He tried writing. However this was never his forte. Whenever I visited him, on each occasion I became concerned that he had not recovered his zest for living. Giselle was ever the optimist. She took Bart off to Baden Baden for rest, treatment and recuperation. At her request Marilyn and I accompanied them. Our hope was to give Bart a lift and to replicate those memorable few days we had enjoyed with them in Alsace on the banks of the Rhine when none of us had yet succumbed to marriage. But even though Bart was happy to be reacquainted with the Baden wines, putting on a brave face and even joining in the raucous singing of those ever tuneful songs such as "Einmal Am Rhein" and "Ein Treuer Hussar", the effects on his well-being appeared short-lived. I would have liked to share Giselle's sunny faith that all would eventually get sorted but was unable to do so.

Yet I was wrong. Despite the tragedy from which Owen had so miraculously escaped, Giselle succeeded in persuading Bart that a cruise might be the answer. She was sure he would find sufficient of interest to reawaken his zest for life. Only reluctantly did he agree at which point she wondered whether Marilyn and I would accompany them again. We were tempted but other priorities were to the fore. In the sizzling summer of 2010 they flew to Venice. From there they sailed along the Croatian coast to Split, Dubrovnik and the bewitching bay of Kotor, then on to Sicily, Naples, and Ajaccio before finally berthing at Nice. Giselle was right. Bart just relished it. However, first she had shown a measure of cunning. In cahoots with Rupert and his wife Joanna she encouraged them to come along too. Bart had always got on well with Rupert, as indeed he did with most people. And Joanna was a good foil for Giselle and had similar taste. What is more Joanna was a keen photographer and well read. Whenever they took an excursion onshore she was interesting and informative in a gentle rather than a knowing way. It was all quite strange for Bart but it bucked him up. In the evenings he dallied at the casino on board and twice at roulette the croupier called out his number "sixteen red". The winnings paid for champagne. Never was this tonic put to better use. Gradually Bart recovered his appetite for life that for too long had lain dormant.

He now had shoes made up so that both legs gave him an equal balance. This meant golf was at last a possibility since mercifully his anguished shoulder was becoming bearable thanks to strong pills that were a mixture of paracetamol and codeine. I was thrilled both for him and Giselle. When Jeremy heard that Bart could be on the way to partial recovery he had a word with Noel. The two came up with an idea. As the demonstration model of a single seater golf buggy they had acquired from McCarthys of Melbourne had achieved its immediate marketing objectives, they decided to put this to even better use. With Giselle in agreement they offered it to Bart. Indeed, to all intents and purposes it was brand new. If champagne had proved a tonic, the golf buggy was now to prove itself in magnums!

At the outset Noel called me. He explained what he had in mind and asked if I would write an article that the Kent Essential would accept. 'This could be an opportunity for a little publicity to help get the single seater buggy well on its way. Perhaps an article in a golf magazine could follow later. Are you still friendly with your old employers?' he enquired.

'Absolutely,' I answered, 'for the editor these days is Leonard Fry, a good chap and the grandson of old Bob Fry who owned our local fish and chip shop. In 1940 it was from him my brother Eric bought supper that fateful day when he was blasted off his bicycle by a bomb on the village school and forever lost the hearing in his right ear. This was the incident which gave rise to my arrival mid-term at Barley Farm that November. It's a funny old world.'

With Bart becoming reinvigorated by his comeback to golf, I could not refrain from remarking to Jeremy that those days spent studying the swing's technique under Leslie King in Knightsbridge would no longer now go to waste. Jeremy smiled and agreed.

'Even in my case Leslie's method has stood the test of time. So I am delighted that Bart feels sufficiently up to it to have another stab at the game. You know he has a certain innate if latent talent. In getting back onto the links in company he enjoys and relishing the fresh air, this could be the best possible form of recuperation for him'.

Twice I joined him in a game at Knole Park where a buggy was distinctly desirable due to the steep escarpment that comes into play both early and late in the round. It was heartening to see how right Jeremy was in his assessment and to witness the renewed fun in life that Bart was once again hell-bent on obtaining. Frankly, he had suffered enough.

By now Marilyn and I were retired and living at Iden in Sussex. Within a few months almost our nearest neighbours happened to be Rupert and Joanna. It was not exactly by chance since when a charming property came up for sale I got in touch with them. Consequently they were the first to see it "before the particulars were even dry". We were simply delighted that the two of them had taken the step to downsize and come to live within close proximity of Rye Golf Club, where for much of his later working life Rupert had been a country member despite having owed his original allegiance to Royal St George's, Sandwich. Marilyn found Joanna's company just as agreeable as Giselle had done and, in playing golf there once or twice a week instead of maybe twice a month, Rupert and I enjoyed an easy companionship without in any way feeling guilty.

Next April I received a phone call from Noel with a surprising invitation. He was as irrepressible and generous as ever. Sensibly he gave us good warning. 'Can you come up on Thursday 17 June and bring not only Marilyn, but Bart and Giselle and Rupert and Joanna also? If so I shall send two cars to York station for on the Friday there is the fathers match at the Hall against the boys. And Nigel, you won't credit this when I tell you the boys cricket team looks to be composed entirely of our grandchildren from that team of '47. Jeremy has just updated me on this for he is still chairman of the governors. Naturally you are all welcome to stay with Evie and me at Langbourn Manor. We have plenty of room for you southerners. Tip can enlighten you on those horses running into form and Owen and Penny will be staying with us too. They could do with a change of air. We have no shortage of excuses for a party and I am more than happy to say Owen will be up for it as he fully understands it will do him good.'

Indeed I could scarcely believe my ears. Granted that Harry, Claude, Slim and Vince were not around, it was extraordinary that their own sons had sent their lads to Ruabon Hall, even more so that all were of appropriate age to compete with the grandchildren of those of us still in the land of the living. Bart and Giselle were more than happy to make the trip as were Rupert and Joanna. Rupert had a great nephew at the school and was glad to link up with Noel for the first time in ages. And of course he always had the time of day for Jeremy. But again who did not? I recognised just how privileged I had been not merely to have been a member of that special cricket team but, once again, how so many of them had helped me massively in my career.

On the morning of the match I caught up with Mark. He was not as doddery as I had feared since the regular company of Mavis was working wonders. Alongside Mark and Mavis was a young Nigerian called Simon Chidobem. It transpired he was the nephew of his old tennis playing friend Richard – the veterinary surgeon so needlessly and cold-bloodedly assassinated in his homeland – being the sixth son of Richard's youngest brother. Simon was an authority on Nigerian music and Mark, looking for a sequel to his book on Tudor music, was now turning his hand to both folk and modern music from Nigeria with the help of Simon. It challenged his intellect and kept him motivated.

As expected we oldies met the fathers over coffee before play commenced. I knew most of them up to a point but those I scarcely knew or did not know at all included Claude's son Kit, Slim's son Douglas, and Vince's son Bruce. As for the lads in the cricket team, I was more or less aware of them through my grandson Nicholas, son of Francis. It was only when I saw the batting order for the school that my eyes stood out on stalks. The grandchildren replicated the batting order we had had in 1947. Not only that, but apart from one the initial of each and every boy's first name was the same as their grandfather's. Well, that made it easy to remember! The odd man out, to coin a phrase, was the slightly brown one they called KV. This I found out stood for Kumar Vincent, grandson of the late Vince.

So, running through the boys side, first in was Martin, grandson of Mark. Then came Tim, grandson of Theo, followed by James, grandson of Jeremy and Hector, grandson of Harry. At number five was Chester, grandson of Claude. At six was Oscar, grandson of Owen, then Neil, grandson of Noel. In eighth position was Nicholas my grandchild. At number nine was Bart's grandson Boris. Then finally at ten and eleven were Sholto, grandson of Slim, and KV.

Jeremy was as amazed as I was and, indeed, all of us still surviving from 1947. He motioned to the headmaster, 'Paul, you would not believe it but history is repeating itself sixty-five years on. Your side replicates our team of '47. Do you realise every one of your players is the grandson of those boys who composed our eleven in that vintage year when we won every match? What is more they are playing in exactly the same order!' He could not help chuckling.

'Jeremy,' he replied, 'this is news to me. I had no idea. But it is very simple. This is the order the sports master has evolved without reference to anyone else and certainly not to me. So far it has seemed to work. As for history repeating itself, I strongly doubt the thesis. This is mere coincidence.'

Jeremy let the matter drop but on reverting to me he wondered whether one day this team would bond just as we had done. I shrugged my shoulders, 'highly lucky if they do,' I replied, 'but plant the seed with young James. You never know. Come to think of it we have been incredibly fortunate.'

I could not resist continuing, 'the cooperation and friendship we have enjoyed has been boundless. I for one might never have broken away to set up my own company without the assistance of pretty well all of you. In fact other than Vince who was always a law unto himself, every member of our vintage year team has entrusted me with work – even Claude, after making his fantastic aviary and feeding me the information for that booklet which Mark found so helpful as a sales tool.'

'Yes, indeed. By the way, strictly between you and me Noel paid for that booklet. You would never have thought when we were nippers that he would grow to have a heart of gold and be so unbelievably loyal. Frankly, overall the ongoing relationships have been astonishing. I never recall even one conflict. Mercifully, both Noel and I even eluded one with Claude. You know, Nigel, the lives of all of us have been the richer for it.'

I nodded and allowed myself to daydream. Had not Gabbitas given me some measure of self-confidence on vaulting the horse in those early days at Heathside so gaining the respect and friendship of Jeremy and Harry, and had I not later run across the two of them on the links at Formby my life would have been so very different. I pulled myself together and paid attention to the match.

The day was fine. The standard of play was like the curate's egg – very good in parts. On the whole the boys batted well even though Martin and Chester scored only five between them. Tim however did rather better with sixteen and James knocked up thirty-six. But Hector hit his own wicket when on eight, while Oscar struck a breezy twenty-four totally unlike his grandfather Owen who had always been always so dour at the crease. Owen of course was thrilled on being regaled with a ball-by-ball commentary. Neil was out for fourteen but in the process scored two sixes. Not so very different from his grandfather! The Tellings genes remained strong. Nicholas, having managed a creditable thirteen was then stumped. Rather unluckily in my view. Boris was caught for five and Sholto notched up eight. But little KV carried his bat and scored eleven. At a hundred and fifty to include ten extras the fathers were clearly set a stiff task. Would they be up to it we wondered an hour or more before tea at 1545?

Some Dads were stylish. Some floundered. All were completely out of practice and of course none had been in that winning team of '47. Whatever talent there had been then was not necessarily passed on. In any case the gently alcoholic libations at lunch – just for the fathers – had been not just generous but copious since Paul did not wish to see his fledglings succumb. With one wicket still to fall and one over remaining, the tension mounted. Facing the bowling was Noel's son Daniel, the MD-in-waiting of Tellings. From afar off one could tell he was a chip off the old block in that he possessed more than a fraction of his father's flair. At the other end of the pitch was Bart's son Stephen. Daniel had only to score two and the fathers would have won. On the final ball, in striving for a four in order to land a knockout blow he slightly mistimed it but dashed forward frantically in pursuit of those two runs that would have ensured victory. But before they managed the second one he was caught on the boundary by little KV. The outcome was therefore a tie.

I heard Jeremy say to Paul, 'maybe you are right and that history does not repeat itself. But it was jolly close, wasn't it. After all till now your team has won every match though, my goodness me, that was a close run thing.'

Paul's brow furrowed as he looked askance. Then he managed a grin.

'Actually I am not so sure after all,' he answered. 'For when we tally the scores at the end of term the match against the fathers is never included. Naturally you will understand we can only count results against other schools. It would be quite wrong to do otherwise.'

As Paul stood up and went over to congratulate KV on his fine catch, I leaned across to Jeremy and Noel for I could not refrain from saying, 'always respect the view of a headmaster even when he shifts his stance.'

Jeremy nodded a bemused smile before murmuring wryly, 'I guess he will have learned something from those years in Down Under.'

Noel looked strangely ambivalent, a characteristic I had never noticed before. After all it was his son Daniel who was caught on the boundary.

Out of Paul's hearing it was left to Theo to have the last word. Ever the imp, his days as a jockey still vivid with memories of badinage in racecourse dressing rooms, he said with that twinkle in his eyes we had come to know so well, 'don't forget, all is fair in love and war. That's just the way it is.'

And on that note we went in to tea.

ABOUT THE AUTHOR

Ian Nalder grew up in Chislehurst, served in Kenya on national service and gained a golf blue at Oxford. Married with three children and six grandchildren he has long been resident in Nairn.

While **A VINTAGE YEAR** is fiction, fact becomes intertwined as fifty people well known in their day are introduced who the author either knew, or met, or knew of through the Press. They appear in character but in a fictional setting.

His other books are:

A Glance Along The Tracks, Patten Press

One in a series of ten books from writers she admired that were commissioned by Dr Melissa Hardie. In this case – personal recollections along with fables of great golfers.

Scotland's Golf In Days of Steam, Scottish Cultural Press

A fascinating insight into how the initiative of railway Barons encouraged golf in the days of Queen Victoria.

Golf & the Railway Connection, Scottish Cultural Press

An equally fascinating insight into how Victorian railway entrepreneurs encouraged golf in England, Wales and Ireland.

Pride In the Pedigree, Gopher Publications

The story of Nairn Golf Club and tales of the famous who came to play.

Nightmare In Paradise, Librario

A Scot's dream to create a golf course in Sri Lanka comes true. But the dream is shattered when disharmony arrives.

ISBN 978-1-78808-960-9